DiTCHiNG DAViD

Fidelity Investigations #1

JENNA BENNETT

When Gina Beaufort Kelly's husband leaves her for a woman young enough to be his daughter, Gina doesn't get mad... she gets even.

Or at least she tries to, by targeting David's assets in the divorce. She spent eighteen years of her life with him; it's only fair that he should compensate her accordingly.

However, David doesn't agree, and when he ends up dead, on the evening before they were set to go before the judge, Homicide Detective Jaime Mendoza suspects foul play—and suspects that Gina's behind it.

Now this jilted wife must figure out who else wanted her soon-to-be-ex-husband dead—and why—before she loses everything, including her freedom.

DITCHING DAVID
Fidelity Investigations Case 1

This is a work of fiction. Names, characters, places and incidents either are the product of the author's imagination or are used fictitiously, and any resemblance to actual persons, living or dead, business establishments, events or locales is entirely coincidental.

ISBN: 978-1942939009

Magpie Ink

CHAPTER ONE

They say the wife is always the last to know, and I guess it must be true, because until David told me he'd found someone else and was leaving me, I had no idea he had even thought about straying.

By then, it had gone way beyond thinking about it. Her name was Jackie—I found out later that it wasn't just Jackie, it was Jacquie with a q—and she made him feel young again. Not surprising, when Jackie-with-a-q was younger than his children.

He had two, both of them with his first wife.

I was his second, acquired when Sandra started to show signs of wear and tear. She was pushing thirty-five by then, and had carried and birthed two little monsters, so it stood to reason she wouldn't look as dewy fresh as she had when he married her.

That didn't stop David from dumping her for another nubile twenty-two year old: me.

At that point Krystal was eleven and her little brother Kenny eight. They went to live with Sandra, and I had to deal with them only on the rare weekends when David had visitation rights. They didn't like me and I'm not sure they liked David much, either. No big surprise there, when he had left their mother for me.

David and I didn't have any children. He didn't want any, and since he didn't, I didn't either. In retrospect I may have regretted that, but at the time it seemed like a logical choice. Besides, my experiences with Krystal and Kenny didn't exactly inspire confidence in my abilities as a mother. And it meant I kept my figure and didn't grow old before my time. When I passed thirty and then thirty-five without being traded in for a younger model, I breathed a silent sigh of relief. I guess I may have become a little too complacent, because it was only a few months past my fortieth birthday when David came and told me it wasn't working out and he wanted a divorce.

"I see," I said, as the bottom fell out of the world.

He arched a brow. He'd always had that ability, and when I was younger, I thought it was sexy. Now I found it conceited. "That's all you have to say?"

Well, no. I could have said a lot more. But I wasn't going to give him the satisfaction of hearing me rant. Or worse, beg. "What's her name?"

David flushed, as if I'd put him on the spot. As if he'd really thought I wouldn't realize what was going on. "Gina..."

"Oh, give me a break! You did it to Sandra; it was only a matter of time before you did it to me. I should have known something was up as soon as you brought home the Porsche."

He'd bought it for himself a few months ago: the classic middle-aged phallic substitute, a screaming red convertible sports car.

But no, instead of seeing the car as what it was, the

writing on the wall, I'd chalked it up to midlife crisis—he'd be turning fifty-three soon—and an effort to recapture his youth.

Duh.

"Jackie," David said. "With a q."

Of course. "And how old is she?"

David announced, with barely concealed pride, that she was twenty-five.

Three whole years older than I'd been when he married me. While he'd aged eighteen years since then. By now, he was more than old enough to be Jacquie's father.

"She wants you for your money," I said.

"We're in love," David answered stiffly.

Of course they were. Jackie-with-a-q was in love with David's position and bank account, while David was in love with her twenty-five-year-old body and her no doubt oft-expressed adoration.

And why wouldn't she adore him? He was rich, handsome, and crazy about her. Crazy enough to be willing to divorce his wife of eighteen years.

But there is none so blind as they who will not see, and I knew it wouldn't do any good to argue. So I told him I understood, that of course he could have a divorce if that's what he wanted, and as soon as the door closed behind him, I was on the phone with the best (female) divorce lawyer in Nashville.

The papers were filed the next day, including the petition for 50% of the marital assets plus a few grand a month in alimony. Tennessee is an equitable distribution state—meaning the actual division of assets would be decided by the court—but we made a good case for why eighteen years of marriage, during which David's business grew by leaps and bounds, entitled me to half of what he owned. And since he'd married me before I could finish college, and he had insisted I didn't have to work, I had no way of supporting myself apart from his income.

I stayed in the house in Hillwood while David had bought a penthouse in downtown for himself. Jackie-with-a-q didn't move in; I guess David's own divorce attorney (male) advised him that it wouldn't look good. He didn't stop seeing her, though. She lived in midtown, and he'd go there every night.

Yes, I followed him. So sue me: I wanted to see the woman he'd left me for.

I gave it a couple of days after the announcement to let him relax and get the divorce process started on his end. By then, David was settled into his new apartment and his new routine, still heading to work every day as if nothing was going on. That afternoon, at the time he usually left Hollingsworth & Kelly for the day, I was parked across the street waiting for him. For the occasion, I'd traded cars with Diana, my attorney, since I thought David might recognize the flashy convertible he'd bought me for my fortieth birthday—to assuage his guilty conscience, I now realized. At Diana's recommendation, I had pen, paper, and a digital camera on the seat next to me, to take notes and snap pictures of anything interesting.

Farley Hollingsworth left first. David's business partner and best friend is a thin man with receding hair and glasses. He looks like your stereotypical accountant. Farley is the brains of the business; David the... beauty, I guess. He's handsome and charismatic, and at fifty-two, obviously still has what it takes to turn the head of a woman half his age. Farley, on the other hand, isn't much to look at, but he makes up for it with intelligence.

He's still on his first wife. They got married during college, and have managed to stick it out for thirty years, though sickness and health, three children, and business ups and down.

I sat there while Farley got into his white BMW and drove off. Home to the house in Belle Meade and Martha. Whom, I will say for him, he sincerely seemed to adore.

Rachel was next to leave. She's David's office manager and administrative assistant, and when he first hired her, I admit to being worried. I thought she'd be the end of my marriage, that he'd hired my replacement.

Instead, Rachel turned out to be older than me, and frumpy. Forty pounds overweight, with mousy brown hair, always dressed in a boxy dark business suit. She came to professional life late, after her husband left her, and taking a chance on her is one of the few purely unselfish things David has ever done.

Or perhaps it wasn't entirely unselfish, since he got a hell of an administrative assistant out of the deal, not to mention Rachel's undying devotion. In her eyes, David can do no wrong. She runs the daily workings of Hollingsworth & Kelly with an iron hand, and manages to juggle dry cleaning, golf appointments, and birthday presents to David's kids and his soon to be ex-wife—me—at the same time.

I wondered how long she'd known about Jackie-with-a-q and how Rachel felt about the situation. She might even have helped David keep it from me. We'd never gotten along well, probably because Rachel thinks I'm not worthy of the great David Kelly. I wondered if she thought Jackie-with-a-q was worthy or whether she really, secretly, wanted David for herself.

I watched as she got into her car, a five year old Toyota, and drove away, home to her own lonely apartment and dinner for one. Then I went back to watching the entrance to the building.

David came out fifteen minutes later. I guess he must have taken the time to freshen up before he left, because he looked spiffy. His hair, thick and silver, was freshly combed, and he had changed the business-like white shirt and conservative tie for a lavender shirt open at the collar. He looked damned good for fifty-plus, and in spite of the fact that I was practically angry enough to murder him, I felt that familiar clutch at the heart. Almost twenty years together will do that to a woman, even when the man's a jerk.

I snapped a couple of pictures of him exiting the building and walking through the parking lot, just to get familiar with the camera.

The phallic symbol Porsche was parked at the back of the lot, and I heard the roar of the engine as he started it. A few seconds later the sleek red shape came rolling out into the street. I started my own engine, but waited until he was a block away before I pulled into the street behind him.

And off we went, through Nashville rush hour traffic. It was no problem at all keeping up with the eye-catching Porsche as David wound his way down Music Row into midtown and from there into the lot of one of Nashville's most expensive restaurants. I snapped a few more pictures as he turned the car over to the valet and headed inside, smoothing a hand over his hair as he went.

I found a parking space across the street and settled in to wait. It wasn't like I could leave the car, after all. David would notice me the moment I walked into the restaurant, and he'd guess why I was there. And I had no desire to give him the idea that I was upset about what was going on.

So I waited. And watched the new arrivals as they handed their keys off to the valet and entered the restaurant through the double glass doors. Couples, single men, small groups of women—girls' night out, I guess—and here and there a single woman, as well. Most were older—the place wasn't easy to afford on a twenty-five-year-old's salary—but one or two were in the right age range. I paid special attention to the blondes, knowing David's preferences, and took pictures of everyone I thought might be a likely candidate. Thank God for digital cameras. In the old days, with celluloid, I'd have had to worry about running out of film. As it was, I kept shooting, and the camera kept clicking away.

They came out two hours later, together. By then, I was in desperate need of a toilet, and would have killed for a drink. But I sat up straight in my seat as soon as I saw David exit the building, and aimed the camera at him. When Jackie-with-a-q followed, I was ready.

And damn, I had seen her walk in, but hadn't paid her much attention. She didn't look like I'd expected, or what I thought I knew David's type to be. Far from a tall, cool blonde, she was a short, exotic-looking brunette instead. She barely came up to David's shoulder, even in high heels—Jimmy Choo's; I wondered whether our money had paid for those—and the two of them together looked like father and daughter.

I zoomed in and started snapping pictures, until the valet brought her car around. She drove a VW Beetle, royal blue, and I don't know why that should have come as a surprise. Lord, she looked impossibly young, and I felt older than I had in a long time.

David handed her into the car with a last, lingering kiss. The way he looked at her reminded me of the way he used to look at me a long time ago. It was a look I hadn't seen in years, and it brought back memories I'd just as soon forget.

She zoomed out of the lot and into traffic. I thought about waiting, to follow David instead, but decided I'd be better off discovering where Jackie-with-a-q lived. I already knew David's new address, since he'd told me where to forward his mail, and of course I also knew where he worked. I could always find him. But if I lost Jacquie now, I might not see her again. While the valet went for David's Porsche, I started Diana's Mercedes and pulled out into traffic.

Jackie-Q had gone in the opposite direction on a two-way street, so I had to go up to the next light and turn around. By then, she was a couple of blocks ahead, and I had to hustle to catch up.

Shadowing someone isn't as easy as it looks in the movies, and by now, rush hour was over and there were less cars on the streets. Luckily the Beetle—like the red

Porsche—was rare enough that it made things easier. I'd hate to think what might have happened if Jackie-with-a-q had been driving Rachel's white Toyota.

I trailed her to an older five-story apartment building in midtown, not too far from the restaurant. The building and location were nice enough, although nowhere near as nice as David's new digs. Maybe Jackie-with-a-q chose to spend her money on clothes instead of housing. Or maybe she just couldn't afford any better. He hadn't told me what she did for a living, and I scribbled a note to myself to find out.

She parked in the lot behind the building and came around to the front. I watched as she unlocked the door and disappeared inside. After a minute, a light came on in a window on the third floor. A couple minutes passed while I waited some more. Two people left the building. A young woman with a small, fluffy dog wandered down the street so the dog could do its business against a streetlight, and a minute later, a dark-haired young man in jeans and a short-sleeved blue chambray shirt came out of the building and headed across the street, directly towards me.

My heart skipped a beat. Had Jacquie noticed me following her, and sent a neighbor to warn me off?

But at the last moment he veered off, and unlocked a pickup truck parked at the curb in front of me. He passed close enough that I could see the expression on his face, and it wasn't happy. His jaw was set and his lips tight. Maybe he and the dog-walker had had an argument, and she had cut it short by taking the pooch for a walk. I watched carefully as he passed the two of them, but he made no move to jump the curb and take them out, or for that matter any move to talk to her. She did lift her head to watch the truck drive away, though, which I thought gave some credence to my theory.

Headlights in my rearview mirror caught my attention, and I forgot all about the young man and the girl with the dog as I watched David's red Porsche slow down and go past me, to pull into the parking space the truck had just vacated. David fluffed his hair in the mirror before getting out of the car and walking across the street, setting the alarm on the Porsche with a flick of his wrist. I shrank down into my seat when he glanced around, even though I knew he couldn't possibly see me through the tinted windows. I took a picture of him walking, then another of him ringing the doorbell—it looked like Jackie-with-a-q hadn't trusted him with a key to her apartment—and then I took a third picture as he disappeared inside.

At that point I figured I'd done everything I could do. I certainly wasn't about to ruin my beauty sleep by sitting here in the car all night. It wasn't like I had any questions about what they would be doing upstairs, and I had no desire to photograph it. Unless they got it on directly in front of the window, I wouldn't be able to, anyway. But I waited a couple of minutes to make sure they were settled before I opened the car door and scurried across the street. A quick look at the lighted display of doorbells showed me that Jackie-with-a-q did indeed live on the third floor, probably in the apartment where I'd seen the light go on just after she went inside. Her last name was Demetros. I took a picture of the doorbell too, and then I gave the young lady with the dog a polite smile as we passed on the sidewalk. She turned to look after me suspiciously before heading into the building with the dog. It growled.

After that night, I made a habit of following David around. I also spent some time outside Jacquie's apartment building. I saw the girl with the dog again—although I don't think she saw me—and I also saw the swarthy young man. And I saw David coming and going a lot. I kept taking pictures and passing them to Diana, who was putting together quite a dossier on David's extramarital activities.

While all this was going on, I myself was pure as the driven snow. I dedicated myself to nailing David in court, and I had no time left over for anything else. Diana was the only person I had any contact with. Most of my friends were wives of clients of David's anyway, so of course those relationships fell by the wayside when we separated. It was rather sobering to realize how much of my life had been wrapped up in his. I had no job, no friends, and not much of a life outside David.

Our court date was the first Tuesday in September, the day after David's birthday. I thought long and hard about buying him a gift—we'd been married for eighteen years, and part of me would always love him, and anyway, it was still *our* money—but in the end I decided against it. It would send the wrong message.

I did call him, though. At work. Where Rachel answered the phone. "Hollingsworth & Kelly. Rachel speaking."

"Hi, Rachel," I said. "This is Gina."

There was a beat, and then Rachel found her voice.

"Hello, Mrs. Kelly."

I hadn't expected warmth, since I'd never received any before, but I'd thought that perhaps the fact that David had been cheating on me might have made her a little more kindly disposed. Guess not.

"Is David around?"

"One moment." She clicked off. I heard a few seconds of Muzak, and then David's voice.

"Gina?" He sounded wary.

"Hi, David."

An awkward silence followed, as I wondered what had possessed me to do this. David probably wondered the same thing.

"I just called to wish you a happy birthday," I said.

"Oh. Um..." He floundered for a moment. "Thank you."

That was all I really wanted to say, so another awkward silence descended. I should have sent him a text, I guess, but I'd wanted to hear his voice.

"I guess I'll see you tomorrow," I said. "In court."

"Right."

I was just about to hang up when he spoke again. "Gina?"

"Yes?"

"I'm sorry."

"Sure." Like I believed that.

"I don't blame you for being upset," David said. "I'll talk to the judge, OK?"

Of course he would. We both would. And as for me being upset...

"I'm sorry," I said, in spite of not being sorry at all. "I

must be missing something. You'll talk to the judge about what?"

"The prenuptial agreement," David said, as if it was obvious.

"What prenuptial agreement?"

"The one you signed when we got married."

OK. Yes, I had signed a prenuptial agreement eighteen years ago. But there was a good reason why I hadn't thought about it since then. "That only applies if I'm the one leaving you," I reminded him. "You're the one who wanted the divorce."

"You filed first," David said.

Well, yes. I had. But...

There was a noise on David's end of the line. To this day I'm not sure whether it was a smothered laugh or his version of "Oh, shit." He didn't say anything. And then he hung up. The sound of the receiver being replaced in the cradle was very soft in my ear.

"He's right," Diana said two minutes later.

"What do you mean, he's right? He can't be right!" My voice was shrill, approaching the register where only dogs would be able to hear me. I forced myself to take a breath and calm down. "The prenup only applies if I leave him!"

"And you did," Diana said. "When you filed for divorce first."

"But he's the one who asked for the divorce!"

"Doesn't matter," Diana said. "You're on record as the petitioner. David's on record as the respondent. That means you left him."

"But he'd already bought another place to live! He had a new girlfriend!"

"And if we can prove that," Diana said, "and make a case for abandonment, the judge might agree to throw the prenup out. It's worth a try."

That didn't sound encouraging. Nor did the word 'abandonment' sound very nice. I hadn't really been abandoned, had I?

Had I?

"What does this mean?" I asked, my voice rather small, even in my own ears.

Diana hesitated. "Best case scenario, the judge sees your point and agrees you're entitled to something. Worst case scenario, the judge decides the prenup stands."

"But I'll get nothing! I won't even be able to pay you!" I'd be penniless, living on the street.

"Then we'd both better hope it won't come to that," Diana said.

There was a moment of silence. I said, "He did this to me on purpose, didn't he? Told me about Jacquie, and told me he wanted a divorce, and then waited for me to file. Because he knew I'd want to file first. That it would make me feel less like I got dumped if I could file first."

"That would be my guess," Diana said.

"I'm gonna kill him."

"If you do," Diana said, "don't tell me. If I don't know, they can't force me to tell them."

CHAPTER TWO

It was a few hours later, and I was drawing a bath before bed, complete with lots of bubbles, candles, wine, and soft music, when the doorbell rang. I'd already stripped out of my clothes, and for a moment I contemplated just letting whoever was out there knock until they got tired. There wasn't anyone I wanted to see.

But then I thought it might be Diana, come to tell me she had pulled off a miracle and that that eighteen-year-old prenup wouldn't be a problem after all.

Or maybe it was David, knocking on the door for one last fling before we severed our connection tomorrow. Yesterday, I might have considered it. Tonight, I'd enjoy telling him no.

So I wrapped a robe around myself and padded barefoot down the central staircase to the front door and flung it open, glass of wine still in hand.

Only to find myself face to face with a stranger. A rather good-looking stranger. Tall, dark and handsome, and at least five years younger than me. Probably more.

I wrapped my arms around myself, wishing I'd taken the time to get redressed, or at least that I was still wearing makeup. Without it, I probably looked every bit of forty. "Can I help you?"

"Mrs. Kelly?"

He had melting, chocolate brown eyes in a face that must have made the twenty-somethings swoon. The hair was black, and just long enough to curl over his ears and over the collar of the suit jacket in the back. And then there was the voice: a clear tenor with just a hint of a foreign accent. Shades of Antonio Banderas.

I nodded. "I'm Regina Beaufort Kelly."

"My name is Jamie Mendoza. I'm with the MNPD."

"The...?"

"Metropolitan Nashville Police Department." He pulled a wallet out of his pocket and flipped it open to show me a badge.

I knew that. I just wasn't thinking straight. "Has something happened?"

"May we go inside?"

"Sure. Um..." I didn't move from the open door. "I don't mean to be difficult, but would you mind if I took a closer look at that?"

I gestured to the wallet.

"Of course." He handed it to me. I opened it.

It had an ID card on one side and the badge on the other. I gave both as thorough of a look as I dared. The badge looked legitimate—it was bright and shiny and said Metro Nashville Police Department—and the ID did have his picture and his name as stated. He spelled Jamie the Hispanic way, with the I before the M—Jaime—but pronounced it the way I would.

"Thank you. Come on in." I stepped back. He followed, and I closed the door behind him.

"Nice place." He looked around the entrance hall, at the inlaid Brazilian hickory floors, the gleaming banister and balustrade, the Persian runner, and the artwork. David paid an interior designer a rather large sum of money to make the house look like a showplace when he bought it.

"Thanks." I put the glass of wine on the console table. "What can I do for you, Mr. Mendoza?"

"Detective Mendoza." He turned to me.

Of course. "Sorry, Detective. What can I do for you?"

"I'm sorry, Mrs. Kelly," Jaime Mendoza said, "but I'm afraid I have some bad news. There's been an accident. Your husband's been killed."

"What happened?" I asked.

It was several minutes later. After he'd dropped his bomb on me, and I'd refused to believe him because David had been alive and well just a few hours ago, Detective Mendoza had suggested that we sit down. I'd been in no condition to object. He'd even brought the glass of wine along, and when we were seated at the kitchen table, he placed it in front of me before seating himself opposite. And answered my question, finally.

"He drove through a guardrail on I-440, across the median, and ended up heading into oncoming traffic."

"God." What a horrible way to go. "Was anyone else hurt?"

"He clipped a few cars on the way," Mendoza said,

"but avoided major impact. There were no other fatalities. A couple of people were transported to the hospital with minor injuries. Your husband was pronounced dead on the scene. It was quick."

"That's good." I had tossed back what had been left of the wine as soon as we sat down, and now I was twirling the empty glass between my fingers. I wanted a refill, but although the bottle was less than six feet away, on the counter behind me, it didn't seem like an opportune time to go get one. "So there was no one else with him in the car?"

Mendoza shook his head. "Was he meeting someone after work?"

"He's been seeing a young woman named Jacquie Demetros."

Detective Mendoza blinked. "Seeing? As in dating?"

I nodded.

He hesitated. "But you are his wife, correct?"

"We're separated. We were supposed to go before a judge tomorrow. To get the official verdict on dividing the assets."

"I see," Jaime Mendoza said. "I didn't realize. I'm sorry. His driver's license listed this as his address of record."

"It's OK," I told him. "He moved out a couple of weeks ago, and we were getting things in order. I guess he forgot he had to change his address."

Unless he'd had second thoughts, which wasn't likely. Or unless he expected to get the house in the settlement, and he figured he'd be moving back in soon.

That was a whole lot more likely.

"Do you know where I can find Ms. Demetros?"

Mendoza had pulled a little notebook and a pencil stub out of his pocket, and was ready to write down any information I gave him. I hesitated. If I told him that I knew where she lived, he might realize that I'd been spying on my husband and his new love.

On the other hand, if I didn't tell him and he found out on his own, that would look even worse.

"She has an apartment in midtown." I gave him the address. It was only reasonable that I should want to know about the woman my husband left me for, right? Nobody could fault me for that. "David bought himself a penthouse in the Gulch. In the Apex building."

"Did your husband plan to marry Ms. Demetros?" Mendoza wanted to know, pen poised over the pad.

"He hasn't said." Not to me. "We don't... didn't really talk much." For a while now, I realized. Long before he moved out.

Although he probably did plan to marry her. If he didn't, why would he need a divorce?

"When was the last time you spoke?"

"To David? This afternoon. It's his birthday." My eyes overflowed, but at least I'd taken all my makeup off preparatory to climbing into the tub, so nothing but tears were running down my face. I got up, walked over to the kitchen counter, tore a paper towel off the roll, and sat back down, clutching it.

"What did you talk about?" Mendoza asked.

"On the phone? I just called to wish him a happy birthday. We spoke for two minutes, tops." I dabbed at my face, hiding behind the paper towel while I wondered whether I was required to tell him about the prenuptial agreement and how my husband—late husband—had tricked me into filing first.

"So you'd say the divorce was amicable?"

"As much as they ever are. I didn't cause a fuss. When he divorced Sandra, she was a lot less conciliatory."

"And Sandra is...?"

"His first wife. He left her eighteen years ago."

I could see the light bulb take shape over his head. "You and Mr. Kelly were married... how long?"

I said we'd been married for eighteen years, and I'm sure Detective Mendoza drew his own conclusions. I felt like a big, scarlet A was forming on my forehead. And to add insult to injury, it all probably happened while Detective Mendoza was in diapers.

"What's going to happen now?" I asked. "I mean, I'm still his wife, right, so I guess I'll have to make arrangements for the funeral and everything...?"

"He was taken by ambulance to the hospital morgue. The medical examiner will have a look at him tomorrow. You are still his next of kin, so unless you want to pass off that responsibility to the estate or to his lawyer, you will be notified when the body is ready for release."

I shook my head. "I'll take care of it." It seemed the least I could do, after eighteen years together. Tomorrow morning, I'd call the funeral parlor and make arrangements to have the body transferred when it was ready. "Have you notified David's business partner yet? Farley Hollingsworth?"

"In the morning," Detective Mendoza said.

"Should I call Sandra? So she can tell Krystal and

Kenny?"

"Your husband had children from his first marriage?"

"They're not children anymore. Krystal is twenty-nine, Kenny twenty-six. But yes, he does." After a moment I added, "Did."

"I'll take care of it," Jaime Mendoza said. "Anyone else who needs to know? Are Mr. Kelly's parents still alive?"

Thankfully not. "My mother-in-law died last year. My father-in-law has been dead for a decade. There's a brother somewhere in California. He and David didn't have much to do with one another."

Mendoza made like a Chihuahua, ears pricked. "Was there a reason for that?"

I hesitated, and then decided I might as well tell the truth. It was no reflection on me either way. "David was successful and well-to-do. Daniel wasn't. David got tired of floating his brother."

"His name is Daniel?"

I nodded. "Daniel Kelly. Last I heard, he lived in Santa Barbara or maybe Santa Cruz. Santa Something, anyway. Other than Daniel it's just me, and Sandra and the kids."

"Do you have an address or a phone number for the former Mrs. Kelly? If not, I'm sure I can dig it up."

I was sure he could, too. But I said I thought we had at least Krystal and Kenny's contact information in the Rolodex in David's office, and I left Detective Mendoza at the kitchen table while I headed into the next room to look for the information. When I straightened from the desk and turned around, he was lounging in the doorway.

"This is your husband's home office?"

I nodded, looking around at it, trying to see it through Mendoza's eyes.

It was a good sized room, maybe fifteen feet to a side, with a heavy executive desk in the middle and a bookcase on either side of the window. They were filled with leather-bound volumes David had never read. Between them ran a long, low console that hid a number of filing cabinets.

"Your husband was an accountant," Mendoza said, "correct?"

"Financial advisor," I answered. "Farley was the accountant. David has... had a degree in business. He brought in the clients for Hollingsworth & Kelly. Farley took their money."

Mendoza looked doubtful, and I added, "It's something David used to say. Farley handled the investments while David handled the people."

Mendoza nodded. "Would you mind giving me the name of your husband's lawyer? And yours?"

I minded, sort of. But I didn't think I could refuse. "My divorce attorney is Diana Morton. David's is... was Anton Hess. Why don't I just write down those numbers for you, too?"

I didn't wait for him to respond, just added the names and numbers to the list I had already started.

"And your husband's estate attorney? Was that also Mr. Hess?"

I told him it was. Anton Hess had handled David's divorce from Sandra way back in the mists of time, too. And he had drawn up that prenuptial agreement I'd signed.

"Here." I handed Mendoza the piece of paper, before he could ask for anyone else's number.

"Thank you." He glanced at it before tucking it away in the inside pocket of his jacket. Armani, unless I missed my guess. Fancy duds for a cop.

"I don't have Sandra's information," I told him. "Sorry."

"That's fine. I can find it."

He pushed off from the door jamb, and I trailed him out into the foyer and over to the door. "Krystal or Kenny will be able to tell you where to find their mother."

He nodded and stepped through the front door out onto the porch. I looked past him to the driveway, where a nondescript gray sedan waited, indistinguishable from any of the other cars on the road. *Good.* At least the neighbors hadn't seen a police car camped out outside my house.

"Thank you for your time, Mrs. Kelly. My condolences on your loss." Mendoza headed down the steps without waiting for my response. He was almost to the car when I remembered something.

"Detective?"

He turned. "Mrs. Kelly?"

"Which hospital was my... was David's body taken to?"

Mendoza didn't speak immediately, and I added, lamely, "For the funeral parlor. So they can arrange transportation."

"He's at the St. Jerome Hospital morgue, Mrs. Kelly," Mendoza said, not unkindly.

"Thank you."

He nodded. I expected him to turn and walk to the car, but instead he lingered for a moment at the bottom of the steps. It wasn't until that moment that I realized I was standing on my front porch with my front door wide open, my feet bare, and my body naked under a terrycloth robe, saying goodbye to a strange man.

The blush felt like it started at my feet and rose in a wave all the way to the roots of my hair. My cheeks burned, and Detective Mendoza's lips twitched. Maybe he'd realized the same thing I'd realized, and thought it was funny.

If he did, he didn't say anything about it. He just nodded politely. "Thanks again, Mrs. Kelly. I'll be in touch."

"Thank you, Detective." I didn't wait for him to drive away, just ducked back into the house as quickly as I could, hopefully before any of the neighbors noticed me standing there, looking for all the world like I was sending off a lover after a sweaty session between the sheets. That was the last thing I needed with the divorce.

And with David lying in the morgue.

God. The realization hit me anew, and I leaned forward until my forehead rested against the cool glass of the sidelight next to the door. David was dead. He had left me for another woman, he was planning to leave me destitute and homeless, and now he was dead.

Outside, Detective Mendoza's sedan came to life, and I opened my eyes again to watch through the window as he pulled away from the bottom of the steps and rolled down the driveway with a crunch of gravel. At the bottom of the drive, he lingered for a moment, brake lights bright in the semi-dark, before turning right and merging with traffic headed back toward town. Off to tell Krystal and Kenny that their dad was gone, I guess. Or off to tell Jacquie that her sugar-daddy had died before she could drag him to the altar.

I pushed off from the door and went to get the phone. I no longer wanted to lounge in a bubble bath with my wine and maudlin thoughts about being left by my husband. The water was cold by now, anyway. And Diana needed to hear about this, ASAP.

It was perhaps fitting that when I greeted her with "David's dead," the first words out of Diana's mouth were, "I told you I didn't want to know anything about that."

I sniffed. "Don't be ridiculous. I didn't do anything to him."

"Then what happened?"

"Nothing happened," I said. "It was a traffic accident. He lost control of his car and crashed through the guard rail."

There was a beat. "How do you know?" Diana asked.

"The police came. David's address of record, the one on his driver's license, was the house. They thought he still lived here."

She sounded resigned. "I suppose you set them straight."

"Of course. What was I going to do, lie to the police?"

Diana didn't answer that. "What did they ask you?"

"Just about the rest of the family. Krystal and Kenny

and Sandra. And David's brother in California. And... um... Jacquie."

Her voice rose, became shrill. "You told them your husband had left you for another woman?!"

I resisted the temptation to ask, again, whether she'd wanted me to lie. "Why not? The divorce is a matter of public record, right? You said so yourself, earlier. I'm on record as petitioner, and David's on record as respondent. They'd find out eventually. And why does it matter, anyway? It was a traffic accident!"

"Never volunteer any information," Diana said sternly. "You should have called me."

"Oh, sure. That would have looked great. The police show up at my doorstep to notify me that my husband has been killed, and I won't talk to them without my attorney present. My *divorce* attorney."

Diana didn't respond to that, so I guessed she saw my point.

"About tomorrow..." I said.

"What about it?"

"I guess our appointment with the judge is off?"

"No," Diana said.

"We're still going before the judge? But David's dead!"

"The judge doesn't know that," Diana said.

"Shouldn't someone let him know?"

"It's Anton Hess's responsibility. David was his client. Let him handle it."

Fine. "I'll schedule my appointment with the funeral parlor for the afternoon, then," I said.

Her voice rose into another shriek. "*You* are making

the arrangements?"

"Of course," I said. "He was still my husband."

"Only until tomorrow!"

"A little longer than that, surely." Since the paperwork wouldn't be filed and things made official until after the judge had ruled. "Anyway, I certainly won't let Jackie-with-a-q bury him." She may have taken him away from me while he was alive, but now that he was dead, he was mine again.

"Let me guess," Diana said grimly. "You'll be ordering the cheapest casket they've got. A plain pine box."

It was tempting, but no. Part of me wanted to bury David in a garbage bag, but the other part knew better. "That wouldn't look good."

"No," Diana said. "It wouldn't.

"Don't worry. I'll bury him properly." In a fancy casket and with appropriate music. "You can come with me to the funeral parlor if you want."

"That's OK," Diana said. "It's not really my place."

No, but if she were concerned that I'd put him in the ground to the sound of Gloria Gaynor, she was welcome to come along and make sure I didn't.

"I'll see you at the courthouse tomorrow," Diana added.

I told her I'd be there, and then I hung up and took the rest of the bottle of wine up to bed with me, the better to drown my sorrows.

CHAPTER THREE

I paid for it the next morning, when I faced my bleary self in the mirror. The bags under my eyes could have held groceries for a family of six, and there were lines on my face I didn't remember seeing before. My mouth turned down at the corners, my lips pale and thin, and my hair looked like birds nested in it.

I poked at it. It was like touching straw.

I'm a natural redhead, with brown eyes. However, by twenty-two I was going through a stage where I was sick of answering to Ginger. I'd been experimenting with hair dyes. The week David met me, I happened to be a blonde. And because David liked me that way, I stayed a blonde for him. Over the years, I'd gone from platinum to a more natural-looking wheat, but I was still blond.

For all the good it had done me. My husband had left me for a Salma Hayek lookalike.

It was too late to stick it to David now, but maybe it was time I went back to my own hair.

Maybe that would be a first step in taking a little of my own life back.

Hell, forty wasn't any age at all. I may not look twenty-five anymore—and damn Jackie-with-a-q anyway—but forty isn't what it used to be. I still had my figure—mostly—and I still had my looks, when I wasn't looking like death warmed over.

Maybe I couldn't expect to turn the head of someone like Detective Mendoza, but there were plenty of older men out there who looked great well into their forties and fifties.

A workout would have been nice, but I didn't think I ought to indulge on the day after my husband had died. And so it was that my first call of the day was to the spa, to book an emergency haircut and color, and a facial to deal with the fact that I looked my age today.

That done, I contacted the funeral parlor—the one David had used to bury his mother last year—and told them what had happened. We set up an appointment for later that afternoon, so I could sign the paperwork—and the check—and pick out the casket and the funeral music.

Then I got dressed—in a demure black-and-gray dress and jacket combo Diana had told me would work well for the hearing—and headed out to the spa.

When I walked into the courthouse three hours later, I was a redhead, for the first time in two decades. My natural color had probably faded some since I was a girl—although who knew, when I hadn't seen it *au naturel* since then?—but I had told the stylist I wanted short and strawberry red, so that's what she'd given me. I still surprised myself every time I looked in the mirror, but overall, I rather thought I was going to like being a redhead again. And the facial had helped with the bags and pale skin, so by the time I pushed open the door to the courthouse, I was looking a lot better than I had this morning. I may even have looked a bit too good, because as soon as Diana saw me come through the doors, she hissed at me. "You couldn't have waited until after the funeral?"

"We were getting divorced," I said. "He left me for a girl young enough to be his daughter. I'm sorry he's dead, but I'm not going to pretend to be grieving."

"I don't expect you to pretend to be grieving. But do you have to look like you're celebrating? That—" she glanced at my head, "is almost as bad as showing up at the funeral in a red dress."

"I would never do that. And I'm appropriately dressed."

She nodded approval of my gray-and-black ensemble. "You should wear it to the funeral, as well."

"I bought it for David's mother's funeral last year," I said. "Are you sure I don't need a new outfit to bury my husband?"

"I don't care. Just as long as it's black. And not too short." She glanced around. "Are you ready to go in?"

"We might as well get it over with."

"My thoughts exactly," Diana said and led the way to the judge's chambers.

Anton Hess must have moved his appointment up, probably so he could inform the judge of the new situation—David being dead, I mean.

More of a surprise was that he wasn't alone with the

judge in chambers. Detective Jaime Mendoza was there, as well, dressed in another killer suit. And for a second, when we first walked in, I'm not sure he recognized me. Then his eyes widened, and he stared at my hair for a second before dropping his gaze to my face again, just to make absolutely sure it was me. Aside from the surprise, however, I have no idea whether he approved or disapproved.

Anton Hess clearly disapproved.

Unlike Mendoza, he's neither tall nor handsome. He's only about my height, a year or two older than David, and shaped like a frog, with a wide mouth and protruding brown eyes. They looked at me with disfavor.

"Your Honor," Diana said, and I turned to the judge. He hadn't seen me before, so he had no way of knowing that my hair was different. "Mr. Hess. Detective Mendoza."

The judge and the lawyer nodded politely. The corner of Jaime Mendoza's mouth quirked.

Diana turned back to the judge. "I assume you've heard the news, Your Honor."

Judge Miller, pushing seventy and with soft, white hair standing up in a cock's comb above the black robe, nodded. "We're postponing."

"Of course." Diana sounded like she'd expected no less. I had assumed we wouldn't be moving forward today, either, but I wasn't sure I could have sounded so blasé about it.

The judge turned to me. "My condolences, Mrs. Kelly."

Anton Hess snorted. Softly enough that the judge

couldn't hear him, or maybe Judge Miller just decided to ignore the snort.

"Thank you," I said, graciously ignoring the snort, as well. Detective Mendoza was watching me, brown eyes bright, and I avoided his gaze.

"Terrible thing." Judge Miller shook his head. "We'll have to find a time to reschedule."

He consulted his schedule, then looked up at Diana and Anton Hess. I guess it was simply assumed that I would be available. "How about two weeks from today? Will that give the police enough time to investigate?" The attention moved to Mendoza.

Who opened his mouth, but before he could speak, someone said, "Investigate?"

It wasn't until everyone turned to look at me, that I realized I was that someone.

"Suspicious death," Mendoza said.

"You told me it was a traffic accident."

"Last night, that's all we knew."

Uh-oh. "Do you know something different this morning?"

It looked like Mendoza hesitated a second, or maybe it was just my imagination. "The brake lines of the car were compromised."

"Compromised?"

It was still my voice asking the questions, in spite of Diana's scowl and unspoken order to shut the hell up.

"Split," Mendoza said. "When the brake fluid drained, the brakes ceased to work."

"But he'd only had that car a few months."

"We don't think it was a factory flaw," Mendoza said.

I blinked. So if it wasn't a flaw in the manufacturing, and it wasn't an accident— "You're saying someone cut David's brake lines? Why?"

I don't know whether Mendoza would have answered or not, or what he would have said, because Diana had had enough. "Why don't we continue this somewhere else?" she said, in a tone that made it clear it wasn't a question at all; it was an order. "With your permission, Your Honor?"

Judge Miller nodded. "I've heard all this already."

Of course he had. That's why Mendoza had gotten here early.

They set up their new appointment and then we walked out of the judge's chamber and into the hallway. Anton Hess waddled off without a word, before I could extend my condolences on his loss. He and David had been friends, or at least associates, for a long time, and I'm sure he was sad to hear about David's death. Diana was about to hustle me to safety, too, when Mendoza spoke up.

"A word with you, Mrs. Kelly?"

"Not without me," Diana said.

Mendoza smiled. An actual, honest-to-goodness smile with teeth and dimples and all. I shouldn't have been affected by it—not with my husband lying in the morgue—but it was hard not to feel warm and squishy inside. I'm sure even Diana melted, under the icy exterior. "I'm not gonna pull out the thumbscrews and rubber hoses, Diana."

"I don't care," Diana said. "If you're going to talk to my client about her husband's death, you'll have to talk through me."

"You're not a criminal lawyer."

"I don't care," Diana said. "If she needs one, we'll get her one. But for today, she has me."

Mendoza shrugged. "Fine by me. I just wanna talk."

"Lunch?" She mentioned a restaurant on Fourth Avenue in Germantown, pretty much right around the corner from the Ferncliff and Morton offices, and a half mile north of where we were standing. "Thirty minutes?"

"I'll see you there." Mendoza turned and walked away. Diana turned to me.

"This isn't good."

"He just wants to talk," I said, still watching him walk away.

Diana huffed. "He thinks David was murdered."

Mendoza disappeared out of sight, and I turned back to her. "That's ridiculous. Who'd want to kill David?"

She arched her brows, and I shook my head. "You're crazy. I'd never hurt anyone."

"Just yesterday you told me you wanted to kill him," Diana said.

"But I didn't mean it."

She didn't answer, and I added, "Come on. Can you really see me crawling around underneath the Porsche, cutting the brake cables? I'd get dirty, for one thing, and I wouldn't know what they looked like, for another. It's not like I change my own oil, you know."

"There are books," Diana said. "Listen to me, Gina. Yesterday, you were looking at a prenuptial agreement limiting you to whatever gifts David gave you during your marriage. Today you're looking at inheriting everything."

Yes, but...

"You had every reason to kill David. If he survived until today, you might have lost everything but the clothes on your back and the car you drive."

"Do you think the police know that?"

"If he didn't yesterday, I'm sure Anton was happy to tell him this morning," Diana said grimly.

I lowered my voice. "So Detective Mendoza thinks I'm a suspect?"

Diana snorted. "Of course he thinks you're a suspect. You're the most obvious suspect. That's why I don't want you talking to him on your own."

I hesitated. "You... um... seemed to know him already."

"We've met," Diana said, in a tone that discouraged further questions.

"I assume he's good at his job?"

"He wouldn't have his job otherwise." She looked at my expression, and relented, just a little. "I didn't meet him in his professional capacity. But if he didn't close cases, he wouldn't keep his job."

OK, then.

"So don't tell him anything. Nothing."

I shook my head.

"Let's go," Diana said.

The Germantown Café is a lovely little establishment in the middle of a neighborhood that used to be Nashville's meat packing district, and is now one of the urban hotspots. If David hadn't already bought a condo in the

Gulch, Germantown would probably have been next on his list. There was even a view of downtown and the Capitol from the windows of the restaurant.

Mendoza wasn't there yet when I arrived. Diana was, and had gotten us a table. She was busy tapping on her phone—sending a text or taking notes—but slipped it into her purse when she saw me coming.

"Any problems?"

"You saw me fifteen minutes ago," I said, sliding onto my chair. "I didn't get lost on the way. And there's obviously still money in the bank account, because my debit card worked in the parking machine."

Diana didn't look amused, and I added, "Do I have to worry about the police or the courts putting a lien or something on my account?"

"Keep in mind that I'm not a wills and estates attorney," Diana said. "But David's will will have to go through probate. That happens every time someone dies, whether they're married or divorced or somewhere in between. It's possible his accounts will be blocked until the estate is settled."

"What about any shared accounts?" If I only had access to the account with my own monthly allowance, I'd be spending some pretty frugal weeks until David's estate was settled. And perhaps from here on out, if Judge Miller decided to uphold the prenup.

"I'm not sure," Diana admitted. "Jaime may be able to tell us."

Jaime, was it?

"Just how well do you know Detective Mendoza?" I asked.

"None of your business," Diana said. "Remember, Gina. He's handsome and charming, but he's a cop. Don't—"

"Tell him anything. I know."

The waiter stopped beside the table, and I asked for a glass of wine. Diana arched her brows at me, and I huffed. "Fine. Sweet tea, please."

Diana smiled approvingly. I rolled my eyes. "My husband died yesterday. You don't think I'm entitled to a drink?"

"Sitting here sipping a Cosmopolitan when the police walks in is likely to give them the wrong idea," Diana said severely, as the waiter withdrew, but not without a startled glanced from her to me and back.

"Detective Mendoza already knows I drink. I had a glass of wine in my hand when he knocked on the door last night." And found me in my bathrobe with bare feet.

"Jaime gave you the news?"

I nodded.

"I wish you would have mentioned that," Diana said.

"Would it have mattered?"

"You would have had some advance notice that they suspected foul play. Homicide detectives don't usually do the notifications for traffic accidents."

I had no idea how she would know that, but I'd take her word for it. "It has to be a mistake. Who'd want David dead? Other than me, of course."

"Of course," a voice said behind me.

Diana closed her eyes in disgust. "Jaime."

He grinned. "Diana. Mrs. Kelly."

"Call me Gina," I managed, resisting the temptation

to fan myself with my napkin. That grin was something else. Ten years too young for me, but killer.

Diana frowned, and Mendoza chuckled. "Perhaps we'd better keep this professional, Mrs. Kelly."

Perhaps that would be best. My rampant, middle-aged hormones to the contrary.

He put his hand on the back of the chair between us "Mind if I sit?"

"I suggested it," Diana said, "so naturally I don't mind."

Mendoza pulled his chair out. "I wasn't sure you'd finished talking."

It was my turn to close my eyes. "About what I said..."

He turned to me, brown eyes dancing. "Yes?"

"I had nothing to do with it. I'd never hurt David. I'd never hurt anyone, but especially David."

Mendoza nodded graciously, but without giving the least indication that he believed me.

"We were married for eighteen years," I said. "And two months after my fortieth birthday, he told me he wanted a divorce because he had a new girlfriend. Oh, and by the way, she's twenty-five."

Mendoza winced. I wasn't sure whether I wanted to kick him or not. He might have meant to be sympathetic, but in reality, he just reinforced that I had a right to feel old.

Twenty-five was probably right up his alley.

"I was angry with him," I said. "Anyone would have been. But I'd never hurt him. He was my husband. I..."

I stopped before I could blurt out that I'd still loved

him. It wasn't something Jaime Mendoza needed to hear, and besides, I wasn't entirely certain it was true.

Sure, part of me would always love David. We'd shared a house, and a bed, and Christmases and birthdays, for the best part of two decades. I'd become an adult while I was David's wife. When he married me, I hadn't been much more than a girl, easily swept off my feet by a rich and handsome older man.

Probably a lot like Jackie-with-a-q was right now.

And maybe that was the problem. The love hadn't died, because it hadn't been there in the first place. He'd bamboozled me with charm and presents, and I'd fancied myself in love with him, but it hadn't been Love, with a capital L.

But none of that was any of Mendoza's business. I shook the thoughts off and came back to the present, just as the waiter stopped beside the table with Diana's tonic and my tea. "Sir?"

Mendoza said he'd stick with water, and the waiter departed. Mendoza turned back to me. "You were saying?"

"I can't remember," I said, sucking on my straw until my cheeks were hollow.

"You'd never hurt your husband because...?"

"He couldn't help it that he fell out of love with me. I'd never blame him for something like that."

"That's very big of you," Mendoza said while Diana rolled her eyes. I guess maybe I was laying it on a little too thick. "Tell me about Ms. Demetros."

I glanced at Diana, who nodded. "You probably know more about her than I do," I told Mendoza. "She's twenty-five. She lives in midtown. She's pretty. She looks nothing like me. David left me for her. And that's all I know. I've never spoken to her. And David didn't tell me much."

"Would she have any reason to want your husband dead?"

"If she did, I can't imagine what the reason would be. David must have been a lot more valuable to her alive."

Mendoza cocked an eyebrow, and I expounded. "He was going to marry her, right? Or why else would he divorce me? If he was just going to keep screwing her—"

Diana winced—a slight Freudian slip there—but I had no choice but to keep going and brazen it out, so I did, "—he could have done that while he was still married to me. And once they were married, all the money would be hers. I'm sure he was generous—he bought me a lot of presents while he was married to Sandra, too—but it's not the same thing as marriage."

Mendoza shook his head. I think he may have been too fascinated—in the manner of someone watching a piano falling in slow motion and knowing the outcome but being unable to do anything to stop it—to speak. Watching as I dug my grave deeper and deeper.

"So unless there's something going on I don't know about, I can't imagine that she wouldn't rather have him stay alive. At least until the wedding. Now she's not getting anything."

"What about his business partner? Mr. Hollingsworth?"

"Farley?" I shook my head. "He and David have been friends since college. He was best man at our wedding. And I'm sure David was much more valuable to Farley alive, too."

Mendoza tilted his head. "How come?"

"I told you last night," I said, taking a sip of tea and wishing it was something stronger. "Farley isn't good with people. He's a numbers-person. David is... David *was* the people-person. He brought in the clients while Farley handled the money. Without David, I'm not sure the business will survive."

Mendoza nodded. "And Mrs. Hollingsworth?"

"Martha. If the business goes under, Martha's cushy lifestyle does, too. Although she was born to money—old Belle Meade family—so she's probably got plenty tucked away from her parents and grandparents."

"The children?"

"They get money once David's estate is settled," I said. "Anton Hess would be able to tell you how much. But David was their father. They wouldn't hurt him."

Mendoza didn't look convinced. I guess he lived in a world where children occasionally killed their parents, for money or other reasons. "And the ex-wife?"

"She won't get anything. And doesn't need anything. She went back to school after David dumped her and got a degree. She's got her own income."

Unlike me. And while I'm sure Sandra hadn't particularly enjoyed reentering college at thirty-plus and with two kids at home, it beat doing it at forty-plus, which was what I was looking at doing. David had married me before I graduated, so all I had on my résumé was eighteen years as a trophy wife, and the ability to arrange business dinners. Not exactly something that would keep me in wine and clothes going forward.

"I spoke to your husband's brother," Mendoza said. "He lives in Santa Monica."

So neither Santa Barbara nor Santa Cruz. However, if he was in California and not in Tennessee, he couldn't have sabotaged David's brakes.

The realization must have crossed my features, because Mendoza nodded. "I'm afraid it down to you, Mrs. Kelly. Unless you can help me out with some viable suspects, it looks like your head will be first on the chopping block."

CHAPTER FOUR

Mendoza didn't end up staying for lunch after all. He dropped his bombshell, and then he got up and walked out, after saying goodbye to Diana. I was still too stunned to speak, if not too overcome to enjoy the view as he departed.

"This isn't good," Diana told me, calmly, when we were alone.

I shook my head.

"I don't suppose you have an alibi for last night?"

I didn't suppose I did. I opened my mouth and then had to clear my throat before I could get my voice to work. "I spoke to David around four. That's when he mentioned the prenup, and when I called you."

Diana nodded.

"I spent some time digging out and reading through the prenup, to see if there was any chance I wouldn't lose everything. I drank some wine while I worried about what I would do if I did. I couldn't afford to keep the house, and I don't have an education, so I have no idea what kind of job I could get. All I've ever been is David's wife."

Diana nodded.

"Eventually I decided I'd wallowed in self-pity long enough, and I decided to take a bath. But I didn't have any wine left, so I had to make a trip to the liquor store first. And when I came back, that's when Detective Mendoza showed up."

"While you were in the tub?"

"I hadn't gotten in yet," I said, even as I thought guiltily about the fact that I'd answered the door in my robe and with a glass of wine in my hand. To anyone who didn't know me—like Jaime Mendoza—it might almost look as if I were celebrating.

Diana took a sip of her tonic. "This isn't good, Gina."

"You already said that," I told her. "On the bright side, if I get arrested for murder, I don't have to worry about being homeless or about making a living."

"That isn't funny," Diana said.

"It's a little funny."

"There has to be someone else who'd benefit from David's death."

Someone else, as in someone other than me? "Lots of people would benefit in some way. Krystal and Kenny would get money. So would Daniel, I think. Farley would get complete control of the business. There's a gift to the cancer society in David's will, since my mother-in-law died from cancer..."

"I don't think the cancer society cut David's brake cables, Gina," Diana said.

"I don't think anybody cut David's brake cables. Daniel's in California. Krystal and Kenny would probably rather have their father alive than dead. And I can't think of any reason why Farley would want to oust David. The business is only as successful as the clients it brings in, and that was David's job. Farley won't be able to do it."

Diana nodded. "There has to be someone, though, Gina. Because if there isn't, you're looking at wearing Day-Glo orange every day for the rest of your life."

A fate worse than death. I shuddered.

After lunch, I headed for the funeral home. By myself, since Diana had to get back to work, and since she didn't really want any part of picking out David's coffin and funeral music, anyway.

I didn't want any part of it myself, but someone had to do it, and I wasn't about to leave it to Jacquie. If I did, David might go in the ground to the tunes of Dropkick Murphys and *Going Out In Style*. Which I suppose was nothing more than he deserved for taking up with someone barely out of her teens, but I couldn't bring myself to let it happen. Besides, I was still his wife, and if it happened that way, someone might blame me for it.

So I walked into my appointment with the funeral director aiming for maturity and good taste. Only to have all my good intentions go straight to hell when I came face to face with my stepchildren.

That was the first time I'd seen them in a year, when we'd all been at my mother-in-law's funeral.

As I had told Detective Mendoza, they weren't children anymore. Krystal was twenty-nine, dressed in a black power-suit with a pencil skirt and four inch heels. Her hair, a natural dirty blond, was bleached to the consistency of straw, and teased into a high bun on the back of her head. I'd seen that same look in the mirror this morning. It was what had necessitated the trip to the spa.

Kenny was dressed down, in black jeans and a T-shirt under a blazer. The blazer was leather, and he was wearing snakeskin cowboy boots. Both of them eyed me with disfavor through identical, ice-blue eyes.

David's eyes.

"We'll take care of this," Krystal informed me.

I smiled, or perhaps it would be more accurate to say I showed teeth. "I'm so sorry for your loss."

Krystal's eyes narrowed. "Like I said, you're not welcome here."

"I made the appointment," I reminded her.

"He was our father!"

"And he was my husband."

"Not for long," Kenny muttered.

I turned to him. "Be that as it may, as of yesterday we were still married. This is my responsibility. Not yours." And certainly not Jacquie's.

"You've done enough!" Krystal informed me.

Kenny added, "More than enough!"

They'd always been close, and looked more like twins than siblings born three years apart. Same blond hair— Kenny had bleached his, too—same blue eyes, same narrow face and delicate features, and same pouty bottom lip. Same nasty attitude, as well.

"I guess you've heard the news," I said. "The police think David's accident wasn't an accident after all."

"That's why we're here," Krystal said, sticking her hands on her hips. Her nails were an inch long and blood red. "If you think that after murdering our father, we'll let you arrange his funeral—"

"—you've got another think coming!" Kenny said.

They nodded in unison.

"That's ridiculous," I told them, even though my mouth was so dry I had a hard time getting the words out. Rage, mostly. And shock. It was one thing for the nasty, suspicious mind of Detective Mendoza—the professional crimebuster—to suspect me of murdering my husband, but I hadn't thought anyone who knew me would leap to that conclusion. "I had nothing to do with what happened to David. Why would I kill him?"

"You only married him for his money," Krystal said, tossing her head. Since her hair was gathered into that birds-nest bun on the back of her head, it swayed and almost fell. She put up a hand to steady it. "Now that you're losing the money, you had no reason to keep him alive."

It wasn't like I'd been keeping him alive up until this point. He'd been doing a pretty good job of that all on his own. And I hadn't married him for his money, either. Although I won't deny that the amount of cash he'd lavished on me during our courtship had done its part to woo me.

"Speaking of money—" I said, eyeing Kenny.

He bristled defensively. "What?"

"What are you doing these days? Krystal's still working in the music industry, right?" I glanced at her. She didn't deny it. "But what about you?"

"I'm a bartender," Kenny said.

"Is there a lot of money in that?"

He shrugged. I took that to mean no, there wasn't.

"I suppose you have an alibi for last night?"

"I was working," Kenny said, not without a glance at Krystal.

"And you?" I asked her.

She sniffed. "I'm not telling you anything."

"That's fine. Just be prepared to tell the police." She'd probably like Detective Mendoza. He might like her, too. Last time I heard, she was still unattached, and just the right age for him.

"The police won't suspect *us*." She tossed her head again. The birds-nest bun swayed.

"I don't see why not," I said. "I'm sure you could use the money. And he was planning to marry a girl younger than both of you. That had to be embarrassing. Not to mention that he might change his will in her favor and leave you with nothing."

"He wouldn't do that," Kenny said, glancing at Krystal.

She added, "He didn't when you married him."

"He was thirty-five then. Now he's in his fifties, and bedding a twenty-five year old. Who knows what he'd promise her. She wasn't with him for his good looks and stamina in bed."

"You don't know that," Kenny said.

Actually, I did. Or at least I knew about the stamina. Unless he popped a pill first, David couldn't keep it up long enough to have a normal session between the sheets. And believe me, he hadn't liked being dependant on that little blue pill.

Come to think of it, maybe that had been part of Jacquie's appeal. He could take the pill before leaving work, and keep an erection through dinner and through having sex with her. She might not even know he needed it. Unlike me, who knew he couldn't get it up without pharmaceutical aid. Something which probably made sex with me a turnoff for him. The fact that I knew he wasn't a young, virile stud anymore.

Maybe he hadn't been planning to marry Jacquie after all. It wasn't like he could keep a dependence on Viagra quiet once they shared the same bathroom.

More to the point, maybe he hadn't gotten tired of me so much as he'd wanted someone who didn't know quite so many intimate details about his failings. Jacquie probably fawned over him. She probably told him he was the most wonderful man in the world. I'd stopped doing that a long time ago. Living with someone 24/7 for a couple of decades has a way of ripping those rose-colored glasses right off.

But that was neither here not there—other than that I will admit it made me feel better to realize that maybe he hadn't found me lacking after all. It wasn't that I'd cared all that much, or like it even mattered anymore, but still, the realization lifted a burden from my shoulders I hadn't been aware I'd been carrying.

And it made the smile I turned on Krystal and Kenny almost genuine. "I was your father's wife for eighteen years. We were still married when he died. I've earned the right to bury him. If you'd like to stick around to make sure the service is acceptable to you, that's fine with me. But I'm not leaving."

They exchanged a glance, and for a second I thought they were going to refuse to cooperate. But eventually

Krystal tossed her head. "I'm not going anywhere."

"Me neither," Kenny added, ungrammatically.

"Then I guess we're in this together." I sat down in one of the somber navy armchairs and crossed one leg over the other. Kenny gave me an appreciative glance, until Krystal elbowed him. They settled down a few chairs away.

Mr. Anselm Howard, the funeral director, came to the lobby and retrieved us a few minutes later, and we started our tour of the facility, which ended in his office. With Krystal and Kenny's help, the appointment took twice as long as it would have otherwise. They objected to every suggestion I made. If I mentioned a cherry wood casket, Krystal wanted mahogany and Kenny blue steel. And if I mentioned carnations, Krystal wanted lilies and Kenny "something peppy, like... I dunno... those yellow things with the black middles?" My suggestion of traditional church music—*Amazing Grace* and *How Great Thou Art*—was vetoed in favor of contemporary Christian offerings.

But he'd been their father, and I wanted them to be happy, so I let them have their way, overall. The music was contemporary—with some modern renditions of older songs—and the flowers a compromise of everything we'd talked about, including a blanket of daisies that would drape over the mahogany casket.

"Thanks for your help," I said insincerely when it was all over and we parted ways on the front steps.

Krystal sniffed. "Don't think this means we like you."

"Of course not." I was under no such illusions. They hadn't liked me for the past eighteen years; I had no reason to think they'd start now. Especially if they thought

I'd had something to do with their father's death. "I'll see you Friday."

I didn't wait for them to answer, just walked down the steps and over to my car. When I drove out of the parking lot, they were both folding themselves into a sleek, black BMW. Krystal was driving, so I guess it must be hers.

Back at the house, I kicked off the heels and peeled out of the gray dress. I hadn't liked it last year, when I wore it to David's mother's funeral, and I liked it less now. After Friday, I might just donate it to Goodwill.

Barefoot and dressed in yoga capris and a pink camisole—one that David had said made me look twenty-eight back when I was a blonde, but which probably clashed badly with my new strawberry red hair—I made my way back downstairs and to the kitchen, where a bottle of Cabernet was waiting. It wasn't even four o'clock, but after the day I'd had, I figured I deserved it.

However, the powers that be must have had other plans. I hadn't even gotten the cork out when the doorbell rang. I put bottle and corkscrew down, and padded in the direction of the front door.

When I pulled it open, and found myself looking at Jaime Mendoza—for the third time in less than six hours—I was tempted to slam the door in his face.

And the thought must have shown, because he grinned. "Hello again, Mrs. Kelly."

I sighed. "Detective."

"I have a few more questions, if you don't mind."

"Would it matter if I did?" I opened the door and

stepped aside. "Come in."

I led the way into the formal living room—because I didn't want him to see the wine bottle on the kitchen counter and think I had a drinking problem—and sat down on the sofa. Mendoza took the chair opposite. When I crossed one leg over the other, he didn't even blink.

"This won't take long," he told me, pulling a battered notebook from the inside pocket of his suit jacket.

"I'm not busy," I answered. "I'm just sitting here waiting to bury my husband. Or waiting to be arrested. Whichever comes first."

He looked up, brows arching. "Did you do something I should arrest you for?"

"I didn't kill David," I said. "Although I know you think I did."

"I don't particularly think you did. I just think you might have."

If that was intended to make me feel better, it failed.

"I don't even know where he was last night." How could I cut his brake cables if I didn't know where he and his car were?

"Having dinner with friends. Celebrating his birthday."

Mendoza opened the notebook. I waited for him to lick the point of the pencil and start writing, but he didn't. "Mr. and Mrs. Farley Hollingsworth," he recited. "Mr. and Mrs. Harold Newsome. Mr. and Mrs. John Oliver. And Ms. Demetros."

"The Newsomes and Olivers are clients." And Mrs. Newsome and Mrs. Oliver did actually have first names, Mendoza's listing of them as appendages to their husbands notwithstanding. Mrs. Newsome was Heidi and Mrs. Oliver Gwendolyn, respectively. There was a time—before Jacquie, before David left me—that the three of us had been friends. We'd had lunch together and done volunteer work together and taken Zumba classes together at the Y.

And now they were dining with Jacquie.

"So Mr. Hollingsworth told me," Mendoza said.

"You've talked to Farley? How is he doing?"

"As expected," Mendoza said. "Shocked. In disbelief. Grieving. Can't imagine why anyone would want to kill his business partner. Mr. Kelly didn't have an enemy in the world."

He sounded just a touch sarcastic.

"Do you hear that a lot?" I asked.

"Every time someone's murdered," Mendoza answered.

"It's true, though. David really didn't have any enemies. If someone's investment went belly-up and they lost all their money, they'd be more likely to blame Farley than David. Although I haven't heard of that happening. And nobody kills someone else just because they beat them at golf."

Mendoza shrugged.

"I guess you've spoken to everyone by now," I added. "I don't suppose there's any chance Jacquie did it?"

Mendoza's mouth curved. "She doesn't have much of a motive. As you said, your husband was worth more to her alive. But she did have means and opportunity. She left the table between dinner and dessert, and didn't come back for what Mrs. Hollingsworth said was 'a long time.'"

He made air quotes with his fingers. "She might have had time to run to the parking lot, slide under the car, slice the brake cables, and run back inside."

I'd love it if she had, but unfortunately, I couldn't quite see it. "What was she wearing?"

"I didn't ask," Mendoza said.

Typical man. "Probably a dress. Something sexy and slinky." Something like what she'd been wearing every other time David had taken her to dinner. "Where did they dine?"

"Fidelio's," Mendoza said. "On Murphy Road."

I nodded. Definitely a dress. Something short and skimpy. Bare legs and high heels. "If she'd been crawling around under cars, her dress would have been dirty and her hair a mess. One of the other women would have noticed her looking disheveled when she came back."

And would have commented on it. I doubted Martha, Heidi, and Gwendolyn had taken to Jacquie. And not because they were feeling any loyalty to me. No, they were all trophy wives—except Martha, but she was secure in Farley's adoration—and Jacquie would have been their worst nightmare. If she could happen to me, she could happen to any one of them.

"No one mentioned that," Mendoza said, consulting his notebook. "Mrs. Hollingsworth assumed Ms. Demetros had been in the restroom touching up her makeup."

Then she'd surely not looked disheveled. And she probably hadn't had time to both cut the brake cables and touch up her makeup. "Damn," I said.

Mendoza's lips twitched. "Sorry, Mrs. Kelly."

He didn't sound sorry. "I don't suppose there's any point in asking what you thought of her?"

"Me?" He sounded sincerely surprised that I asked. "The same thing every other man who saw her thought, I suppose."

I grimaced. *Great.* "Not sure that's something you should tell the grieving widow."

"You asked. And you're not grieving."

Since saying I was grieving would be lying, I didn't. "How do you know?" I asked instead.

He used the pencil to point to my head. "That doesn't look like grief. That looks more like a statement."

"I can't wear red to the funeral, so I colored my hair instead?"

He shrugged. Very nicely, too. Good shoulders.

And I had no business noticing that, since he was roughly the age of my stepchildren.

"I started life as a redhead," I told him. "David liked me as a blonde, so I stayed blond for him. This morning I woke up and realized I didn't have to be a blonde anymore."

Mendoza nodded. "Can you tell me where you were yesterday?"

"All day?"

He nodded.

"But..." I bit back my objection that I'd only found out about the prenup in the afternoon; that until then, I'd had no reason to kill David. If Mendoza didn't know about that little wrinkle, I wasn't about to point it out to him. "Is it possible that the brake cables were compromised during the day?" I asked instead. "Wouldn't the accident have happened sooner?"

"The car was parked outside the Hollingsworth & Kelly offices for most of the day," Mendoza told me. "The parking lot isn't monitored. At five o'clock, Mr. Kelly drove directly to Fidelio's. The valet parked the car. The lot is a self-park as well as a valet-park, so anyone has access to the cars."

I nodded. "I'd been to Fidelio's. I knew the setup."

"The others arrived within the next twenty minutes. Ms. Demetros parked her own car. The Newsomes arrived separately, with both using the valet. Ditto for the Hollingsworths. The Olivers arrived together, and also used the valet."

So they'd all had cars in the lot, and they'd all had excuses, if they needed one, for going outside during the meal. "Did you ask the valet whether any of them went into the lot during dinner?"

"There were a couple of valets," Mendoza said, "and they both stayed busy. They couldn't say for sure one way or the other."

Too bad.

Mendoza eyed me. "Do you have a reason to think someone at the dinner wanted Mr. Kelly dead?"

Well, no. I just wanted to make sure he knew I wasn't the only suspect.

"If you know the setup," Mendoza said, and I grimaced. Maybe it would have been better not to tell him that, "you know that someone from outside could easily have accessed the lot while your husband was inside at dinner."

I was well aware of that. It was just a few months

since David and I had been to Fidelio's, for my fortieth birthday.

Mendoza twitched his pen over the notebook page. "If you'd give me a rundown of your whereabouts yesterday, Mrs. Kelly? Including last night after five?"

CHAPTER FIVE

I told him I had no alibi for last night between talking to Diana on the phone and his own showing up on my doorstep to tell me David was dead. Mendoza thanked me and left, and I headed back to the kitchen and my bottle of Cabernet. I needed it more than ever.

He had admitted that while David's brakes could have been tampered with during the day, while the car had been parked behind the Hollingsworth & Kelly building on Music Row, it was more likely any tampering had happened later, in the parking lot at Fidelio's Ristorante.

There were a couple of different reasons for this. Someone might have felt nervous about sabotaging someone's brakes in broad daylight in a well-trafficked area, in a parking lot surrounded by business buildings. There was no telling who might happen to come by, or who might be watching from out of an office window. The lot behind Fidelio's is secluded, and it was dark by the time David got there. Much safer to do that kind of damage at night.

Also, the drive from Music Row to Murphy Road had been on secondary roads during rush hour. There'd been a lot of other cars, and a lot of stop and go. David's brakes must have gotten a workout. It was Mendoza's opinion that if the brakes had been compromised at that point, it was likely they would have failed before David made it all the way to Fidelio's.

He also made the point that an accident in those circumstances was unlikely to be fatal. With bumper-to-bumper traffic and low speeds, failed brakes between Music Row and Sylvan Park were more likely to result in a fender-bender than death. And if someone had deliberately cut David's brake cables, a fender-bender probably wasn't the desired result. That was a lot of trouble to go to for very little payoff.

I think that was the first time it really sank in that someone had deliberately tried to kill David. I knew he was dead, and I knew the police thought it wasn't an accident, but until Mendoza said that, it hadn't felt real.

Someone had killed David.

The problem, I reflected, as I guzzled Cabernet with unladylike eagerness, was that even with that knowledge, I had no idea who would have wanted him dead. Sure, I might have joked that I did, but I certainly wouldn't have done anything to kill him. And I hadn't been kidding when I told Diana I wouldn't recognize a brake cable if one reached out and bit me. I'd be just as likely to cut the fuel lines, and end up with gasoline all over me.

Also, I'd been home last night, other than that quick trip to the liquor store—the one I had camouflaged as a trip to the grocery store when I spoke to Mendoza.

Heidi, Gwendolyn, and Martha weren't likely to know the difference between a brake cable and a fuel line, either. Not that either of them had a reason for wanting David dead. Nor their husbands. As far as I knew, the business was going well and everyone was happy.

Unless David had diddled one of the wives, and her husband had found out...?

Just a couple of months ago, I would have laughed at the idea. But that was before Jacquie. Now I was willing to acknowledge that if he had cheated on me with her, he might have cheated on me with someone else. Including someone I might consider a friend.

But if he had, he wasn't doing it anymore. I'd been following him around for weeks, and the only woman he ever saw—other than Rachel—was Jacquie. So why would a jealous husband want to kill him at this point?

Unless it was Jacquie's jealous husband, of course. I wondered whether Mendoza was looking into that possibility.

Or unless David had had an affair with someone else, and she was upset about being supplanted.

I tried to imagine one of my friends—former friends—sleeping with my husband, and couldn't. If either of them wanted to have an affair, surely they wouldn't pick another old fart just like their own husbands. They'd find some gorgeous young stud in his twenties or early thirties—someone like Jaime Mendoza—and get their money's worth.

For a moment or two—or three or four—I enjoyed the mental image of Detective Mendoza undressed and sprawled across a big bed: his hair rumpled, his skin glowing against cool cotton sheets, his eyes smoldering, and his grin wicked.

And then I derailed the train of thought before it could go any farther. Aside from his age—too young for me—he was most likely attached. If not actually married, then he probably had a girlfriend. At his age, and looking like that, I couldn't imagine he didn't have someone in his life. And I wasn't about to commit adultery, not even in the privacy of my own mind.

But yes, if I had wanted to cheat on David—or on Harold Newsome or John Oliver or Farley Hollingsworth—that's what I'd do. Find someone like Jaime Mendoza and make it count. I certainly wouldn't choose to cheat with someone who had anything in common with David. What would be the point?

This was all speculation, though. I had no proof, and not even a reason to suspect that David had cheated before he took up with Jacquie. And anyway, if he had, surely he wouldn't have invited her and her husband to his birthday dinner. Would he?

Which brought me back to the money. The money that was the only logical reason why anyone would want to do away with David.

I had the best motive of everyone, but I hadn't done it. Jacquie had no motive at all. Krystal probably made a decent living. The suit she'd had on this afternoon had been expensive, and the car she drove more so. Unless David had bought both for her—and I didn't recall that he had—she was obviously capable of keeping herself in style.

Kenny was a different story. He'd always drifted from

one thing to the next, looking for God knew what. His backbone, maybe. He'd dabbled in drugs in his teens, and David had had to bail him out more than once. He'd gotten kicked out of no less than two colleges for partying instead of studying. He'd never graduated with any kind of degree, so it was no wonder he couldn't get a decent job. Whatever settlement he was getting from David's will might make a big difference to him. And he'd probably know the difference between a brake cable and a fuel line, too.

He'd said he'd been working last night. He might have been telling the truth. I had no way of knowing, since I hadn't asked him where he worked.

If I called and asked, he'd probably refuse to tell me. But it was still fairly early. Not quite five o'clock. Maybe he hadn't left home yet.

Maybe I could catch him before he did, and follow him. And then I could call there and ask someone else whether he'd worked last night.

There was no time to waste, so I didn't change, just slipped my feet into a pair of shoes and headed out the door.

Kenny lived in a condo complex on Hillsboro Road, near Green Hills. David bought the apartment for him half a dozen years ago, before Kenny got kicked out of Belmont College for excessive partying.

It's an expensive area, but the condos were old and not very well maintained. They also weren't gated. I was able to drive right into the lot and find a parking space across from Kenny's building, where I could park and slide down in my seat and keep an eye on his door in the rearview mirror.

If memory served—and I hadn't been here since he moved in—Kenny lived on the second floor. There were two stories to each building, with four apartments on each floor: two facing the front of the building and two facing the back. The staircases were exterior. Because of the location—close to the universities and the hospital district—and the fairly reasonable prices, the complex was popular with students and young professionals, who couldn't afford anything better.

As cars came and went, depositing and picking up men and women in suits and jeans, I watched Kenny's door. It didn't open.

There were parked cars in the lot that could belong to him, but since I had no idea what kind of car he drove, I didn't know if any of them did. Or maybe he didn't have one. He'd been riding with Krystal this afternoon.

Hard to believe, in a town as lacking in public transportation as Nashville. Then again, there was a bus line right around the corner.

As dusk settled, the apartment windows stayed dark. I glanced at the clock. I'd been here an hour, and there'd been no sign of Kenny. He was either holed up inside, in the dark—not a very likely scenario—or he'd gone out before I got here.

Bummer.

I turned the key in the ignition and backed the convertible out of the space. I was just on my way out of the lot when I met a car coming in through the same fairly narrow gate. I and the other driver were less than four feet away from each other as we passed, and because I feared for my mirror, I glanced out. And stomped on the brake.

The other driver rolled past without glancing at me. I watched as he pulled into a parking space in front of Kenny's building and got out. And then I watched as he climbed the stairs and let himself in through Kenny's door. After a few seconds, the light went on in what I knew to be Kenny's kitchen.

I left the complex while I fumbled for my phone.

My first call was to the police switchboard in downtown. When the phone was answered, I asked to talk to Detective Jaime Mendoza and was transferred to homicide. There, another voice answered, and I asked for Detective Mendoza again.

"He's gone off duty for the night," the voice on the other end informed me.

"It's kind of an emergency," I said apologetically. "Or not really an emergency, I guess. Nobody's in danger or anything like that. But it's something he should know now, not tomorrow morning."

The voice hesitated. Or the person it belonged to did. "What's this about?"

"The Kelly homicide," I told her. "I'm Regina Kelly. The wife. Widow."

There was another pause. Then— "Hold, please."

I heard a click, and dead air. Then another few clicks. She was either transferring me, or hanging up.

Then there was a ringtone, cut short. "This is Jaime," a voice said.

"Detective?" There was music in the background. I

couldn't have sworn to it, but it sounded like the theme song to Scooby-Doo. But while Mystery, Inc. may have been appropriate entertainment for a detective, wasn't it a little juvenile?

He didn't say anything, and I was so busy trying to identify the music that I didn't realize immediately that he probably didn't recognize my voice. "I'm sorry. This is—"

"Mrs. Kelly." He sounded resigned. Or maybe reluctant was a better word.

"I'm sorry to bother you at home," I said.

"That's OK." His tone of voice made it very clear that it wasn't. And when he spoke again, to someone on his end of the line, I understood why. "Daddy won't be long, Elias. I'll get you your juice in a minute."

Argh. He was at home, with a child. And probably a wife somewhere around. Good thing I hadn't gotten past covering him with sheets in my fantasy earlier.

"I'm sorry," I said again. "I just wanted to tell you something."

"It couldn't wait until tomorrow?"

Argh. "No. Or probably not. Tomorrow might be too late."

"Too late for what?"

"I'm not explaining this right," I said. "I was sitting outside Kenny's apartment just now—"

"Why?"

"Looking for him. Because I thought he might not have gone to work yet."

"What did you want to talk to him about?"

"I didn't want to talk to him," I said. "I wanted to see where he worked."

There was a beat. "So you were sitting outside your stepson's apartment, waiting for him to go to work, so you could tail him there. Why?"

"Because I don't know where he works. And I wanted to know whether he worked last night. He said he did, but I thought he might be lying. So I was going to follow him there, and then call and ask someone whether he'd really been there last night—"

"Let me save you the trouble," Mendoza said, while the kids from Mystery, Inc. started talking behind him. "He works at Murphy's Law. It's a bar."

"I know that." Not only because Kenny had told me he was tending bar, but because I was familiar with it. And its location. "It's just a block from Fidelio's."

"I'm aware of that," Mendoza said. "I was there today. And before you ask, yes, Kenneth Kelly worked the evening shift last night. Five to closing."

Five to closing? "So he was a block away when David's car was sabotaged."

I waited for Mendoza to make some kind of sound to acknowledge my point. When he didn't, I drove it home. "He could have taken a five minute break to run down the street and cut his father's brake lines."

"Yes," Mendoza said, "but why would he?"

"I'm sure he needs money. He always needs money. David was making noises about cutting him off if he didn't settle down to keep a job longer than six months at a time."

"You didn't mention that earlier," Mendoza said.

"I didn't think about it." But it opened up new and interesting vistas. Vistas that drew me in completely. I pictured the scene last night: Kenny ducking out of the bar for a smoke break and hoofing it down the alley to Fidelio's, where he slithered under his father's car, cut the brake lines, and hoofed it back to Murphy's Law without anyone being the wiser.

"Is that all you wanted to talk to me about?" Mendoza's voice cut through my ruminations, and I came back to myself with a jerk.

"I'm sorry. No."

He sighed. It wasn't very loud, but I heard it.

"I'm sorry!"

"I heard you. Listen, Mrs. Kelly, I'm alone here with a thirsty five-year-old, so if you could hurry it up..."

I was tempted to stick my tongue out at the telephone. But since I figured he wouldn't have been rude unless he really did need to get back to the kid, I spoke fast instead. "I was sitting outside in the parking lot waiting for him to leave. But he never came out. So I gave up and started to drive home. And as I was exiting the condo complex, another car drove in. A big, rusty pickup truck with California plates."

"OK," Mendoza said.

"I got a look at the driver. It was my brother-in-law. Daniel."

He didn't speak.

"You said you'd spoken to him, right? Was he in California then?"

"I assumed he was," Mendoza said. I arched my brows. A pretty big assumption, wasn't it?

He couldn't have seen me, but when he continued, he sounded defensive. "I called him on his landline. And he answered. It seemed like wasted time and resources to have the local police check and make sure he was where he said he was."

"Well, maybe you should do it now," I said. "Because I'm pretty sure he's in Nashville at the moment. And if he drove here in the truck I saw, he didn't leave California this afternoon."

It takes a bit longer than four or five hours to drive from the West Coast to Nashville. I wasn't even sure he would have had time to fly here in the time since Mendoza spoke to him.

Mendoza sighed. "Anything else?"

"Yes. You should send someone over to Kenny's apartment to talk to Daniel. The sooner, the better. I don't think he noticed me, but I could be wrong about that. And anyway, if he's here, and he killed David, he probably won't stick around too long."

"I'm..."

"Home alone with a five-year-old. I know. Isn't there someone else who can go?"

"Yes," Mendoza sighed.

"Thank you."

"For what?"

"Being open to the possibility that maybe I didn't kill my husband. Will you do me a favor?"

"What?"

"Will you let me know what you find out? Whether that really was Daniel? Or whether I've totally lost my mind?"

Mendoza sighed again—deeper this time. "Yes, Mrs. Kelly. I'll let you know. But tomorrow, OK?"

"OK," I said. "Someone will go over there tonight, though. Right?"

"Yes, Mrs. Kelly. You can leave it to me."

"Thank you," I said. And then I hung up before I could exasperate him any more than I already had. And since I was out driving around anyway, and since I'd rather be doing this than sitting at home with my glass of wine and my thoughts, I turned the nose of the convertible in the direction of midtown and Jacquie's place. Might as well see how the other woman was spending her time.

By now rush hour was over, and driving was a breeze. It was less than fifteen minutes before I was parked in my usual spot outside Jacquie's building.

Yes, I had been there enough to pick out a usual spot. Unlike the first time I'd followed her home, when I'd ended up parking in a metered space on the street, I had since found a nice little loading dock down the street, where nobody bothered me this time of night. All the deliveries had been done for the day, and I had the place to myself. So I backed in, killed the engine and the lights, and pulled out the binoculars I kept in the glove box for these occasions.

Yes, I had gone to the trouble and expense of purchasing a pair of high-powered binoculars for these occasions.

You may think I'd gone a little overboard, and you may be right.

In my defense, I didn't actually look into the apartment. I couldn't have, even if I'd wanted to—and I didn't particularly want to. I knew what David and

Jacquie were doing up there; I didn't need to see them in action. And anyway, I was on the ground while the apartment was several stories above me, so I wouldn't have been able to see much anyway. Mostly it was just ceiling. I only saw people if they stood in front of the windows.

Today, someone happened to be standing in front of one of the windows. I trained the binoculars on her, and adjusted the sharpness.

It was Jacquie, and she was braced on her hands, looking down at the street. As I watched, she turned in my direction, and I slid down in my seat, heart jumping. But then I told myself she couldn't have seen me. Sure, my car was somewhat distinctive—a pale blue convertible—but she couldn't see me. Not in the dark.

Then I saw what she'd been looking at. A pickup truck rolled past me and came to a stop across the street from Jacquie's building. The horn honked once, and Jacquie lifted a hand before disappearing from the window. After a second, the light turned off upstairs.

I assumed she was on her way down, so I turned my attention to the truck. It was a nondescript dark pickup, black or blue or dark green, like ten thousand others driving around Nashville. It wasn't Daniel's truck, though. Too new, too shiny, and too well-kept.

I couldn't see the driver in the dark, and he—or she; let's not be sexist—didn't turn on the interior lights. Or light a cigarette or make a phone call or anything else, that might enable to me to catch a glimpse of his or her features.

Thirty seconds later, the door to the building opened,

and Jacquie came mincing across the street. I sharpened the binoculars and zoomed in on her.

I had plenty of time to stare. It took her a small eternity to cross the street. Her heels were easily four inches tall, and she was balanced on what looked like a one-and-a-half inch platform. The rest of her curvy little body was poured into a pair of jeans that rode low on her hips, and a skin-tight top that showed her belly button plus a lot of cleavage. Her boobs jiggled when she walked. Her hair was blown out, and her lips lacquered red. If she was mourning David, she did a good job of hiding it.

I glanced guiltily down at myself. It was years since my boobs had done anything that came close to jiggling. These days, they needed help staying up. And I had no room to talk about clothes inappropriate for mourning, since I was wearing pink with sequins. If Jacquie was on her way out to drown her sorrows in a pitcher of margaritas with her girlfriends, who was I to judge? I only wished I had girlfriends of my own to share a pitcher of margaritas with.

I watched each agonizingly slow step across the street and around the truck to the passenger side, and it was when she opened the door and the ceiling light came on, that I got my first look at the driver.

Not female. A young man with dark hair.

The same young man I'd seen come out of this building once before, just before David went in.

The interior light went out again when Jacquie closed her door, and they pulled away from the curb with a roar of the engine. The streets were fairly empty, so I gave them some time to get ahead of me before I turned my own lights on and followed.

I think I may have mentioned this before, but it's a lot easier to follow someone when there's a lot of traffic. When traffic is sparse, you have to stay much farther back so the people you're following don't see you. And because you have to keep a good bit of distance between your cars, you run the risk of losing your quarry.

In this case, I did. After only a block, they zoomed through a light on yellow. I got caught by the red, and by the time I got going again, the truck was nowhere to be seen.

CHAPTER SIX

I thought about calling Detective Mendoza, to tell him I'd seen Jacquie head out in the company of another man, dressed to kill, and did he think there was any chance that she had a jealous ex-boyfriend who might have killed my husband... but I figured I'd already exasperated him enough for one night, and besides, I didn't really want him to know I was following Jacquie around. So I figured I'd just go home instead, and finish my Cabernet and watch TV until I fell asleep.

But first I decided to take a tour of the neighborhood, just in case I'd missed the truck somewhere, and they'd parked and gone inside a building while I was lingering at the red light a few blocks back.

And that's when I hit pay dirt. There was a dark blue truck parked in the lot behind Rotier's—a little hole in the wall on Elliston Place, that is said to serve some of the best burgers in Nashville—and the hood was still ticking. I pulled into an empty parking space a few slots away, and got out. When I placed my palm flat on the front of the truck, the metal was still warm.

It might have been someone else's truck, but I figured it couldn't hurt to take a look inside. So I hitched my purse more securely over my shoulder and headed for the back door.

Here's the thing. I didn't grow up wealthy. When David met me, I was a struggling college student, waiting tables at night to make ends meet while I tried to keep up with the studying for a marketing degree. The color I'd used to turn my hair from red to blonde back then had come out of a box, because trips to the spa were out of the question. It was years—decades—since I'd been inside a dive like Rotier's, but walking through the door brought back memories. The low light, the dingy floor, the smells. The neon beer signs decorating walls covered in ugly 1970s paneling.

It was a narrow space. A row of booths against one wall and the bar against the other, with a line of small tables between the two. The waitresses were dressed in jeans and T-shirts, and so were most of the patrons.

I stopped just inside the door to let my eyes adjust to the gloom, and to see if I could see Jacquie and her date.

And lo and behold, there they were, in a booth in the corner. Jacquie had her back to me, but I recognized the guy. When I came in, he looked up, and then looked me up and down for a moment before turning his attention back to Jacquie. I wasn't sure whether to be flattered that he looked, or offended that he didn't look at my face, but since it was for the best that he didn't recognize me, I guess I should simply be grateful that he was a lout.

"Help you?" one of the waitresses asked.

The table next to Jacquie and her companion was

occupied, and so was the one on the next row. There was no way for me to get close enough to hear what they were talking about. The best I could hope to do, was keep an eye on them for a while.

I smiled at the waitress. "I'd like to order a hamburger to go."

"On French bread?" When I didn't answer immediately, she added, "It's our signature burger."

"That's fine," I said. I'd just have to do another twenty minutes on the elliptical tomorrow.

"With some sweet potato fries?"

I really shouldn't, not if I wanted to keep my girlish figure—and seeing Jacquie in those painted-on jeans and that skimpy top had brought home with a vengeance just how far beyond twenty-five I was—but that did sound good. And anyway, it was probably another specialty. I would offend her if I said no.

I threw caution to the wind. "Sure." An extra hour. But it would be worth it.

"I'll go put in the order. Why don't you have a seat at the bar while you wait?"

Why not?

I wandered over to the bar and scooted up on a stool. In the mirror, I could see the corner with Jacquie and her companion. She was leaning forward stabbing the table in front of him with her finger. He was leaning back with his arms folded across his chest.

Classic defensive posture. While hers was classic offensive. I saw her lips moving, but of course I had no idea what she said. Lip-reading isn't a skill I've cultivated. I could tell he didn't like it, though. He was pouting.

He was a good-looking guy, other than the pout. Young, of course. Jacquie's age, or maybe a year or two older. Dark-haired and brown-eyed. They might even be siblings.

"Get you something?"

The bartender's query dragged my attention away from the couple in the corner. "Sure. Um..." It didn't look like a place where the wine would be good. And anyway, I was driving. "Sweet tea?"

He nodded and moved away. A minute later he was back with a glass. "I'm waiting for a to-go order," I said. "I'll pay for it all together when the sandwich comes."

He just shrugged, so I assumed that was going to work.

In the minute or two I'd been busy elsewhere, the dynamics in the corner booth had changed. Now it was Jacquie's companion who was leaning forward, stabbing the table, while she was leaning back, pouting. Her folded arms pushed her breasts up and out, and I'm sure it wasn't an accident. The guy kept getting distracted from what looked like a tirade. Every so often his eyes would drop into her cleavage and he'd stop talking for a few seconds while he just stared.

"Friends of yours?" the waitress asked, and I jumped. She chuckled and put the bag with my hamburger on the counter in front of me. "Total's $10.91."

Not bad for a burger and fries. At Fidelio's, even the appetizers are in the fifteen-dollar range. And of course there are no burgers. "And the tea," I said.

She eyed it. "On the house. I don't feel like amending the bill." She took my credit card and turned to the register.

I waited until she'd finished punching in the numbers and had laid the receipt in front of me with a pen. And then I asked, "Do you know them? Have they been here before?"

She glanced over my shoulder. "The couple in the corner? I've seen them before, but it's been a while. His name's Nick."

I scribbled my name on the receipt and added a hefty tip, to cover both the drink and the information. "How do you know?"

"He wears a uniform sometimes. With a name patch." She took the receipt and glanced at it before sticking it in the cash drawer. "Thanks."

"No problem. Do you know what kind of uniform?"

"The Body Shop," the waitress said. Or maybe she said Body Shoppe.

"What's that? Gym? Or cars?"

"Cars. There's one over on Charlotte Avenue. He might work there."

He might. Or he could be from the other side of town, and just be hanging out in this neighborhood because of Jacquie.

I slid off the stool. "Thank you."

"Don't mention it," the waitress said and wandered off. I took my to-go bag and did the same.

The hamburger was delicious, and so were the sweet potato fries. I ate both with one hand while I drove home with the other, and there wasn't a single fry left by the time I got to Hillwood. I would have to up that time on the elliptical by another fifteen minutes. I was so full and happy I didn't even want the rest of the Cabernet. I just crawled into bed and went to sleep.

It wasn't until the next morning that I thought about what I'd discovered, and what it all might mean.

First of all, Daniel was in Nashville, and staying with his nephew Kenny. I had assumed Daniel was above suspicion, by virtue of being on the other side of the country—and obviously Detective Mendoza had thought the same thing—but now he was firmly in the mix. Either he or Kenny could have killed David, alone or together. They both stood to gain financially, and they both had opportunity and know-how. While I'm sure they loved David, neither had been particularly close to him. He'd been exasperated with them both, and their spending and inability to keep a steady job.

And Jacquie was already getting dressed up and stepping out with another man, not twenty-four hours after her fiancée was murdered.

Not only that, but they'd been going out before, too. Not for a while, the waitress had said. I wondered whether that 'not for a while' happened to coincide with Jacquie's relationship with David.

And Nick—whether he was her brother or former boyfriend or something else—worked at a car place. He'd definitely know where to find the brake lines in David's Porsche. He probably owned a pair of coveralls he could have worn to wiggle under the car in Fidelio's parking lot, while Jacquie was keeping David busy inside. As Detective Mendoza had pointed out, there was no reason to suspect the killer had been in the restaurant having dinner with David. He'd been suggesting that I might have been the guilty party, of course, but the same thing applied to Nick.

So was Nick acting on his own, or were he and Jacquie working together?

On his own, I decided, as I huffed and puffed on the elliptical. If they'd planned it together, surely they'd have had the good sense to make sure that Jacquie was married to David and would inherit the money before they did away with him.

So maybe Jacquie threw Nick over for David's money and position. And Nick had decided to take care of things before she married David and was lost to him forever.

Or at least lost to him until David died. And that might have taken some time. Years. Decades, even. David was more than twice Jacquie's age, but he was in good shape. He worked out, he played golf, he watched his diet. He would have lived another thirty years, God willing, if someone hadn't snuffed him out before his time.

I couldn't see the Newsomes or the Olivers as murderers, and Farley was better off with David alive and bringing in new clients. The idea of Martha crawling around under the Porsche was nothing short of ludicrous. Krystal had her own income and, as far as I knew, no grudge against her father. I suppose it was possible she'd do something stupid to help her brother, but I couldn't see her deliberately set out to murder David. She'd be more likely to float Kenny herself. She probably already did. And Jacquie wouldn't have killed David before she got her hands on his money.

That left Kenny, Daniel, and Nick as possible

suspects. Unless the killer was someone who hadn't even crossed my radar yet.

By now it was Thursday morning. David had died on Tuesday night. The first twenty-four hours had gone by without an arrest. I wondered whether that was good or bad. Don't they say that most crimes are solved in the first twenty-four hours?

Or maybe that's seventy-two hours? If so, Mendoza had until Friday evening around eight to come up with the killer. I guess I should be grateful he hadn't settled on the most obvious suspect and arrested me.

I hadn't told him about seeing Jacquie and Nick together. I'd thought about it, both last night and this morning, but I hadn't been able to bring myself to contact him. He already knew about Daniel; let him worry about that. I'd just go to the Body Shop on Charlotte Avenue myself, and see what I could find out.

I was on my way across the parking lot to the convertible when my phone rang. The number was vaguely familiar, but not one I could place immediately.

"Mrs. Kelly?" a voice said. Same thing there: vaguely familiar, but not someone I knew right off. "Anselm Howard at Boling & Howard Funeral Home."

Of course. "What can I do for you, Mr. Howard?"

"It's what I can do for you," Anselm Howard said. I arched my brows; not that he could see me. He must have realized on his own that the touch of levity was misplaced, because when he continued, he was back to business. "I wanted to let you know that your husband's remains were delivered this morning."

Oh. "Thank you." No problem with having the

funeral tomorrow, then.

"There was a bag of his personal effects included. I thought you might want to stop by and retrieve it."

I might do that. I hadn't actually thought about it—I guess I hadn't been as calm and collected yesterday as I imagined I'd been—but someone had to take care of things. Things like cancelling the utilities for the new apartment, and making sure the insurance company knew he was dead.

"I'll have the effects ready for you," Mr. Howard said. "Along with a preliminary copy of the death certificate. Once the original has been filed, you can request a certified copy from the vital records office."

I told him I'd be there in twenty minutes, and instead of heading toward Charlotte Avenue and the Body Shop, I headed toward Woodbine and the funeral home instead.

It didn't occur to me to go home and change first. When I walked in—still in my yoga pants and sneakers and a fitted T-shirt—Mr. Howard gave me a funny look, and that's when I realized that perhaps I should have put on something tasteful and black, like I'd worn yesterday.

"You caught me coming home from the gym," I said. "I thought I might as well stop by now, instead of going home and going out again later."

Mr. Howard nodded, but looked unsure. And I guess he must have felt my presence diminished the quality of his establishment, because he thrust the clear plastic bag filled with David's belongings at me. "Here." He didn't add, "Now go," but he might as well have.

"Thank you," I said, peering at it.

It was a good sized bag. I could see fabric, some of it

dark and woolen, some thinner and pale blue. Pants and shirt, I assumed. What David had been wearing when he died. There was a pair of black dress shoes at the bottom of the bag, and a jingle when I shook the plastic experimentally. Must be David's keys or loose change. Maybe both.

For the first time, it occurred to me to wonder what had happened to David's car. It must have been towed somewhere, I guessed, and someone must have looked at it, to have determined that the brake lines had been compromised... but what would happen to it now?

"I'm afraid I can't tell you that," Mr. Howard said when I asked. "I would recommend you inquire of the police. They would have arranged for it to have been towed."

That would necessitate another call to Detective Mendoza. Maybe I'd just wait until he called me—which he'd said he would, to tell me what had happened with Daniel—and I'd casually drop the question then. It wasn't like I cared about the Porsche. I had my own car. And besides, it was probably totaled anyway. If the accident killed David, it must have killed the car, as well.

Mr. Howard cleared his throat. "I'm sure you would like your husband to go in the ground appropriately dressed, Mrs. Kelly."

I suppose I would. Putting him in the coffin stark naked would be satisfying, but wrong. "You need something to bury him in, don't you?"

Mr. Howard nodded.

I glanced at the bag. "These clothes..."

"Destroyed."

Ah. Better not to think too hard about that.

"I'll find something and bring it to you," I said, seeing my trip to the Body Shop dwindling into the afternoon.

Mr. Howard inclined his head in something that was halfway between a nod and a bow. "Thank you."

I might as well get started. "See you later," I told Mr. Howard. He looked relieved as I walked toward the front door. I tried not to take it personally.

Once in the car, I opened the plastic bag and turned it upside down over the passenger seat. The heavy things tumbled out first: David's shoes, his keychain, his wallet. I had to shake the bag to get the clothes out.

As Anselm Howard had said, they were destroyed. The doctors must have cut them off David's body at the hospital. And they were stiff with blood. I pushed them onto the floor with my fingertips, fighting back a shudder of revulsion and an unexpected urge to cry. Poor David. I'd been angry with him, but nobody deserved to die like that.

Had he suffered? Or maybe—hopefully—he'd died on impact, and there hadn't been time for more than the realization that he was going to crash. And fear. I'm sure there'd been fear.

I wiped my eyes with the back of my hand—thank God for waterproof mascara—and picked up the keychain. There was a little blood on that too, but I girded my loins—or rather, my quivering stomach—and dealt with it.

There was the key to the Porsche, with the factory emblem on it. Useless now, most likely. The key to the Hillwood house, where I lived. And where David had lived up until a couple of months ago.

Keys to the office: the front door, David's own office, and the storage room where the hardcopies of the files were kept.

Three keys I didn't recognize. One, at least, must be to the new apartment. Maybe two. Maybe all three. Front door, apartment door, and mailbox.

There was only one way to find out. I'd have to go to David's apartment and see which keys fit where. And while I was there, I could pick out a suit and bring it back to Mr. Howard, as well.

But first I'd go home and take a shower. I look pretty good for forty-plus—and I intend to stay that way—but Mr. Howard was right: I shouldn't be walking around in my workout gear.

CHAPTER SEVEN

I got to David's apartment building just before eleven, lucked out and found a parking space on the street outside, and walked in to find a fifteen-year-old doorman behind a desk giving me the beady eye. "Can I help you, ma'am?"

"Not really," I told him in passing. "I know where I'm going."

If he hadn't called me ma'am, it's possible I might have been nicer, but no woman enjoys being ma'amed, and I wasn't so used to it yet that it didn't still rankle.

He jumped up and ran after me. "You can't go upstairs!"

"Of course I can." And he wasn't man enough to stop me. In my heels, I was taller than he was, and he wasn't old enough to shave yet. If he laid a hand on me, I could easily take him.

"I have to announce you!"

"The person I'm going to see is dead," I told him, and stopped him in his tracks. He rocked back on his heels. His eyes widened and his skin blanched, and for a second

I was afraid he'd faint.

"Dead?!" he squeaked.

I took a breath. Perhaps I was being too hasty, and too upset by the *ma'am*. I was being unkind to this poor young soul who was obviously overcome by the news. "My name is Regina Beaufort Kelly. David Kelly was my husband."

"Was?" The young man swayed.

"He passed away Tuesday night," I said.

"Mr. Kelly's dead? Upstairs?!" His eyes rolled upward, to the ceiling.

"Of course not upstairs. He's at the funeral home. I have to pick out a suit for him to wear when he's buried."

The young man looked faintly sick.

"I have his keys," I said, lifting them. "And a copy of the death certificate, if you'd like to see it."

"No." He shook his head, and kept on shaking it. "No, that's OK. I trust you. You... just go on up."

It seemed to be a day when men I encountered couldn't wait to get rid of me. Lovely.

"I'll do that," I said. "Thank you for your time."

He didn't answer, just staggered back to the desk and dropped into the chair. I got into the elevator and pushed the button for the top floor.

I'd never been to David's new place before. I'd driven by the outside, so I knew what the building looked like—big and expensive-looking, like a giant phallus pointing to the sky—but this was the first time I'd been inside. So far I was impressed. The doorman was barely out of high school and easily bowled over, but there was a doorman. The foyer was all granite and marble, and the elevator was a nice: industrial steel with lots of mirrors. It moved quickly and silently, with no jerking and not much illusion of speed. We ascended fourteen stories before I'd even realized it. The car came to a stop with the slightest of bumps, and the doors slid soundlessly apart. I stepped out into the hallway.

There were four penthouse apartments in David's building, one on each corner. I'm sure it's much more exclusive when there's only one, but the building was huge; it wasn't like one person could afford the entire top floor. Or would need that much space.

David's apartment was Penthouse 3, on the northeast corner. I inserted the most likely-looking key on the keychain into the lock and jiggled it. The lock tumbled, and I turned the knob and pushed the door in.

And... hot damn!

The place was gorgeous. If nothing else, David had had good taste in apartments.

The front door opened into a hallway that ran the length of the apartment. All the doors were on the left; the right was a flat gallery wall that, I was willing to bet, matched the wall in the mirror-image apartment next door. That way, the only shared wall with the other apartment was this interior hallway, while none of the actual living spaces butted up against one another.

The first door on the left was a coat closet. Nice and big. The next was a laundry closet. It must have come with the matching front-loader washer and dryer, since I doubted David had bought them. He probably had everything dry cleaned, including his socks and underwear.

After that came a lovely little half bath, with a marble vanity and fake orchid in a pot.

The master bedroom was next, down a separate hallway. Oversized, with a wall of windows looking out over downtown, and a master bath that would have looked at home on one of HGTV's Luxury Living segments. The closet was big enough to hold a square dance inside. David's wardrobe—and he did like to dress well—only took up half the space.

I looked around for anything of Jacquie's, but there was nothing I could see. If she'd been here—and I'm sure she had—she had left wearing what she'd arrived in.

I had to pick out a suit for David to wear tomorrow, but first I wanted to see the rest of the place. So I went back into the hallway and continued east.

The next room was the last room, and it didn't have a door. The hallway opened up into a gigantic living room/dining room/kitchen combination that took up an entire corner of the building. There were windows on two sides here: overlooking downtown to the north, and the Cumberland River and the Adventure Science Center to the east.

It was stunning, and would probably be even more fantastic at night, when all the lights were lit outside, outlining streets and interstates.

The kitchen was gourmet all the way. Stainless steel, granite, six-burner gas stove...

Wasted on David, who I'm sure didn't do his own cooking any more than he did his own laundry. A quick look inside the oversized fridge and walk-in pantry confirmed this supposition. The pantry held a box of instant oatmeal and one of microwave popcorn, along with a box of Cheerios. In the fridge was a half-empty container of almond milk, a six-pack of imported beer with a bottle missing, and a lot of bottled water. The only well-stocked thing in the kitchen was the wine-cooler.

The dining room set was all glass and chrome; very different from the heavy, dark wood in the house in Hillwood. And the sectional sofa was white leather with black piping. It faced a TV almost as big as the wall itself.

Looking around, I realized I had apartment-envy in a very big way. I love our house in Hillwood, and the idea that David might have been trying to take it from me in the divorce had filled me with worry and anger, but at the same time, I could totally get into something sleek and modern and sexy, like this. It must have made David feel very young and hip.

The kitchen had a built-in office area, and I sat down and pulled out the top drawer on the right. Pens and pencils, rubber bands and paper clips were jumbled together in an unholy mess. The drawer below had been intended for hanging files, but when I opened it, I saw that David had just tossed any mail he wanted to keep into the drawer unopened. The top envelope was from a bank, and not the bank where our joint accounts were housed.

I picked it up and slit the envelope. It contained a statement, and when I unfolded it, I realized that David had a few hundred thousand dollars sitting in an account I knew nothing about.

A few hundred thousand dollars I assumed he'd wanted to keep out of the divorce settlement.

I dialed Diana's number, of course, and when she answered, told her, "I'm at David's place. His new place."

There was a beat of silence. "What are you doing there?" Diana wanted to know.

"I'm thinking of moving in."

"Gina...!"

I rolled my eyes. "I'm kidding. The funeral home needs a suit to bury David in, and I had to go get one. And since I was here anyway, I figured I'd take a look around."

"Of course," Diana said. "Nice place?"

"Very." Part of me would certainly move in if I could. Unfortunately, the condo might not be mine. If the judge ruled for the prenup, I'd lose not only the condo, but the house as well.

I tried to imagine Kenny moving in here, and Krystal into my house in Hillwood, and shuddered. "Do you know anything about a brokerage access account at Second Community Bank? With a quarter million dollars in it? In David's name?"

"No," Diana said.

"It's not listed among the assets for the divorce?"

"No," Diana said. "Tell me about it."

I told her about it; where it was and what it said, and how I'd found out about it. "The balance was just under two-fifty at the end of the last statement cycle two weeks ago."

"Bastard," Diana said.

Yes, indeed. "He's hiding assets, isn't he? Just in case the judge throws out the prenup and I'm entitled to half of everything."

"Uh-huh," Diana said. "Send me copies of everything

you can find pertaining to that account, and to any others he may have had. If he had one, he probably had several. Send me anything that doesn't look familiar to you. Anything in David's name only. Or David's with someone else. Someone other than you."

I glanced around. "There's no office equipment here. No copier, no scanner, no fax machine. I can take pictures with my cell phone and send them to you. Or is it OK to take the paperwork out of the condo and back to the house? I can scan them from the office there."

"At the moment," Diana said, and she sounded ready to chew nails and spit them out, directly at Anton Hess, "everything David owns is yours. The judge hasn't ruled yet, and you're still married. Take them anywhere you want."

Excellent.

"I'll see what I can find," I told her, mentally rubbing my hands together. "I don't suppose you've heard anything about anything?"

Diana said she hadn't. "What about you? Anything new on your end?"

Rather a lot, actually. I told her about Jaime Mendoza stopping by yesterday afternoon, and my discovery that Daniel was in Nashville and not in California. "I called and told him. Mendoza. He said he'd look into it."

"Then I'm sure he will," Diana said.

"He said he was alone with a five-year-old."

"He has a son." Her tone of voice was a clear warning to stop asking questions. "Anything else?"

"After I spoke to him, I saw Jacquie having food and drinks with a guy named Nick. The waitress at Rotier's said she'd seen them together before. And I've seen the guy, Nick, come out of Jacquie's building once."

"Did you tell Jaime that?"

I told her I hadn't. "I'll slip it into the conversation the next time I talk to him. He sounded busy last night." Not to mention exasperated. I hadn't wanted to try his patience any further. "I figure I'll hear from him sometime today. He told me he'd let me know what happened when he spoke to Daniel."

"Then I'm sure you'll hear this afternoon," Diana said. "Get me that paperwork, Gina."

"Yes, ma'am." I don't know why I ma'amed her—she's only a couple of years older than me. It was probably the tone of her voice: brisk and businesslike. "I don't know how long it'll take. It depends on how much junk is in this drawer. And then I have to take the suit down to the funeral home, before I can go back home."

"Take your time," Diana said. "We're not going back in front of the judge for a couple of weeks. That'll give me plenty of time to dig into things." She sounded like she was looking forward to it.

I told her I'd get her everything as quickly as I could, and went back to digging through David's non-existent filing system.

Thirty minutes later I had statements not only for that account, but for a couple of others. David had a retirement account with almost a million dollars in it that I never knew existed, as well as a time deposit with another two hundred thousand. I had no idea where the money had come from.

Or rather, it had come from the business, obviously. I'm sure David had earned it, fair and square. He isn't the cheating type, not in that way. His salary was more than sufficient—obviously, since he'd managed to squirrel so much of it away without me noticing it was missing.

And now I had my explanation for why he never wanted me to take an active hand in any of the household finances. I would have been happy to do the budgeting and balancing—I'd been handling my own meager finances before David married me, and you can take my word for it, a college student putting herself through school by waiting tables, knows all there is to know about stretching a dollar—but David had had an accountant who took care of things so I didn't have to, and I didn't question it. I just took the allowance they gave me, and spent it. Now I wished I'd paid more attention.

But at least Diana knew about the extra money now. And David's trying to keep it hidden might be enough to make the judge throw out the prenup. At least I hoped so.

I tossed all the papers I wasn't interested in back into the drawer and took the stack I did want with me into the bedroom, where I placed it on the king sized bed before going over to the closet.

There was no paperwork here. I guess David hadn't lived in the apartment long enough to accumulate more than a drawer's worth of mail. I was surprised he'd had time for that much.

The suits were hanging in a neat row, color coordinated from black to gray and then to navy. David had never been a brown person. Same thing for the shirts: from black to white, via shades of purple and blue, with the occasional pink or pale yellow thrown in for good measure. Some were discretely striped, but most were solid. The ties had a built-in rack of their own, and so did the shoes.

For a second, I felt overwhelmed—how do you choose an outfit for your husband to wear into the ground?—but then I told myself it didn't matter. He wouldn't know the difference anyway. And we weren't planning to have an open casket visitation. As Anselm Howard had pointed out, delicately, David hadn't died peacefully in his sleep.

In the end, I went with a tasteful, charcoal gray suit— the same one David had worn when he told me about Jacquie—with a deep purple shirt and checked tie. I grabbed a pair of black socks and shoes, and hesitated for a moment over the underwear drawer. Did Mr. Howard expect me to bring underwear?

It wasn't like the suit would chafe without it, under the circumstances.

Then again, better to bring something he didn't need, than for him to need something I didn't bring. I pulled a pair of black briefs out of the drawer and added them to the pile.

And then I gathered up the clothes, and the paperwork, and my purse, and left David's love shack.

I had planned to drop off the clothes with the funeral home's front desk and beat a hasty retreat, but when I walked in, Anselm Howard was right there in the lobby, saying goodbye to another grieving family. A middle-aged mother and two grown children, all of them with swollen, red eyes and quivering lips, clutching tissues.

A far cry from Krystal, Kenny, and myself yesterday.

I averted my eyes, feeling guilty. Both about seeing their grief, and about not showing enough of my own.

Mr. Howard sped them on their way and then turned to me, his eyes on the bag. "Is that for me?"

I nodded, extending it. "Suit and shirt, socks, shoes, and underwear. I wasn't sure whether you needed that, but..."

"Better safe than sorry," Mr. Howard said. He gestured me to follow him through the door at the end of the lobby.

I did, although I had no idea why. My heels clicked on the concrete floors as we headed down the hallway, bypassing the offices, until Mr. Anselm pushed open a set of double, steel-reinforced doors at the end of the hall. Frigid air rushed out, and my skin prickled. A sickly sweet odor was almost, but not entirely, obscured by the smell of chemicals.

I stopped dead, if you'll pardon the expression. Mr. Howard stopped too, and looked back at me. When I didn't speak, he said, "I thought you might want to see Mr. Kelly. Since the service tomorrow will be closed casket."

Oh, God.

"Do I have to?"

Mr. Howard blinked. "No. It's optional."

But if I didn't, he'd wonder why. Most wives probably wanted to say goodbye to their husbands. That was probably what the sobbing family in the lobby had just done.

"Is he..." I hesitated, "presentable?"

"As presentable as we could make him," Mr. Howard said. "With a violent death, there is sometimes visible damage. That can't be helped. But we cleaned Mr. Kelly up as best we could. I wouldn't recommend changing tomorrow to an open casket viewing, but I believe you won't see anything too disturbing."

Wonderful.

There was no real way around it, though—not without looking like a very bad wife—and David's and my private life, including the fact that we'd been separated when he died, wasn't really any of Mr. Howard's business. So I squared my shoulders and marched forward, into the cold smell of the embalming room.

In the end, the experience didn't turn out to be quite as bad as I'd feared. The room had a couple of big steel tables in the middle of the floor, and David was lying on one, covered by a sheet. Mr. Howard dropped the bag of clothes on the floor next to the table and folded back the top of the sheet. Or rather, the bottom. A pair of naked feet sporting a toe tag appeared.

Mr. Howard clicked his tongue and put the sheet back, but not until I'd seen David's name on the tag.

Then the process was repeated on the other end of the table. David's head appeared, with silver hair brushed back from his face and his complexion faded to a sickly gray.

Other than that, he didn't look too bad. At least not the parts of him I saw. Mr. Howard only folded the sheet back to just below his chin, so I guess most of the damage was farther south.

There was some bruising on David's forehead, mottling the skin; I guess maybe he'd hit his head against the steering wheel or the windshield in the collision. His eyelids were sunken and his lips thin and pale, but other than that, he looked like my husband.

He didn't look like he was sleeping. I've heard people say that, and it isn't true. He looked dead. Quite definitely dead. And the part of him that had been David, was gone. There was no spark inside, to animate the features or raise and lower the chest under the sheet.

"Here."

It wasn't until I glanced over, and saw that Mr. Howard was extending a box of tissues, that I realized I was crying.

"Thank you." I took one and dabbed my eyes.

"I'll give you a moment alone," Mr. Howard said, turning away.

"No!"

He turned back, looking surprised, and I added, a bit more calmly, "That's not necessary. I've... seen enough."

And the last thing I wanted, was to be stuck here by myself with the bodies. There was another corpse on the other table, covered by a sheet—probably the one the grieving family in the lobby had visited.

Mr. Howard looked doubtful, but said, "If you're sure."

"I'm positive, thank you." I took one last look at David, and turned away.

"My pleasure," Mr. Howard said. I could hear the rustling of the sheet behind me as he re-covered the body.

"Let me show you out."

"I can manage." And he probably wanted to get David dressed. I knew I'd like him to. "Through the double doors and straight down the hallway, right?"

Mr. Howard nodded.

"I'll see you tomorrow," I said.

He inclined his head. And waited beside the table, with his hands folded, until I was out of the room. The last thing I saw, when I turned in the doorway, was what looked like Mr. Howard praying over David's profile.

CHAPTER EIGHT

I had to get home to scan the various account statements to Diana so she could get to work proving to Judge Miller that David had been hiding assets from the estate. But on my way across town, the route took me fairly close to Music Row and the Hollingsworth & Kelly offices, and it occurred to me that no one might have told Rachel and Farley about the funeral arrangements.

I knew they knew about David's death, because Detective Mendoza had spoken to Farley and Martha. I assumed he'd spoken to Rachel, as well, although he hadn't specifically mentioned it, and I hadn't specifically asked. But unless they were in communication with Krystal or Kenny—and I doubted it—nobody might have told them when and where the memorial was to take place.

I turned the car in a northerly direction and headed toward Music Row.

I hadn't been inside the Hollingsworth & Kelly offices for months, maybe as much as a year. I had no real business there, and the knowledge that Rachel didn't like me, made me reluctant to invade her domain. In fact, David had explicitly asked me not to, because it made her crabby for the rest of the day whenever I went there. Since I'd had a look at her by that point, and knew that she wasn't a threat to my marriage, I was fine with it. I didn't particularly care about the business, or only insofar as it provided David's—and by extension my—income.

It still looked the same. A cozy lobby with sleek, gray sofas and vintage black and white photographs of the country music greats. Hank Williams Senior, Patsy Cline, Jim Reeves, Johnny Cash. David and Farley had never worked for or with any of them, but the pictures gave the impression they had. They also gave the impression that Hollingsworth & Kelly had been in business a very long time, when in fact, David and Farley had started the company twenty years ago. Patsy, Jim and Hank were all dead by the mid-1960s, which was about the time David and Farley started kindergarten.

The front door was hooked up to a bell that rang in Rachel's office, which guarded the sanctuary of David's office, and it didn't take long at all before she walked out into the lobby.

She didn't look good. She had always been a bit frumpy, but now her round face was paler than usual and her makeup had smudged. She was clutching a tissue. "I'm sorry..." she began, and then she recognized me and stopped mid-apology. "Mrs. Kelly."

The words sounded like they were squeezed out between two millstones.

"Rachel. I'm sorry for your loss." She seemed to be

taking it harder than me. And I'm sure that's why the look she gave me was full of dislike.

"I wanted to tell you about the funeral," I added. "I wasn't sure anyone had."

She blinked. "No." I guess maybe she'd expected me to be rude right back.

"The visitation is tomorrow at ten. The service is at eleven. The graveside service is at one. The funeral home is Boling & Howard in Woodbine. The same place where David's mother's funeral was last year."

Rachel nodded.

"He'll be buried at Spring Hill Cemetery. Where his mother is buried. And his father."

Rachel nodded.

"There's a reception afterward, at the house. Three to five."

Rachel nodded.

"I should probably tell Farley myself." I glanced at the door to the inner sanctum. "Is he here?"

Rachel hesitated. For a second, I wondered whether she'd refuse to let me go in. But then she nodded. "I'll take you back."

It was tempting to tell her I knew the way—which I did—but I squashed the impulse. This was her domain. David's home had been mine. I could let her have this. "Thank you," I said.

She led the way into the bowels of the building, her sensible heels clicking on the floor. I followed, my less sensible heels clicking also, while I wondered why Rachel didn't make a little more out of herself.

She wasn't a bad-looking woman. A few years older

than me, and quite a few pounds heavier, but she had nice, thick, still-brown hair that she kept pulled back from her face in the most unattractive way imaginable for someone with a round face who's carrying an extra forty pounds. It wasn't a bad face, though, when she wasn't scowling at me. She'd probably been a very pretty girl. Her eyes were big and green—they only seemed small because her face was puffier than it ought to be. And because she didn't use any makeup to make them look bigger, I suppose. But she had good skin, and good hair, and good teeth, when she bothered to show them. It was a shame that she spent her life in ugly business suits with an ugly haircut to top them off.

Naturally I didn't say so. It was none of my business why Rachel chose to live her life the way she did.

She stopped in front of Farley's door and knocked. I waited for her to push the door open and announce me, but she waited until he'd told her to come in, and then she opened the door and stuck her head through. "Mrs. Kelly is here to see you."

There was a beat. Then— "Gina?" Farley's voice said. He sounded shocked.

"Yes, Mr. Hollingsworth." Rachel stepped aside and waved me in.

"Thank you," I told her and crossed the threshold. She closed the door behind me with a soft click.

There are only the three offices in the building. David's and Rachel's on one side of the hallway, and Farley's on the other, along with the records room. He doesn't want an administrative assistant, and I guess he doesn't really need one. David had a social schedule that kept Rachel busy. Golf and power lunches with clients, and meetings with people he was trying to woo into becoming clients. Business dinners and charitable events. And of course Krystal and Kenny and Jacquie and me.

While Farley pretty much spent his life right where he was now: behind a big cherry wood desk piled high with papers and a computer, before going home to his wife every day at five o'clock.

He blinked at me through wire rimmed glasses. Rachel had told him I was here, and I couldn't imagine that she was someone who regularly pulled his leg with inaccurate information, but he seemed surprised to see me. "Gina?"

"Hi, Farley," I said. "Do you mind?"

I gestured to one of the two visitors chairs in front of the desk.

"No. Of course not. Sit down."

I did, after moving a pile of papers off the chair and onto the floor. Farley watched me sit and then kept watching.

"I stopped by to tell you about David's funeral," I said when it became obvious that he wasn't going to speak first. "I wasn't sure you were in contact with anyone who had that information."

He shook his head.

"Kenny and Krystal and I went to the funeral home yesterday afternoon. The service is tomorrow." I repeated the specifics I had told Rachel.

"So soon," Farley said.

Was it? David had been dead three days. The police

were finished with him, or so I assumed, since they'd released the body to Boling & Howard. I didn't feel like I was rushing to get him in the ground. Anselm Howard had asked whether we'd like to try to have the funeral this week, or wait until after the weekend, and it was the one thing we'd all agreed on: we wanted to do it sooner rather than later. Why wait?

"The reception is at the house afterwards. Three to five."

Farley nodded, but didn't say he'd be there. I wondered whether he would be, or whether he and everyone else thought I'd murdered David, so they were shunning me. I might be sitting there all alone, with a catered spread for fifty, while everyone David had known gave me the cold shoulder.

"I don't suppose you have any idea who would have wanted David dead?"

Farley looked startled. He opened his mouth, and then closed it again. And then he took his glasses off and polished them on a cloth he had lying on the desk. I have no idea why he didn't just start wearing contacts—David did—instead of the glasses that made him look like an old fart.

Then again, it wasn't just the glasses making Farley look like an old fart; it was everything else, as well.

"Was anything going on here at work?" I pressed. "A disgruntled client? Someone who lost money and blamed David? Did David diddle someone's wife?"

Farley looked nauseous. "Gina..."

"Someone must have had a reason to want to get rid of him."

"You," Farley said.

"Other than me."

Farley shrugged. Either he couldn't think of anyone, or he wasn't going to share his thoughts with me.

"What happens to the business now?" I wanted to know.

Farley's voice was calm. "David's interest in the business reverts back to the business."

I already knew that, but I wanted to see his reaction. "So you get it?"

He nodded.

"How nice for you."

Farley's pale face flushed. "I don't appreciate your tone, Gina."

"I'm sorry," I said, not bothering to sound it, "but it *is* nice for you."

Farley put his glasses back on his face and leaned forward across the table. "David was my oldest and best friend. I would never have murdered him for his share of the business!"

It was tempting to ask what *would* have made Farley murder his oldest and best friend, if not the controlling interest in the business, but I knew he hadn't meant it that way. Before I could say anything, however, Farley continued. "The business probably won't last long without David. I'm not a rainmaker. I handle the investments. Without someone to bring in new clients, we'll die within a couple of years, most likely."

"That's sad."

Farley shrugged. "It's life. Of course, I might be able to find someone else, but it won't be the same. It won't be a partner."

No, it wouldn't. He'd have to hire his rainmaker: someone who could go out and press the flesh and bring in the cash, the way David had done. Farley didn't have it in him. And he was right, as I had been all along: he was better off with David alive.

He tilted his head to look at me, vaguely birdlike. The light from above hit the lenses of the glasses and made them opaque. "You're not meddling in the investigation, are you, Gina?"

"Of course not," I said. All I'd done was order a hamburger to go from the restaurant that makes the best hamburgers in Nashville yesterday. It could have happened to anyone. And for my snooping through David's mail in the penthouse... well, that had nothing to do with his murder, but everything to do with my divorce.

"Did you happen to know that David had a second set of bank accounts and an IRA he never told me about?"

Farley blinked. "I'm afraid I have no idea what David told you about and what he didn't, Gina."

Oh, smooth. And it was all the confirmation I was going to get. I got to my feet. "It was good to talk to you. I hope to see you and Martha at the service tomorrow. And at the house afterwards."

Farley got to his feet, as well. "It was good to see you too, Gina. Take care of yourself."

He didn't offer to walk me out. And I noticed he still didn't commit to attending either the funeral service or the reception.

Rachel was nowhere to be found when I walked out of

Farley's office, so I found my own way to the front door. Her Toyota wasn't in the lot, either, so instead of reiterating my hope that I'd see her tomorrow, I just got in my car and started driving.

I had to get home to scan Diana the statements for David's hidden accounts, so she could start working on them. And I suppose I could have done it from the office. There was plenty of office equipment there: scanners and fax machines and computers. But it felt safer to do it from home, even if it would take longer. And I figured once I got there, I wasn't going to want to leave again immediately, so instead of going directly home, I drove clear across town again, over to Charlotte Avenue and the Body Shop. Might as well take care of that while I was out. My car could use an oil change, anyway.

I don't usually use quick lubes for my oil changes. David had a mechanic he liked to use, who charged a lot more, but who was experienced in dealing with foreign cars. So it was a while since I'd been through a quick lube.

The Body Shop looked much like I expected it to. It was a long building with a half dozen bays. Inside, men were busy changing tires and using blow torches. Two of the bays were dedicated to quickie oil changes. I pulled in behind an older model Chevrolet that was waiting in line, and looked around.

There were five cars ahead of me. And a dark blue truck parked in the corner of the lot, out of the way of the line of cars, with a couple of others.

As the line crept slowly forward, I determined that Nick was here, and that he worked in the bay on the right. As the line split into two closer to the building, I positioned myself in that line, and waited. Eventually, the car in front of me drove into the bay, and I moved up into first position. And that's when Nick noticed me.

He was standing there talking to the driver of the Volvo in front of me. Probably a woman, because he was smiling and leaning on the top of the window. And then he looked up, and froze. The smile slid right off his face.

After a second he pulled it together, and went back to talking. And he went to work doing whatever he was supposed to do, under the car and under the hood, but he kept shooting glances in my direction. I couldn't be entirely certain it was my presence that had rattled him, but there wasn't anything going on behind me that might account for the frequent looks.

When the Volvo got the go ahead to leave and maneuvered slowly out of the bay and into the sunshine on the other end of the building, I prepared to move forward. But then Nick walked away, toward the little office and waiting room beside the next bay. I hesitated with my foot on the brake.

He disappeared inside. A minute passed. I could sense restlessness in the drivers behind me. The guy in the Lexus directly behind mine was frantically texting on his phone.

After a minute, a man came back out of the office and began waving me inside the bay. It wasn't Nick.

I rolled down my window. "What happened to the other guy?"

"Lunch break," the new guy said. He was older than Nick, approaching my age, with a bald head and a beer gut under the overalls. His name patch said Bud.

"Whatcha need done?"

"Um... oil change?"

"Full service or basic?"

"Oh. Um..." Full service sounded like it would take longer, and so give me more time to ask questions. But if Nick wasn't here, I should probably just cut my losses and get home. "Basic."

"Turn the car off and pop the hood," Bud said.

I did, and as he started tinkering with things, I looked out the rearview mirror. And saw Nick skulking across the parking lot to his truck. As I watched, he got in, reversed out of the parking space, and headed out of the lot. The last I saw of him, was when he took off down Charlotte Avenue in a cloud of exhaust. And I'm not entirely sure, but I think he might have given me the finger.

The insult added to the injury came after the oil change was complete and Bud had processed my credit card. He handed it back through the window with a clipboard and a pen for me to sign the receipt. And when I had, he said, "No offense, lady. I don't know you from Adam."

Or Eve, as the case may be. "But?"

"But ain't you a little too old to be chasing after Nick?"

I blinked. The sheer audaciousness of the question took my breath away. Not only that he asked it, which was rude in and of itself. But that he called me old, not to mention that he thought I was chasing after Nick. Romantically, I assume.

I sputtered, but before I could speak, Bud continued.

"I mean, you're not bad-looking, for an older broad. I'd throw you a bang."

"Big of you," I said, my voice half-choked. As if I would ever—ever!—have anything to do with someone like this. *Ever!* "But—"

"But Nick's taken. And no offense, lady, he ain't gonna throw over that sweet little piece of tail he's got for you."

"I thought Nick's piece of tail dumped him for someone else," I said.

Bud shrugged. "That's off. The old dude died."

The old dude, as in my husband.

"That's too bad."

"Not for Nick," Bud said.

Famous last words.

"Thank you," I told Bud.

"Sure." He winked. "You let me know about that bang, y'hear?"

When pigs fly.

I forced a smile. "I'll do that."

And then I drove away from there as if the bats of hell were on my tailpipe. Bud, I'm sure, was laughing.

CHAPTER NINE

All I wanted by the time I got home was to open a bottle of wine and crawl into bed. After I sent the various bank statements to Diana, naturally.

However, such was not to be. When I came up the driveway, I saw I had company. A nondescript gray car was parked at the bottom of the steps. It might have belonged to anyone, except for the couple of extra antennae sprouting from the roof. I wasn't surprised when the driver's side door opened and Jaime Mendoza stepped out.

I *was* surprised at the way he greeted me. "Where have you been?" accompanied by a scowl.

"Running errands," I said, reaching into the backseat for the paperwork for Diana. "Why?"

His eyes narrowed. "Where?"

I wanted to ask him what business it was of his where I'd been, but I didn't dare. He was the police. He could make anything I did his business, and probably would, if I annoyed him. So I rattled off the list of places I'd visited so far today. "The gym, the funeral home, David's apartment, the funeral home, David's office, the Body Shop on Charlotte Avenue..."

Mendoza's scowl deepened. "We need to talk."

"I thought we were talking," I said.

"Inside."

Fine. "Would you like to come inside, Detective?"

"Yes," Jaime Mendoza said, "I would."

"Follow me, please." I closed the car door with a tilt of my hip—my hands being full—and led the way up the stairs to the front door. Mendoza followed, so close on my heels I could practically feel his hot breath on my neck. It was ridiculous. What did he think I was going to do, make a break for it? In the shoes I was wearing, I'd make it fifteen feet down the driveway before he caught up. And then he'd probably tackle me to the ground, and that would hurt, not to mention ruin my outfit. So no, I wouldn't run.

Yet he stood there, close enough to smell, while I juggled papers and inserted the key in the lock.

He smelled good. Not strongly—probably not aftershave or a spray-on fragrance—but clean and fresh. Shampoo and soap, at a guess, with an undertone of spice.

David had been partial to Nautica. I wasn't. This was nice, though.

The door unlocked, and I shifted the papers over to the other arm and pushed it open. "Come in."

I left Mendoza to close the door, and headed into the dining room, where I dropped the statements on the table for later. No sooner had I stepped away than Mendoza picked up the top sheet and perused it. After a second, he glanced at me.

"David was hiding assets," I said, shrugging out of my jacket. "I found the statements this morning. I'm sending them to Diana."

He didn't comment, just put the piece of paper back down on top of the pile before plunging his hand into his jacket pocket. He was wearing another designer suit today: a nice charcoal with thin, black stripes that emphasized broad shoulders and narrow hips. The shirt underneath was fuchsia. A lot of men wouldn't be able to pull off the combination, at least not without looking ridiculous, but Mendoza looked great.

"Here." He pulled out his own folded piece of paper and handed it to me.

I unfolded it. And felt my breath catch and my capacity for speech leave me yet again. "What—?"

"Restraining order," Mendoza said.

"I can read." I didn't need him to translate for me. I hadn't actually questioned what I was holding. It was more that I was wondering why I was holding it. "Someone filed a restraining order against me?"

"Jacquie Demetros," Mendoza said.

I took a breath. And then another. And finally managed, "Why?"

"She said you were stalking her."

The unfairness practically choked me. She had seduced my husband and ruined my marriage and perhaps left me destitute, and now she had the nerve to complain that I was bothering her? "I'm not stalking her! I've never even spoken to her."

"She said you park outside her apartment building for hours," Mendoza said. "And that you follow her when she goes out."

Oh, for... "I've never parked outside her place for hours. Ever. Yesterday I hadn't even been there five minutes when Nick showed up and they left."

Mendoza sighed. "And naturally you followed."

I tossed my head. It didn't work the same when I had no hair to toss. "For your information, I lost them after two blocks. They went through a yellow light, and I got stuck on red. By the time I could move again, they were gone."

Mendoza's brows arched. Clearly he didn't believe me. "She said you followed her into Rotier's."

"I was hungry," I said. "I wanted a hamburger to take home, because I didn't feel like cooking. I had no idea that's where they were until I got inside."

He looked at me. Down and up again. "You don't look like someone who eats hamburgers."

"I don't usually. I'm getting older, and I'm trying to stay healthy." And keep my figure. "But I did an extra thirty minutes on the elliptical this morning to atone."

"So it was a total coincidence that you happened to be there at the same time as Ms. Demetros."

"Yes." I did my best to look like I was telling the truth.

He tilted his head. "I'm not sure I believe you."

"I can't help that," I said.

He took a deep breath. It expanded an already nice chest under the gray jacket. "Mrs. Kelly."

I returned my attention to his face. Nothing wrong with that, either. In fact, every part of him was a pleasure to look at. "Detective Mendoza."

"You'll have to leave Ms. Demetros alone from now on. No sitting outside her apartment with binoculars. No following her around."

"She was sleeping with my husband," I said. "I had a right to know what he'd left me for."

Mendoza didn't disagree with that. "If you come within a hundred feet of her," he said instead, "I'll have to arrest you."

I stuck my bottom lip out. "Fine. How far is a hundred feet?"

"From here to the backyard," Mendoza said. "Farther than across the street from her apartment building. And you can't go inside the same establishment that she goes into. No more to-go orders from Rotier's."

Fine. "What am I supposed to do if she shows up at David's funeral tomorrow? Leave?"

He blinked. "You think she will?"

"She was his girlfriend," I said. "I think she might."

Mendoza thought about it. "If she shows up here, or at your husband's funeral, then she's breaching the restraining order. Not you. As long as you don't go near her, you should be fine."

Good to know. "But if she shows up tomorrow, I can't pull her hair out by the roots, right?"

"No," Mendoza said. "That would be assault. I'd have to arrest you for that, too."

Figures. "There isn't much I can do, is there?"

He didn't answer, and I added, "She came into my life and stole my husband, but I can't keep an eye on her. She can come to my husband's funeral and to my house, but I can't throw her out."

"You can ask her to leave. You just can't lay a hand on her. And it would be better if you got someone else to do the asking."

"If she shows up here," I asked, "can I file a restraining order? Or some other kind of report? Like, can I sue for emotional battery?"

His lips twitched. "Probably not."

"That's a damn shame."

We stood in silence for a moment. "Can I offer you anything, Detective?"

"Nothing I'd be able to accept," Mendoza said. And added, "I'm working."

"Coffee? Tea? Bottled water?"

"I'm fine."

Yes, he was. But I wasn't about to say so. I shouldn't even be noticing, since he had a five-year-old at home, and probably a wife to go with the kid.

"We can at least sit down. And you can tell me about Daniel."

Mendoza arched inquiring brows at me, and I elaborated. "You said you'd look into him and get back to me."

"Oh," Mendoza said. "That."

I pulled out a dining room chair and planted myself. After a moment, and a bit reluctantly, Mendoza did the same. And folded his hands on the table. He wasn't wearing a wedding ring. Not that that meant anything. Lots of men don't wear them, and as a cop, maybe it was a safety measure. He probably upset some people, and the less they knew about his private life, the better. It didn't mean it was OK for me to ogle.

"Well?" I prompted when he didn't say anything.

He sighed. "I knocked on Kenneth Kelly's door this morning. Daniel Kelly was there."

"I knew it!"

"He admitted that when I spoke to him on the phone the other day, he was already in Nashville."

"That's suspicious, isn't it?"

"Yes and no," Mendoza said.

"He lied to the police. That has to be suspicious."

"He had a good reason," Mendoza said.

It was my turn to arch my brows at him, and he added, "By the time I spoke to him, his brother was dead. He knew if he admitted to being in town, he'd become a suspect."

"So why didn't he leave again? Why is he still here?"

"For the funeral," Mendoza said. "He wants to bury his brother."

Great. Not only did I possibly have Jacquie to look forward to, I had Daniel, as well. And of course Krystal and Kenny and any number of David's friends and associates who no doubt believed I'd killed him. Nothing but good times ahead.

"How long has he been here?" I asked.

"Since the weekend," Mendoza said.

"Does he have an alibi for Tuesday night?"

"He was staying with your stepson. He said he was tired and spent the night in the apartment. It's a long drive from Santa Monica to Nashville."

No doubt. "But Kenny was at work. So Daniel could have gone out and Kenny wouldn't have known about it."

Mendoza nodded.

"So he's a suspect, too."

"Everyone's a suspect," Mendoza said, which was a relief. Even if that 'everyone' included me. At least I wasn't alone under suspicion.

"Do you know anything about the guy Jacquie was having dinner with?"

"His name is Nick Costanza," Mendoza said, a bit reluctantly. "She said they're friends."

"That's not what the guy at the Body Shop on Charlotte Avenue said."

Mendoza looked at me.

"Nick Costanza works at the Body Shop on Charlotte Avenue. The Rotier's waitress told me." He didn't speak, so I added, driving the information home, "He'd know how to cut David's brake lines."

"Everyone in the world would know how to cut your husband's brake lines," Mendoza said.

"I wouldn't."

He just arched his brows at me, so I decided not to pursue the subject any further. And anyway, Mendoza added, "That's somewhere you said you were today. The Body Shop on Charlotte Avenue."

I nodded. "Nick saw me and ran. He left someone else to do my oil change. A guy named Bud. And Bud said Nick and Jacquie were involved."

"Hearsay," Mendoza told me.

"I told him I thought Jacquie was involved with someone else, and he said that ended when the old dude died."

There was a beat. "That's not proof that Costanza had anything to do with it," Mendoza said.

"But it's possible he might have, if Jacquie left him for David, and he wanted her back."

Mendoza didn't say anything to that. "Anything else?" he asked me.

I thought about it. David had been hiding assets, Nick had run away from me—there was no need to tell Mendoza that Bud thought I'd been chasing after him—and I'd talked to Rachel and Farley. "I don't think so. I assume you know that David's share of the business goes to Farley."

Mendoza nodded. "But he'll have to replace your husband with someone else, or he won't be able to keep the business going. He needs a constant influx of clients with money to manage."

"It's like I told you. David was worth more to him alive than dead."

We sat in silence for a moment.

"So did you get your kid fed last night?" I asked, when it became clear that we had nothing more to say about David's murder.

Mendoza nodded. "Without burning down the kitchen and before his mother came home." He grinned. "I got brownie points for both."

Good for him. He'd probably gotten sex after the kid was asleep, too. I tried not to think about that, or about how long it had been since I'd gotten any. It was before I knew about Jacquie, although I was pretty sure David had slept with us both for a while. He could hardly stop sleeping with me without arousing my suspicions that he was getting his needs met elsewhere, and I hadn't suspected a thing.

Anyway, it had been a while. And I definitely didn't need to be thinking about that now.

I came back to myself in time for Mendoza to say, "You and your husband didn't want any children?"

"David didn't. He was in his mid-thirties when we got married, and he already had Krystal and Kenny with Sandra. I guess maybe he didn't want them to feel like he was replacing them, too. Bad enough that he was replacing their mother."

Although that was crediting David with a level of sensitivity I wasn't sure he had possessed. It was more likely he'd simply realized that he didn't like children very much, and he didn't want any in addition to the two he had.

"How did you feel about that?"

"I went along with it," I said. After a pause, I added, "If I'd been older when we got married—you know, a little more sure of myself and who I was—I might have said something, but I didn't. It's my own fault."

Mendoza tilted his head to look at me. "How old were you when you married Mr. Kelly? He was in his mid-thirties and you were...?"

"Twenty-two," I said.

Mendoza muttered something. It was my turn to arch my brows, and he said, "That's a big age difference."

"Not as big as David and Jacquie."

Since there was nothing Mendoza could say to that, he didn't try. "I should be going," he said instead.

He probably should. Since he had a wife and kid at home, and all. Not that I hadn't enjoyed sitting here looking at... I mean, talking to him.

"The funeral's at eleven tomorrow," I told him as he headed for the front door. "At Boling & Howard funeral home in Woodbine."

He nodded.

"Visitation's at ten. The graveside ceremony at one. And the festivities start at three. Here."

"I'll try to stop by," Mendoza said.

"Do you think the murderer will show up at the funeral?"

He grinned, and damn near blinded me. "I wouldn't be surprised. Your husband was killed by someone he knew. Anyone who isn't there, will move to the top of the suspect list."

"I'll make sure nothing stops me," I said.

"I can't imagine much would," Mendoza said, and walked out, leaving me to stare after him, not quite sure whether he'd just complimented or insulted me.

CHAPTER TEN

Nobody didn't show up. At the funeral, I mean. Everyone who was anyone was there.

I walked in at ten o'clock sharp, and found Sandra already present, brooding over the casket.

I hadn't seen David's first wife all that many times in the eighteen years he and I had been married. At first, naturally, she'd been upset with me for stealing her husband. Never mind the fact that he'd told me their marriage was over but for the formalities.

Later on, of course I realized he'd been lying, but at the time, I bought into the assertion that his wife didn't understand him and was too busy with the kids to want to have sex.

And yes, I'm sure he'd told Jacquie the same thing. Minus the kids. But as far as explaining why his and my relationship was no longer working, he'd probably told her I'd lost my libido when I turned forty, and that I wasn't interested in sex anymore.

Whatever it took, to get whichever woman he had his eye on into the sack.

Anyway, there was Sandra, standing by the casket. When I walked in and saw her, I thought she might be having a moment, so I stopped. But it was too late; she'd heard me, and turned. For a few long seconds, we stared at one another. Then she opened her mouth, and I braced myself.

"Nice hair."

Oh. My hand flew to it, automatically. "Thank you."

"It isn't a red dress, but it's the next best thing."

Yes, it was. Although it was a little disconcerting how everyone I knew thought my new color was an attempt to stick it to David, when all I'd done was go back to the hair I was born with.

And for the record, I was appropriately dressed, in the same gray and black ensemble I'd worn to court on Wednesday morning. Sandra was likewise appropriately dressed, in a black skirt and white blouse with a jacket, and her hair pulled back from her face into an elegant chignon. Unlike me, she's a natural blonde, who gave her coloring to her children.

Anyway, as I mentioned, I hadn't had much to do with her during the time David and I had been married. They'd had the children in common, so they had to talk once in a while, but I stayed out of it as much as I could. They weren't my children, and they didn't like me— Sandra didn't like me either, and wouldn't welcome my interference—so I left those problems to David to handle. And as Krystal and Kenny grew up and needed less parental intervention, the contact between Sandra and David (and me) had become less, too. She'd stopped by David's mother's funeral to pay her respects last year, but other than that, it must have been three or four years since I'd last seen her.

You can imagine my surprise when she told me, "I slept with him, you know."

"Yes," I said. "I know. Krystal and Kenny are a dead giveaway."

"Six months ago," Sandra said.

My mouth opened. I closed it again.

Six months ago I hadn't even turned forty yet.

And although I had realized that if David had slept with Jacquie, he might have slept with someone else too, I had never considered that he might have slept with Sandra.

Hell, she was older than me by a good ten years!

While I stood there gaping like a goldfish, Sandra continued, "He said your relationship was on the skids. He told me I still looked as good as when he married me."

I closed my mouth again, on the words I wanted to say. It wouldn't be constructive to tell her that he'd been lying through his teeth; that while she looked good for fifty-plus, she didn't look twenty-two anymore, and that's what she'd been when they got married.

"I'm sorry to hear that," I managed eventually. "And I'm sorry for your loss."

If she'd been sleeping with him as recently as six months ago, she must be taking this harder than I was. Not that I hadn't been sleeping with him six months ago... but it was different.

"Mostly," Sandra told me, "I'm just sorry I didn't kill him first."

Oh. Um...

There wasn't a whole lot I could say to that, so I didn't try. "I didn't kill him either," I told her instead.

She looked at me for a moment. "I'm sure you didn't."

Somehow, it didn't sound like a compliment.

Other people started coming in at that point, so I went and sat down. Mostly my job here was just to be present, to look like a loving wife and to field any condolences—of which there were few. Most people had probably figured out that since we were in the middle of a messy divorce, and since David had left me for Jacquie, condolences weren't in order.

Or perhaps they just didn't feel they could condole me on the loss of a husband I was widely rumored to have murdered.

They showed up, though. All of David's clients and their wives. Farley and Martha. Krystal and a long-haired young man in jeans and a black blazer whom I supposed was the boyfriend—and probably some sort of client. Kenny and Daniel. Rachel. Anton Hess.

Jacquie Demetros and Nick Costanza.

He cleaned up well, in a dark suit and tie. If he had engine grease under his nails, it didn't show.

Jacquie, meanwhile, looked like a caricature of a Hollywood widow. She was dressed all in black: a shiny satin dress that hugged every curve and showed off a totally unsuitable amount of cleavage. The shoes were the same pair she'd worn to dinner two nights ago: sky-high and sexy, with ankle straps. On her head was a big, black hat with a veil, and she clutched Nick's arm with one hand while the other pressed a handkerchief—black-rimmed—to her nose.

Nobody moved. We just watched her mince over to the coffin on those crazy heels. It was sort of like a train wreck: I couldn't look away.

Sandra turned to me. "Is that the bitch?"

The room was fairly silent, and she didn't bother to moderate her voice. I'm sure quite a few people heard her, in addition to me. I don't know about Jacquie. If she did, it didn't slow her undulating progress toward the daisy-draped casket.

I nodded. "That's her."

Sandra's mouth twisted. "He got what he deserved."

I wouldn't have gone quite that far—I'm not sure anyone ever deserves being murdered, even a cheating husband—but I could understand her feelings. Looking at Jacquie—young and beautiful and fresh, and did I mention young and beautiful?—it was hard to feel any sympathy, for her or for David.

"That takes a lot of nerve," Sandra added, "showing up here."

Indeed. "She might really be grieving for him."

"For the money," Sandra said. "That girl's got gold-digger written all over her. In big letters."

Well, yes. "Nobody forced him to get involved with her."

She glanced at me. "He was a prick. They deserved each other."

No argument here.

While we'd been talking, Jacquie and Nick had reached the casket. We all watched, surreptitiously and not so surreptitiously, while she reached out a small, gloved hand and put it on the shiny wood.

Yes, gloved. She was actually wearing fingerless gloves in black lace; the better to let her tasteful black cherry nail polish show, I assume. And I'm sure every man in the room was shifting uncomfortably in his seat as that gloved hand slowly stroked the wood.

Sandra muttered something unprintable. "Are you going to let her do that?"

"I can't stop her," I said. "She's sworn out a restraining order against me. If I approach her, I'll be arrested. But you can go tell her to stop if you want."

Sandra cursed and stalked off. But not, I noticed, up to Jacquie. Instead, she homed in on Krystal and started haranguing her daughter to do something about the situation instead.

Movement at the door drew my attention in time to see Detective Mendoza slip through and into the room. He was wearing the same suit as yesterday—and filling it out just as nicely—this time in combination with a crisp white shirt and a subdued gray-blue tie. And just as all the men had stiffened noticeably watching Jacquie caress the casket, now a fair few of their wives sat up a little straighter as they watched Mendoza make his way inside.

Good to know I wasn't the only one who reacted to the man's overabundance of testosterone.

He watched Jacquie for a moment. I saw his lips tighten, but I wasn't sure whether he was trying to hide a grin or something else. After a second, he began scanning the rest of the room.

I headed for the door. I might not be able to do anything about Jacquie, but I could greet Mendoza. It was pretty much all I was good for anyway.

"Detective."

It might have been my imagination, but I felt like everyone in the room was watching me. And I wondered how many of those people knew he was the cop in charge of David's case, and how many assumed—or wondered whether—he was some sort of romantic entanglement of mine instead.

Just in case, I made sure to stay at a very professional distance. Not that I'd be rubbing up against him if we were alone. Wife and kid, remember? Not to mention that he was practically a baby.

He nodded politely, but with a hint of amusement. As if he knew what I was thinking. "Mrs. Kelly."

"Everyone's here. All the suspects."

He glanced around. "Looks that way."

"I don't suppose you're here to make an arrest?"

Part of me was hoping he'd say yes. I was ready to get out from under the suspicion hanging over me like a cloud.

Of course, the other part was terrified he'd arrest me. I knew I hadn't killed my husband, but I also knew what it looked like.

Mendoza shook his head. "Afraid not."

"Any news?"

"Nothing I want to talk about here," Mendoza said, perusing the room.

Understandable. I cleared my throat. "Thank you for coming. I'll just... um... go sit over there. And wait for the service to start."

Mendoza nodded. "I'll stay in the back of the room.

And keep an eye on things."

I glanced over my shoulder. "I don't suppose that includes detaching Jacquie from the coffin?"

Mendoza squinted at her. "Is she... stroking it?"

I nodded, biting my lip. "It's a bit unseemly. I'm sure everyone's wondering why I'm not doing anything about it. And of course I can't, because—"

"Of the restraining order." Mendoza sounded resigned. "I'll go talk to her."

"Thank you." I turned to watch him walk away, and then reconsidered when I realized that half the room was still watching me. The other half was watching Mendoza, their eyes glassy.

No, I was definitely not the only woman responding to the sex appeal.

So Mendoza detached Jacquie and made her sit down. And then he went and took a seat himself, at the back of the room. On his way past, he gave me a wink. I was so surprised my mouth opened, and I probably looked like an idiot standing there gaping after him. Until I realized, once again, that people were staring and—by now— whispering. I was blushing as I went to find my seat.

The service got underway after that, with Anselm Howard delivering the eulogy. It relied heavily on David's accomplishments and philanthropy, and on the suddenness of his passing, with no mention of the fact that he was in the process of divorcing his wife of eighteen years because he'd found himself a twenty-five-year-old mistress.

After Mr. Howard had wound down, he invited anyone else with something to say to stand up, and

Krystal jumped to her feet to give a touching speech about her daddy and how much she'd miss him. Kenny followed, less verbose and obviously more ill at ease. I thought Sandra might have something to contribute, but she didn't, so instead it was Daniel's turn next.

This was my first chance to really get a good look at David's brother. We'd met before, obviously, but it had been years. Maybe as much as a decade. He hadn't come back for their mother's funeral last year. His excuse had been something about the distance and lack of money, but I think their mother had always liked David best, and Daniel probably knew it.

He was older than David by a couple of years, and looked his age. Unlike David, who had worked hard at staying in shape and looking young, Daniel didn't look like he cared. He kept his gray hair long—it was pulled back into a ponytail for the occasion—and the black suit was years out of date. The jacket pulled across his stomach.

It wasn't new, and it clearly didn't belong to Kenny, so Daniel must have brought it with him from California. I made a mental note to ask Detective Mendoza what Daniel thought he'd need the suit for here in Nashville. It wasn't like he could have known he'd be going to a funeral.

Daniel sat down, and Farley took his place. He spoke about the business and about his long friendship and relationship with David. After him came Anton Hess, who did the same. A couple of clients and golfing-buddies of David's also had their say. As the last one sat down, Anselm Howard gave me the eye. I prepared to get to my feet to thank everyone for coming out, and to explain about the graveside service and subsequent reception at the house in Hillwood. But just as I braced myself to get up, Jacquie stood.

I subsided back into my seat. Mr. Howard blinked. The audience gasped. Whispers broke out as Jacquie undulated her way up to the podium; her posterior, as the saying goes, moving like two puppies under a blanket. I think I even heard growling, but it probably wasn't the puppies. It was more likely to be one of the men, or perhaps Sandra giving vent to her feelings.

Jacquie stopped behind the podium and leaned into the microphone. In a breathy Marilyn Monroe voice— *Happy Birthday, Mr. President!*—she said, "My name is Jacquelyn Demetros."

I don't think anyone had been in any doubt about who she was, but I suppose it was nice of her to introduce herself.

"David and I were engaged."

The room buzzed, and more than one head turned to look at me. I smiled tightly. *Yes, David and I were still married when he died.*

"We were happy," Jacquie sniffed, raising that black-rimmed handkerchief to dab at her nose under the black veil. As if she'd really do anything so uncouth as to develop a runny nose in the middle of her big moment. "Until *she* killed him!"

She shot out a quivering finger, directly at me. My jaw dropped, and my skin felt like it shriveled as everyone in the room turned in my direction.

Part of me wanted to jump up and scream that it

wasn't true. The other part was glued to the chair, in a mixture of mortification and shock.

Determined steps came down the aisle toward the front. I turned my head, jerkily, like a marionette on a string, and saw Detective Mendoza making his way to Jacquie, who had subsided into a sobbing heap draped over the podium. The microphone broadcast her sniffles to every corner of the room.

Mendoza didn't look at me, but a glance at Nick brought the latter to his feet. They approached Jacquie one from each side.

"Time to go, Ms. Demetros," Mendoza said calmly. He took her elbow and removed her from the podium. She staggered, and Nick grabbed her other arm. Between them, they supported her to the back of the room and out the door. She was wobbling on the high heels, and hiccupping under the veil. Mendoza shot me a look on the way past, something halfway between sympathy for my ordeal and an eyeroll over Jacquie's behavior. Or at least that's what I hoped it was.

What happened was a tough act to follow, and I didn't try. After a glance at me, Anselm Howard made the announcement that the memorial service was over. The action would pick back up at Spring Hill Cemetery at one o'clock, he said—not in those exact words—and anyone who wanted to come to the graveside ceremony was welcome to attend. Maybe I should have stood up at that point and added that there'd be a reception at the house in Hillwood at three, but to be honest, I didn't care if I ever saw any of these people again. If I ended up with a spread for fifty and nobody to share it with, that was just fine with me.

I should have known better.

The graveside ceremony went off without a hitch. Daniel and Kenny, Farley and Krystal's boyfriend, plus two of David's clients and golfing buddies, carried the coffin from the hearse to the grave. I guess Anton Hess was either too short or too old to pitch in, but he was there. Jacquie wasn't, so I didn't have to worry about her throwing herself on top of the box as it was lowered into the ground. Even the weather cooperated. It was a drizzly, dreary day with gray skies and intermittent showers, but the twenty minutes that we spent in the cemetery, watching David go into the ground, were dry. The air was misty, but it didn't rain.

Anselm Howard had handed everyone a white rose to toss into the grave on top of the coffin, and we did, to the tune of *Amazing Grace*, sung by Krystal's boyfriend, who sounded like he smoked a lot. After that, we each grabbed a handful of earth from the pile next to the hole in the ground, and threw it in. The rattle of dirt and stones on top of the coffin sounded very final.

I was the first to walk away. Not only did I have a party to get to, and caterers at the house, but I had no desire to commiserate with Krystal and Kenny and Sandra and Daniel about David's death. They were all hugging one another and brushing away tears, and the idea of taking part in it made my stomach clench.

I had my hand on the handle of the car door when I heard the slosh of a foot on the soggy ground. I spun around, expecting... I wasn't even sure. But it was just

Rachel, in one of her boring, black suits with a boring white shirt under it.

"Sorry," she said. "I didn't mean to startle you."

I took a breath. "It's OK. Just the situation."

She nodded, but didn't make reference to the clutch of people hovering over the grave, or Jacquie's accusation back at the funeral home. "There's a reception at your house in an hour?"

I acknowledged the accuracy of this. "You're welcome to stop by. I'm sure David would have wanted you to. And Farley, too."

Something moved across Rachel's eyes, but too quickly for me to see what it was. "I was wondering whether you might like some help," she said.

"Oh. Um..." Not something I'd ever thought I'd hear from Rachel. I was pretty sure she didn't like me.

Although maybe this was the last thing she could do for David, and she felt like she wanted to do something.

"Sure," I said. "There's a team of caterers at the house right now, setting up, but once they're done, they're going to leave. I didn't want to have waiters circulating with trays of hors d'oeuvres, you know? It might make the occasion look too much like a party. So when the buffet gets empty, I'm going to have to refill it. I wouldn't mind some help with that."

Rachel nodded. "I know where you live. I'll meet you there."

"Thank you," I said.

She squished off across the wet ground to her Toyota, and I got into the convertible and wished, not for the first time, that it had a proper roof. A trickle of rain had found a weakness in the joint between the metal and the canopy, and had dropped onto my seat. I was sitting in a puddle of water. It put the cherry on top of what had been one of the worst days of my life so far.

And it was only halfway over.

CHAPTER ELEVEN

The catering team had come and gone. The dining room table was set with trays and platters filled with food—stuffed mushroom caps, deviled eggs, tiny rounds of French bread topped with salmon and caviar—while the buffet had been transformed into a serve-yourself bar of wine and liquor.

I gave it a quick look on my way past—the kitchen counters were heaped with extras, too—before hustling up the stairs to the master bedroom, peeling off my clothes as I went. The back of my tasteful black and gray dress had a big spot across the bottom—it looked like I'd wet myself, perhaps when Jacquie made her accusation—and I had to get out of it and into something else before Rachel knocked on the front door. The last thing I wanted, was for anyone to take it as a sign of guilt.

Three minutes later, wearing a pair of black slacks and a cobalt blue blouse, I headed back down the stairs, just as the knock came. I yanked the door open, only to take a step back. "Oh."

It wasn't Rachel. It was Daniel. "You goddamn bitch,"

he told me, in a very conversational, calm tone.

He had yanked off the tie and left the suit jacket in the truck, so he looked a little more comfortable than before. The expression on his face didn't reflect any increased comfort level, though.

"What do you want?" I asked.

He took a step toward me. I, perforce, took one back. Not because I wanted him in my house—I didn't, although it wasn't like I could stop him. He was David's brother, and if anyone had the right to attend the reception, it was David's family. But he was a big guy— six-one or two, and correspondingly broad—and the way his face twitched was disconcerting.

"You sicced the cops on me."

"Your brother was murdered," I said, trying my best to stand my ground and sound calm as he loomed over me. "You should be glad they're looking at all the possibilities."

Daniel's eyes narrowed. They were David's eyes, cool blue and penetrating. "We all know who murdered David."

Me, I assume. I decided not to dignify the remark with an answer.

"What I'd like to know," I said, "is how you knew you'd need that suit you're wearing. It's obviously not new, so you must have brought it with you from California. What made you think you'd need a suit on this trip?"

He flushed a very ugly shade of puce. "You accusing me of something?"

"I'm wondering what you're doing here," I said. "You

don't live in Nashville. You didn't even come to your mother's funeral last year. But now you've driven all the way here, just in time to put your brother in the ground. A brother who was alive and well when you left the West Coast. And coincidentally, you just happened to bring your funeral suit."

"I don't like your tone," Daniel growled.

I didn't like his, either. And I wished he'd leave. He was scaring me. He leaned over me, and his fists kept clenching and unclenching. Also, his breath was bad.

"I didn't have nothing to do with what happened to David. And don't think it's gonna work pointing the finger at me so as the cops forget about you. We all know you did it."

"Then you have nothing to worry about," I said, taking another step back, "do you?"

He followed, and reached out a meaty paw to wrap around my upper arm. "Listen, bitch—"

But whatever he'd planned to say was lost when there was a crunch of tires on gravel. Daniel turned his head and I peered over his shoulder to see Rachel's white Toyota make its way up the drive to the house.

Daniel cursed and let me go. He pushed past me and disappeared into the dining room. I assumed he was attacking the hors d'oeuvres, or more likely the liquor, so I didn't bother to follow him. Besides, I needed to greet Rachel.

She came up the steps looking half suspicious, half apprehensive. "Was that Daniel?"

I nodded.

"What's wrong?"

"He thinks I killed David," I said. "I think he might have."

Rachel squinted at me. "Why?"

"Someone did. He's here."

She didn't respond to that, just peered past me into the house. "What do you want me to help you with?"

So she didn't want to discuss Daniel. Fine. "Let me show you around," I offered.

"I've been here before," Rachel said.

Had she really?

Sure, David entertained at home—dinner parties, cookouts, and the like—but his administrative assistant wasn't invited to those shindigs.

"You weren't here," Rachel added.

"Where was I?"

She shrugged. "Shopping or something."

Shopping. Right. "What was David doing?"

"He was busy," Rachel said, avoiding my eyes. Although I suppose it's possible she was just having a look around. "He gave me his key and had me drive out here to pick up something."

"Something, what?"

"A change of clothes," Rachel said. "He was going to dinner."

With Jacquie, I assume. If he had scheduled dinner with a business associate, he'd just wear the same suit he'd worn to work all day.

Or maybe with Sandra. Or—hell—someone else. Someone I didn't even know about.

While I tried to figure out whether it would do any good to ask, or whether I even wanted to know the answer, Rachel moved past me into the house. I shrugged and followed.

We stayed busy after that. I showed Rachel the spread in the dining room, and the extras stacked on the kitchen counter and in the fridge. If nobody showed up, I'd be eating well for a long time.

Although plenty of people did show up. About fifteen minutes after Rachel walked in, they started coming up the driveway. Farley and Martha, Sandra and Kenny, Krystal and the boyfriend. All the business associates. Anton Hess. They were all milling around my house, chatting and laughing, eating and drinking. Rachel and I had our hands full, keeping the trays stocked.

Even Diana had taken off work early to stop by. She walked in around four, holding a manila envelope. "Big crowd."

I nodded. "I guess they don't want to risk missing it, just in case the police show up to arrest me."

She arched her brows. "Any chance of that?"

"Probably a pretty good chance. I had the best motive of anyone. Although I will say that Detective Mendoza doesn't seem to be in a hurry to slap me in handcuffs."

"That's Jaime," Diana said. "A sucker for a pretty face."

I laughed. "Oh, please." He had a wife at home; what did he care what my face looked like? "If he was sure I'd done it, I don't think he'd have any problem throwing me in jail."

Diana shrugged. "He can't be sure, then."

"There are a few other options. Did I mention that

Daniel's in Nashville?"

"Briefly," Diana said. "Is he here?"

I nodded. "Talking to Anton Hess."

She scanned the room, and then grinned. "Excellent. I have something to give Anton, anyway. I'll go take a look at him."

I eyed the envelope. "What do you have to give Anton?"

"Notice that we know about the hidden accounts," Diana said. "I can't wait to hear what he has to say."

She sashayed off across the room. I watched as she approached the two men—Daniel looming over squat little Anton Hess the same way he'd loomed over me earlier—and stopped beside them. Anton, of course, looked wary. He knew who she was. Daniel didn't, so he gave her a frank and appreciative once-over, top to bottom and back.

Diana's an attractive woman. A few years my senior, with sleek blond hair she keeps pulled back into a chignon that can go from businesslike to elegant in a heartbeat, and a still-trim figure under the expensive business suit. I wasn't surprised that Daniel approved. She's married, though, so that approval wouldn't go anywhere. And anyway, he was hardly Diana's type.

As I watched, she greeted them both, and then addressed Anton. The lawyer's face flushed red, and then paled. When he accepted the envelope, I swear I saw his hand tremble.

Diana came back across the floor with a pleased smile, while both men watched her go. I'm pretty sure Daniel was watching her rear end, while Anton Hess's expression was a mixture of fear and loathing.

"So that went well," I said, when she was close enough to hear me.

She grinned. "I thought he'd have a heart attack on the spot."

Me, too. "You think this will weigh in our favor, right?"

"It should," Diana said. "Nobody likes a cheater."

No, indeed.

"And speaking of cheaters, I don't suppose the Other Woman's here?"

"Jacquie?" I shook my head. "I'm sure Detective Mendoza warned her to stay away. Did I happen to mention I now have a police record? She swore out a restraining order against me."

"You're kidding."

"I wish," I said. "But no. I have to stay a hundred feet away from her at all times. While she can come to my husband's memorial service and stand up in front of everyone and say I killed him."

Diana's eyes widened. "She did that?"

"She most certainly did."

"Would you like to sue her for slander?"

"I'd like to," I said, "but I doubt she has anything I want. And anyway, when the police figure out who killed him, everyone will know it wasn't me."

Diana shrugged. "Let me know if you change your mind. So what happened?"

"After she made her announcement, you mean? Everyone gasped and stared at me. Detective Mendoza removed her. She didn't show up for the graveside service, so I figure he must have put the fear of God in her."

"Or the fear of the law," Diana said. She shook her head. "I don't suppose anyone got a picture?"

Oh, God.

"Now that you mention it, I think the funeral home taped the service. Just in case I wanted to watch it and remember later."

I have no idea why Anselm Howard would think I'd want to do that. There was no part of me that wanted to relive any part of today. Most especially the part where Jacquie accused me of killing David.

"Imagine that falling into the wrong hands," Diana murmured.

Thank you. "I'll make sure to pick it up personally." And burn it.

Diana grinned, as if she knew what I was thinking. "Anything else I should know before I go?"

I thought about it. "I don't think so."

"In that case I'll head home. Steven and I are going on a date."

Steven was Diana's husband. I had never met him, but I knew he was a professor at one of the universities, and that they'd been married a long time. It was nice that they still had date-nights.

"Have a good time," I told her. "I assume you gave Judge Miller a copy of David's paperwork, too?"

"Messengered it over this afternoon. I decided to give myself the pleasure of serving Anton personally." She smiled toothily. "We should hear something on Monday. I'll let you know."

"Thank you," I said, and walked her to the door. "Have a good weekend."

"You, too." She gave me a look. "Don't do anything stupid."

"Like what?"

"Stalking Jacquie and getting yourself thrown in jail."

I hadn't planned to do that. "I'm going to have a nice, quiet weekend while I try to figure out what to do with the rest of my life."

"Famous last words," Diana said, and walked out the door. Halfway down the stairs, she had to sidestep to avoid running into a man coming up. He muttered something—I don't think it was an apology—and pushed past me and inside. "Charming," Diana said, looking after him.

"Krystal's boyfriend." Trailing a reek of marijuana behind him. "I think he's some sort of musician."

Diana didn't comment, just shook her head and continued down the stairs. I waited for her to drive away before I headed back inside the house.

Rachel was in the kitchen, replenishing platters. "Everything OK?" she asked when she saw me.

I nodded. "What can you tell me about Krystal's boyfriend?"

She glanced past me to the door to the dining room. "Problem?"

"Not as far as I know." When I walked through, neither of them had been there. I guess maybe they were huddled in the music room or something. Or maybe Krystal had dragged her boyfriend back outside to air him out and get rid of the fumes. "I think he's been smoking pot."

"He does that," Rachel said, her fingers transferring canapés from one tray to the other. "Mr. Kelly was upset about it."

"David? He didn't approve of Krystal's boyfriend?" He hadn't mention anything to me about that. "Is he a new boyfriend?"

"They've been dating for a year or so," Rachel said, "on and off."

I blinked. "Why didn't David tell me?"

Rachel didn't look at me, just kept her attention on the food. "Maybe he didn't want to worry you."

Or maybe he thought I wouldn't be interested. Krystal and I had never been close.

Or—*hell!*—maybe he was already screwing around with someone else by then, and was unburdening himself to them instead.

I tried to imagine Jacquie taking an interest in Krystal's boyfriend—in any way but the obvious one—and couldn't.

But who better than Krystal's mother?

"Sandra told me she had a fling with him six months ago," I said.

Rachel didn't look up, but her lips tightened.

"Did you know about that?"

"I knew about all of them," Rachel said.

All?

My lips felt stiff. "How many were there?"

She looked up, and when I looked into her eyes, I felt the bottom drop out.

"He's been cheating for years. But most of it was like

with the former Mrs. Kelly. Brief flings. Ms. Demetros was the first time it got serious."

"How many?"

"I didn't keep count," Rachel said.

"But more than the two of them."

She nodded. "Several more."

I took a deep breath and straightened my fingers. They were curled into claws, and I knew it was unfair to attack Rachel. She wasn't who I wanted to hurt. I wanted to hurt David, and barring that, Jacquie and Sandra and every other woman he'd slept with. But mostly I wanted to hurt David.

Wanting to hurt the dead doesn't feel good. Not only because it's impossible to get any kind of satisfaction, but also because it makes you feel bad about yourself.

Although Rachel was standing right in front of me, and I was upset with her, too. "Why didn't you tell me?"

"I needed to work," Rachel said.

And if she'd told me what David was doing, he would have fired her.

I understood that. But I still couldn't keep myself from saying, "Well, I hope you're happy now."

"I'm not," Rachel said. "And anyway, in the end, it was all for nothing."

She lifted the tray and headed for the door to the dining room.

I trotted after. "What do you mean?"

She gave me a look over her shoulder. "I mean now that Mr. Kelly is dead, I'm out of a job anyway."

She passed through and into the dining room, where she placed the tray on the table. Four different people elbowed her out of their way to get to it.

"Farley isn't keeping you?" I asked when she came to stand next to me. "But you run the place!"

"Mr. Hollingsworth prefers to do his own running." Her voice was carefully neutral.

"What will you do?"

Rachel shrugged. "I'll have to find another job. Mr. Hollingsworth gave me a three month severance package, so I have a little time. I won't have to settle for the first thing that comes along."

"That was nice of him," I said stupidly. Rachel gave me a look that told me, eloquently, just how stupid I was. Farley had fired her. He wasn't being nice. "Why doesn't he want to keep you? You were doing a good job. And he'll need someone to answer the phones and greet the clients."

Rachel shrugged. "After today, it's none of my concern."

Wow. So not only had he fired her, but it had taken effect immediately. David went in the ground, and Farley cleaned house.

"I'm so sorry," I said.

Rachel looked at me. "No offense, Mrs. Kelly, but between the two of us, I think I got off easier. At least I get severance pay. According to Mr. Kelly, you're not getting squat."

Oh, really? "Is that what he told you?"

She shrugged.

"Well, I've got news for you," I said. "I found his hidden accounts. And by now both his lawyer and the judge know about them. And my lawyer says we stand a good chance of getting the prenup thrown out, because nobody likes a cheat."

Rachel smiled—a real smile, not the close-lipped professional version she usually gave me. It transformed her face, made her look younger and even a bit thinner. "Good for you."

"Thank you. And if there's anything I can do to help you with the job hunt..."

"No offense, Mrs. Kelly," Rachel said again, "but after what happened this afternoon, I'd say your credibility is pretty low."

Ouch.

"I didn't kill David," I said, raising my voice just enough that those of David's friends and associates who were hovering near the table could hear me. "So the police won't be able to prove I did. Sooner or later they'll find the real killer, and then everyone will know it wasn't me."

And on that note, just like in a TV movie, the front door opened, and Detective Mendoza stood on the threshold. The wind lashed the rain behind him, and somewhere in the distance, thunder rumbled.

"Mrs. Kelly," he told me, "I need you to come with me."

CHAPTER TWELVE

You could have heard a canapé drop.

In fact, one did. Gwendolyn Oliver was holding a shrimp puff, and it hit the floor with a sound halfway between a splat and a soggy thump. The hand that had held the puff flew to cover her mouth, and she stared at me over it, her eyes round.

Everyone else was staring, too.

"Of course, Detective," I said calmly. "Just let me get my coat."

Mendoza glanced around the room. "We're just going to the garage."

Ah. "In that case, I think I'll probably be all right without it." I turned to Rachel. "Will you keep an eye on things here?"

She nodded. "Of course, Mrs. Kelly."

I turned to Mendoza. "Lead the way, Detective."

"After you, Mrs. Kelly." He stepped aside and bowed politely as I brushed past him into the hallway and from there over to the interior door from the house to the garage.

"What's going on?" I asked him when we were inside the garage with the door closed between us and the teeming crowd in the house. I had no doubt that some of them had gravitated to the door and were now doing everything short of pressing their ears to the wood to try to hear what we were saying.

"I need a witness," Mendoza told me, looking around at the dim interior of the two-car space, "and it *is* your garage. Is there a light in here?"

"Of course." Next to the kitchen door. I reached out and flipped the switch. A couple of hundred-watt bulbs came on, bathing the convertible and the empty space next to it—the one that used to be occupied by David's Porsche—in brilliance. At the same time, it probably enhanced every wrinkle and enlarged pore on my face.

I took a step back. No sense drawing attention to those parts of myself. It had been a long day, and I hadn't had time to refresh my makeup. "Would you like to tell me what we're doing here?"

"Looking for something," Mendoza said, still looking around instead of at me. I should be grateful, although I admit it made me feel a little unimportant.

"Looking for what?"

"A pair of grease-stained overalls and a knife."

I opened my mouth, but found I couldn't speak. When I didn't say anything, Mendoza turned to watch me, interestedly. "Cat got your tongue?"

I closed my mouth, opened it, and tried again. "What makes you think there's a pair of grease-stained overalls and a knife in my garage?"

"Anonymous tip," Mendoza said, going back to surveying the room.

"Someone called to tell you there's a pair of overalls and a knife in my garage?"

He nodded.

"Who?"

"We don't know," Mendoza said. "That's why it's called an anonymous tip."

Well, duh. "Don't you have caller ID?"

"Of course we do," Mendoza said. "The call came from here."

"Here?"

"Your house. Your landline."

My landline.

I swallowed. "So anyone in the house could have called."

"Including you."

"Why would I call you to tell you there's a pair of overalls and a knife in my garage? If there's a pair of overalls and a knife here, you're the last person I'd want to know about it."

"Good to know," Mendoza said.

"You know what I mean. You already suspect me. If the overalls and knife are here—" the overalls and knife used to cut David's brake lines, I assumed; and I'm sure Mendoza did, too, "—that'll just make me look more guilty."

"If the overalls fit," Mendoza said.

"Well, if they don't, there's no point in leaving them here, is there?"

I didn't wait for an answer, just stepped off the small

staircase and began walking along the wall. "Did this anonymous tip tell you where in the garage the overalls and knife are supposed to be?"

"It wasn't a long conversation," Mendoza said. "All he said was, 'there a pair of overalls and a knife in Gina Kelly's garage.'"

Great. So the stuff we were looking for could be anywhere.

I went in one direction, and Mendoza in the other.

It seemed to me that there were two explanations for the anonymous call. Someone might have happened to notice the overalls and knife while in the garage on an entirely innocent errand. If so, the stuff must be out in plain sight.

Or the caller might have been the person who put the overalls and knife there—David's murderer—and if so, the stuff could be anywhere.

"Here," Mendoza said.

I raised my head. He was over against the other wall, on the side of the garage where David's car used to be parked.

"You found it?"

He nodded. "Come take a look."

I made my way around the convertible and over to him, in time to see him snap on a pair of thin rubber gloves he must have pulled out of his pocket. "I have to go to my car for a paper bag," he told me. "Don't touch."

I promised I wouldn't, and ended up standing there, with my hands clasped behind my back, while I waited for him to come back.

There was no doubt he'd found what we'd been

looking for. Up against the wall just inside the electronic garage door, was a wooden box with a sloped lid, a bit like an overlarge salt cellar. It came up to mid-thigh on me, and it was full of sand. The house sat atop a hill, with a long, sloped driveway down to the street. And while we don't usually get a lot of winter weather in Nashville, it happens. The sand was there so we could use it on the driveway in case of snow.

Now the lid was propped open, and inside I could see a bundle of utilitarian fabric. It looked a lot like what Bud the lube guy had worn yesterday. I couldn't see the knife, but I figured the overalls were probably wrapped around it, and when Mendoza took the bundle out of the sand box, he'd find the knife inside.

"Here." He nudged me aside. He was carrying a big, brown, grocery style bag that he opened and put on the floor. When he reached into the sand box and lifted the bundle of fabric out, I took a step back. My DNA wasn't on it now—I'd never seen it before—and just in case DNA could transfer over short distances of empty air, I wanted to put more space between myself and the stuff.

Mendoza unfolded the bundle carefully—probably expecting to find the knife inside, too. It started sliding, and Mendoza guided it into the paper bag before shaking out the overalls.

"One thing I can tell you," he told me, "whoever called it in either put the stuff here, or poked at it. The knife wasn't visible until I unrolled the fabric, so no one could have known it was there just by looking."

"It wasn't me."

He shot me a look. "Relax, Mrs. Kelly. If I thought it

was you, I'd have arrested you by now."

Good to know. At least until he added, "Although I could change my mind. So watch what you do."

"Yes, Detective," I said meekly.

The overalls, when unrolled and held up, looked like they might fit me reasonably well. They were too big, of course—a man's size—but I'm tallish for a woman, so I could have rolled up the sleeves and legs and gotten away with wearing them, especially in the dark.

They were bulky, though. If I did want to crawl underneath someone's car in the dark, I might have chosen to wear something that was easier to move around in. Yes, I'd run the risk of ruining whatever I was wearing, but sacrificing a pair of yoga pants and a T-shirt to the endeavor would have been worth it. And I would have had plenty of time to get rid of the evidence on the drive home. There were any number of dumpsters and trash cans between Fidelio's and home, along with a hospital, a college, and several apartment buildings.

Naturally I didn't tell Mendoza any of that. And besides, that wasn't what the real killer had done, anyway. He—or she—had held onto the knife and overalls, to plant in my garage.

Mendoza folded up the overalls and stuffed them into the paper bag. "These will have to go to the lab."

I nodded. "What are the chances you'll find anyone's DNA on them?"

"Pretty good," Mendoza said, "unless they were washed. What are the chances I'll find yours?"

I made sure my voice was steady. "Very slim. If they touched the little shovel that's in the sand box, and I touched the shovel last winter, or if whoever put the stuff here rubbed the overalls against the door handle of my car..."

"Right," Mendoza said, folding the top of the bag over. "We can worry about that later."

Or I could, at any rate. There was no reason for him to worry, either way.

"Thank you for taking care of Jacquie earlier," I said. "At the funeral."

Mendoza's lips quivered. "My pleasure."

"And thanks for convincing her she shouldn't come to the graveside service or the reception. I was afraid she might throw herself on top of the coffin as it went into the ground."

"I wouldn't have put it past her," Mendoza agreed. "We had a little talk. I explained that she was in breach of her own restraining order, and if she didn't go away and stay away, there was nothing I could do to keep you away from her."

"I'm not planning to go anywhere near her," I said. And I wasn't. I knew everything I needed to know about Jacquie. She seemed sincerely, if overly, distraught about David's death—or the loss of David's money—and I didn't think she'd had anything to do with killing him. Nick was another story—I still thought he might have done it—but it wasn't like I would learn whether he had or not by following him around. Besides, if the killer had put the overalls in the garage and called the police from one of the phones inside the house, it had to be one of the guests inside, or someone who had left already. But it couldn't be Nick. He might have found a way into the garage to plant the overalls and knife, but he couldn't have gotten into the house to make the phone call. Someone would have noticed him. Probably me.

"What do you think?" I asked Mendoza. "Whoever did this, probably did it to incriminate me, right?"

He nodded. "Unless..."

"Unless I did it, to make it look like someone else did it, to make it look like I didn't kill David."

He grinned. "Exactly. You have the makings of an investigator, Mrs. Kelly."

"Thank you," I said. "I think. Let's forget about that last one for a second and say it was someone else, and they did it to make me look suspicious."

Mendoza nodded.

"It had to be someone who was here earlier. Or is still here now."

Mendoza nodded.

"So say you did it."

His eyebrows crept up his forehead.

"Just go with it," I said. "You killed David, and you put the stuff in the sandbox to incriminate me. And then you called the police to make sure your plan succeeded."

Mendoza nodded, a tiny wrinkle between his brows.

"Would you leave before the police arrived, or would you stick around to see what happened?"

"I'd leave," Mendoza said promptly. "But most people would stick around. They wouldn't be able to resist."

"That's what I figured." I glanced at the door to the house. "David's murderer is one of the people inside right now."

"Or an accomplice," Mendoza said. "One person could have cut the brake lines, and another could have stashed the evidence."

True. "Nobody's missing, though. Everyone David knew has come through the house today. His children, his brother, his ex-wife, his lawyer. His business partner, his clients. Everyone except his mistress. And we know she didn't do it."

Mendoza shrugged.

"So now what?" I asked.

"Now I take this," he lifted the bag, "downtown and give it to the lab. They don't take weekends off, so hopefully they'll know something by tomorrow."

"DNA evidence?"

He shook his head. "That takes weeks. But if there are hairs or fibers, that'll give us a start. A long, blond hair would eliminate a lot of people."

But not me. "What about fingerprint evidence?"

"Fabric doesn't take fingerprints. Unless our friend got brake fluid on his hands, which isn't impossible. The knife is more likely, but I'm sure he wiped that. Or wore gloves when he used it."

He probably hadn't worn gloves when he put the evidence in my sandbox, though. At least I hadn't seen any of my guests walking around wearing gloves. Except Jacquie, and she hadn't been here.

"Are you going to test the box?" I asked hopefully.

Mendoza shook his head. "The wood's too rough to take prints. I'd have more luck with your doorknobs and phone handles, but with all the people coming and going here today, I'm not sure it's going to be worth it. But I'll send a team out. How many phone extensions?"

I counted on my fingers. "Hallway, kitchen, David's office, our bedroom, the bathroom, all three guestrooms, and the walk-in closet, of all places..."

Mendoza sighed.

"Whoever it was, couldn't have called from the hallway or kitchen," I told him. "There were too many people there. But someone could have snuck into David's office and used the extension there. Or snuck upstairs and used any of the phones on that level. Anyone who knew they were there."

"So someone who knew the house," Mendoza said. "And who knew the chances of someone else accidentally stumbling into an unused second-level bedroom were slim to none."

I nodded.

"I'll take this in and dispatch a CSI team to deal with fingerprints."

My eyes widened. "You aren't going to fingerprint all my guests, are you?"

If he did, David's funeral would be the talk of the season.

Of course, after Jacquie's performance, it probably already was.

Mendoza shook his head. "They'll check the phones. We'll worry about matching prints once we know whether we have any to match."

That made sense. I smiled. "Have a good weekend, Detective."

"You, too, Mrs. Kelly," Mendoza said. "Don't get in any trouble."

"That's what Diana said."

He tilted his head. "She was here, too?"

"Not in the garage. Or in the office. Or upstairs. She just stopped by to serve Anton Hess with papers saying that Judge Miller knows about the money David's been hiding. Mr. Hess wasn't happy."

"I wouldn't have been, either," Mendoza said, moving toward the door.

I followed. "Do you know anything about Krystal's boyfriend?"

"I know he's her alibi for the night her father died. Why?"

"Rachel says David didn't like him. Also, he smokes pot."

"How do you know?" Mendoza wanted to know, interested.

"I smelled it on him. He came around the corner of the garage just as Diana was leaving, and bumped into her. He was reeking of it."

"He has a record for possession," Mendoza said. "He's supposed to have cleaned up his act, but maybe he back-slid."

No maybe about it.

"Anything else you haven't told me?"

I thought about it. "Daniel got in my face. He was upset because I had sicced the police on him. I don't suppose you happened to ask him why he came to Nashville with a funeral suit in his luggage?"

"He said he had an appointment," Mendoza said, "and he needed to look good for it."

"An appointment? With who?"

"Whom," Mendoza said. "Your husband."

With David? "What about?"

"He wanted Mr. Kelly to bankroll a business he and your stepson wanted to start."

I snorted. "I can imagine what David said to that."

Mendoza's voice was bland. "Apparently he wasn't complimentary."

No, I hadn't thought he would be. But before I could ask any further questions—like, when had this appointment taken place, and was it possible Daniel and Kenny had killed David to inherit the money to get their business off the ground?—the door into the house opened. Farley stuck his head through and peered around. "Is everything all right, Gina?"

"Everything is fine," I said. "Detective Mendoza was just leaving."

Mendoza nodded. "Excuse me, Mr. Hollingsworth." He took the stairs up to the kitchen two at a time. Farley pulled his head back inside the house, and Mendoza disappeared through the opening. I followed, to fetch up in the hallway, surrounded by a crowd of people.

"I'll be in touch, Mrs. Kelly," Mendoza told me formally.

I nodded. "Thank you, Detective. Have a nice weekend."

"You too, Mrs. Kelly."

He headed for the door. The crowd parted for him like the Red Sea for Moses. We all just stood there and watched until the front door had closed behind him.

"Well," I said brightly, "I guess that's that."

Everyone stared at me.

"I trust you're all having a good time? Eating and drinking and all?"

A few heads nodded.

"If you'll excuse me," I said, "there's something I have to do."

I didn't wait for anyone to respond, just walked down the hallway to David's office, opened the door, and disappeared inside.

It wasn't until I'd closed the door behind me that I looked around and realized that not only had someone been here before me, and that someone hadn't just used the phone—if the phone call to the police had been made from David's office—but he (or she) had searched the place, as well.

Drawers were open with papers on the floor, the surface of the desk was an unholy mess, and someone had gone through both the bookshelves—dropping books left and right—and David's bank of filing cabinets. One drawer wasn't quite closed, and the corner of a manila folder was stuck in the gap.

I stood just inside the door and looked around, mouth agape. And then I backed out slowly and locked the door behind me. Once Jaime Mendoza's CSI team arrived, they could tackle it. Speaking for myself, I'd had enough.

CHAPTER THIRTEEN

I used a couple of extension cords I found in the garage to block off the stairs to the second floor. I figured whoever had tossed David's office, had probably also made the phone call to the police from there, but just in case two different people were behind the two things, I wanted to protect whatever evidence was upstairs until Mendoza's CSI team could arrive. I have no idea what my guests thought about what was going on, and I didn't care. At that point, I just wanted them all to go away.

Of course they didn't. They hung out for another eternity, grazing their way through the buffet, emptying the wine bottles, and talking about David's many virtues.

By the time the last one of them rolled slowly down the driveway, I was sick enough of people that I wanted to scream. And I still had Rachel to get rid of.

"I'll help you clean up," she told me.

I looked around at the mess—the picked-over platters, the used flatware and silverware, the crumbs—and shook my head. "That's not necessary. The catering company will be here within the hour to pick up their plates and silverware. And packing up the food will give me something to do tonight."

I had nothing else to look forward to. The CSI team probably wouldn't be very entertaining, and Mendoza wasn't likely to come back.

"It's a lot of work," Rachel said, looking around as well.

"That's OK. I don't have much else to do these days."

She nodded, as if she knew what I was talking about. "My husband passed away seven years ago. Heart attack in bed."

God, how awful. Especially if, you know, they'd been in the middle of something. Bad enough to lose David in a car accident, but in the middle of coitus...? "I'm so sorry."

"It wasn't my bed," Rachel said. "Until that happened, I had no idea he was fooling around with someone else."

I winced.

"That's when I went to work for your husband. I didn't have anything to live on. No pension, no life insurance. No savings. I needed an income."

I nodded.

"I didn't want him back," Rachel said. "I wouldn't have taken him back if he came crawling to me on his hands and knees. But I remember how empty the house was. How I realized I had no life apart from him."

Yes, indeed.

"We'd been married more than twenty years. And suddenly I was alone. And I realized I had no idea who I was."

Boy, could I relate.

"Having to go out and find a job was a relief. It kept me from sitting at home with nothing to do."

"I get it," I said. "And I won't brood. I'll clean up, and then I'll probably go to bed. It's been a long day. And then tomorrow I'll find something to do."

Something useful. The judge might still rule in David's favor, and I'd inherit nothing. I'd have to go out too, like Rachel, and find a job.

"Just how easy is it to find a job, anyway?"

"When you're over forty and you have no education?" She shook her head. "Not easy."

"What are you going to do now?"

"I have a little time. I'll figure something out." She sounded confident. Good for her.

"It seems Daniel and Kenny were hoping to start a business together," I said. "Detective Mendoza said they were trying to get David to bankroll them."

Rachel nodded. "Mr. Kelly said no."

"But now that he's gone, they'll probably both inherit something. David made provisions in his will for Daniel, I think, and since I'm not their mother, the estate gets divided upon David's death, and Krystal and Kenny get their shares. If Daniel and Kenny put their money together, they may have enough to start their business."

"Yes," Rachel said, "but what they wanted, was to open a bar. And I don't want to work in a bar."

Hard to blame her for that. "Well, I wish you the best," I said, fervently hoping that I wouldn't find myself in the same position in a couple of weeks or months. "And if there's anything I can do..."

"I'll let you know. Let me leave you my phone

number. Just in case you need anything." She looked around for a pen and paper, and found both hanging on the fridge.

"You're being very nice to me all of a sudden," I said, while I watched her scribble down her number. "Is it because David's dead and you feel sorry for me?"

She shook her head. "It's because while Mr. Kelly was alive and fooling around, I was feeling guilty. I couldn't tell you, because if I did, I'd lose my job, and every time you were nice to me, I felt bad that I was lying to you."

"You weren't lying to me," I said. "David was."

"I might as well have been." She finished writing the number down, and turned to me. "If you're sure you don't need my help, I'll head home now."

"That's fine," I said. "You've been a great help already. The caterers will be here soon. And it's been a long, crazy day. I just want to put my feet up and not have to be nice to anyone."

Rachel nodded. "Totally understandable. Call if you need anything."

She headed for the door with me trailing behind.

"I did have a question," I said. "This meeting Daniel and Kenny had with David, the one when he said no to backing their bar. When did it take place."

"Tuesday afternoon," Rachel said.

And by Tuesday evening, David was dead.

"Do you have any idea how much they were asking for?"

But Rachel shook her head. "He didn't tell me that. And they weren't speaking loud enough that I could hear the details."

"I appreciate it." I opened the front door and held it while she passed through. "Drive carefully."

"You, too, Mrs. Kelly," Rachel said.

"I think by now you could probably call me Gina. David's dead, so he isn't your boss anymore. And Mrs. Kelly makes me feel old."

Rachel grinned. "Of course, Gina. Have a good evening."

"Likewise," I said, and watched her get into her car and navigate slowly down the driveway. When her taillights had turned left at the street, I closed the door and kicked off my heels, and headed into the dining room to pour myself a glass of wine.

By the time the doorbell rang fifteen minutes later, I'd changed into a T-shirt and a pair of yoga pants, and was busy covering the leftovers with plastic wrap and storing them in the refrigerator, between sips of Cabernet.

I expected the caterers, but it was actually the CSI team that arrived first. There were three of them, two women and a guy—not Jaime Mendoza—and I had shown them the sandbox in the garage and was in the process of explaining that my late husband's office didn't usually look the way it did now, when the caterers arrived. So I left the CSI team in David's office to see what fingerprints or clothing fibers they could find, and went to greet the catering team. There were three of them, as well, all women, and we spent the next fifteen minutes in the kitchen, finishing the job of emptying the trays so they could pack them up and remove them.

Once that was done, I headed back to the CSI team,

which was still immersed in David's office.

"This will take a while, Mrs. Kelly," one of the women told me when I stuck my head around the door to see how they were getting on. "There's a lot of upheaval in this room. And Jaime said we have three or four rooms to do upstairs, as well."

I nodded. "I think whoever called, probably called from down here, but I'm not sure. There were so many people in the house that I have no idea where anyone was most of the time. Someone could have gone upstairs for five minutes, and I would never have noticed."

She nodded. "We'll be here for hours yet."

And she must have seen the dismay on my face—all I wanted to do was take my glass of wine and crawl into bed, and if there was a CSI team fine-tooth combing my house, I couldn't—because she added, "Do you have somewhere else you can go for the night?"

For a second, I thought about Rachel, and about calling to ask if I could crash on her couch for the night. But I really didn't want the company. I wanted to be alone. I'd been surrounded by people all day, and I needed some time to myself.

Maybe I could rent a hotel room for the night?

That cost money, though, and I didn't know how much of that I'd have, going forward. And on a Friday night, there were no guarantees that I'd be able to find a vacancy anywhere I'd consider staying. A fleabag motel on Murfreesboro Pike was out of the question. Not on the day I had buried my husband.

It was the thought of David that clarified things. I still had his keychain, and the penthouse was just sitting there in the Gulch, empty. I could spend the night there.

So what if he'd screwed Jacquie in that bed? I could change the sheets.

"Yes, thank you." I smiled at the CSI tech. "I do. I'll just throw a few things into an overnight bag and be out of your way."

"Take your time," the tech said. "And you're not in our way. We'll be busy in here for the next hour, at least."

Wonderful. I headed up the stairs to throw my pajamas and robe and a change of underwear for tomorrow into a bag, before I headed back down and stuck my head into the office. "I'm going. The fridge is full of leftovers from the funeral, if you get hungry. Please help yourselves. I'll probably just end up throwing half of it away if you don't."

They exchanged a glance. "Thank you, Mrs. Kelly."

"You can leave through the garage when you're done. Just make sure the front and back doors are locked, and then hit the button for the garage door and get out before it closes."

"We'll do that," one of them said. "Thank you, Mrs. Kelly."

"Good luck. I hope you find something."

They looked around, at the mess left by whoever had rifled through David's office. "Oh, I'm sure we'll find plenty. Whether it's going to be helpful, is another story."

Right. "My fingerprints are on a wineglass on the kitchen counter, if you need them." As well as all over the rest of the house, obviously.

"Thank you, Mrs. Kelly," the tech said. "That's most helpful."

The subtext was, *now get the hell out of here and let us work.* They probably wanted to go home for the weekend, too.

"See you." I headed out the door to the garage and let them fend for themselves.

David's apartment building looked just the same as it had two days ago: upscale, expensive, and snooty. The same young man was sitting behind the security desk, leafing through a magazine. When he saw me, he turned pale, and the magazine slithered off his lap and to the floor. It might have been deliberate. Maybe he was looking at dirty pictures.

"I'm going up to the penthouse," I told him. "David was buried today. The house is still a mess after the funeral. And I need some peace and quiet."

He swallowed and nodded.

"Does the restaurant—" on the first floor of the building, "—deliver upstairs?"

"Yes, ma'am." His voice squeaked and he had to clear his throat. While he did, he kept nodding. Over and over. "They sure do."

"Wonderful." I gave him my best smile and watched him color. Not bad for an old lady. "Thank you."

"Yes, ma'am." He cleared his throat, and kept clearing it as I headed for the elevator. Sweet boy.

Upstairs, I dumped my overnight bag in the hallway, and headed directly into the living room, where the view at night, through the floor-to-ceiling windows, was everything I'd hoped for. After a quick phone call downstairs, to order a serving of chicken and broccoli to be delivered, I opened a bottle of David's wine and curled up on the white leather sofa and let out a breath I felt like I'd been holding all day.

It hadn't been the worst day of my life—the day I lost my mother was probably at the top of that list, and the day David told me about Jacquie was a close second—but it was up there. Knowing I'd be on display all day, that everyone would keep watching me for signs of grief or guilt, had kept me on my toes, and between Jacquie's performance at the funeral and the confrontation with Daniel when I got home, I'd been a nervous wreck by the time the reception started. And then to have Detective Mendoza show up, to say that someone had made an anonymous phone call essentially accusing me of murder... well, it would have been enough to rattle anyone.

Thankfully, he didn't seem inclined to think I was guilty. I'm sure I was on the suspect list—I would have to be—but although I probably had the most obvious motive, I didn't get the feeling he was gearing up to arrest me. Unless he was just giving me enough rope to hang myself...

It was a disconcerting thought. And quite likely. In fact, why else would he be so nice, and even a bit flirtatious, with me? He couldn't possibly be interested. Not only was he a decade too young, but there was that wife and kid he had. And besides, wasn't there rules about getting involved with suspects? My far-from-vast knowledge of the intricacies of police work had come from watching TV, so it wasn't like I knew a lot, but I could swear that that had been a plot point in a few movies I'd seen: the cop's involvement with one of the suspects, and how unethical it was.

So yes, he was probably just leading me along by the nose, waiting for me to do something incriminating so he could swoop in and arrest me.

If the crime scene team found my fingerprints all over David's office, would that be enough for an arrest warrant?

I mean, they would. It was inevitable. I hadn't spent much time there, but it was just a few days since I'd been standing at the desk, manipulating the rolodex, and writing down names and phone numbers for Mendoza.

Hell, it was just one day since I'd used the fax machine to send David's account statements to Diana. I'd even used the phone extension to call and tell her they were coming. My fingerprints were all over that room. If nobody else's fingerprints were found, would Mendoza arrest me?

The doorbell tore me out of my reverie, and none too soon. I put the glass down and padded barefoot to the door to receive my dinner. And because I was feeling rebellious, and because I'd already cleaned my share of platters and silverware today, I just grabbed a fork from the drawer and ate straight out of the carton while I watched the Millennium Falcon get sucked up by the tractor beam.

Eventually I fell asleep, right there on the sofa, and when I woke up, sunlight was pouring through the floor-to-ceiling windows. Everything appeared a lot brighter than it had last night. The world looked brand new and shiny, and it was the first day of the rest of my life. All I had to do was make sure I didn't end up in prison for murdering my almost-ex husband, and everything would be fine.

But that might be easier said than done, I admitted as I faced myself in the bathroom mirror, with toothpaste foaming about my lips. Someone seemed to be trying to pin David's death on me.

Was it because I was convenient and had a compelling motive, or was it personal? Was someone out to get me personally?

Hard to believe. Not only am I mostly nice, but I didn't think I'd truly pissed anyone off enough that they'd kill David just to ensure I ended up in prison.

Sandra had probably resented me for stealing her husband away. But that was eighteen years ago. A bit long to be holding a grudge.

Although, when she and David had their fling recently, she might have believed he'd leave me and come back to her. And when he didn't...

Well, when he didn't, it hadn't been because of me. It was because of Jacquie. So if Sandra wanted to kill David and frame someone for murder, she should be framing Jacquie, not me.

Except nobody in their right mind would believe that Jacquie killed David. Not before she got her hands on all that lovely money.

And we were back to me, and my extremely compelling motive.

So no, I couldn't think of anyone who hated me enough to want to see me behind bars. It was much more likely that the killer wanted David out of the way, and I was the most convenient scapegoat.

I already knew who the suspects were. Nick, for love of Jacquie. Kenny and Daniel, for love of money. And now, maybe Krystal and/or her boyfriend, because of David's disapproval of the match.

Krystal didn't need David's approval to marry her boyfriend, though. And she had her own income, so even if David threatened to cut her out of the will, she'd survive.

Nick was young, and good-looking. He could just wait for Jacquie to outlive David, or get tired of him. I doubted it would take long. Nick could find someone else to sleep with in the meantime. I didn't think he'd have a problem getting laid.

That left Kenny and Daniel. Money is always a compelling reason to want someone dead, and they had asked David for capital to start a business, but David had said no. How much did they stand to gain when he died?

Enough that it made sense to kill him?

Anton Hess would have a copy of the will on file in his office, although chances were good he wouldn't share it with me. But David must have had a copy, too. Had he taken it with him when he moved out of the house in Hillwood, or was it still in the office at home?

It took me less than an hour to turn David's penthouse upside down. There was no will. I went through the drawer in the kitchen again, and found only what I'd found last time: old mail, paid bills, bank and credit card statements, and the like.

A couple of file boxes in the back of the closet looked promising, until I took the lids off and realized they only contained copies of business files. Something David had brought home during the past couple of months, probably, since he left the house in Hillwood. I flipped through them, but couldn't see anything out of the ordinary. And since David's clients' financial matters are confidential, and certainly none of my business, I didn't look closely. Just close enough to see that there was no copy of David's will in either box.

Back to the house in Hillwood it was, then, for a thorough search of the office there. I had to do that anyway, since the CSI team had told me to look for anything missing. Now I wondered, for the first time, whether whoever had torn the office apart, had been looking for the will. He or she had been looking for something, and the will made as much sense as anything else.

I had lost sight of Daniel after he'd threatened me and then pushed past me into the house yesterday afternoon. I'd gotten busy with Rachel, and then other people had started showing up. But Daniel would have had time to go into the office to look around. And he'd certainly seemed angry enough with me to be willing—or happy—to frame me for murder.

If he knew he stood to inherit something, but he didn't know how much, he might have wanted a look at the provisions. Especially if there was some sort of timeline on this bar purchase he and Kenny wanted to make. Probate can take some time, but if they knew the money was coming, they might be able to keep the deal alive on the assurance. And between the hurry and the temper Daniel had been in yesterday, he might have left the office looking the way it did.

Looked like it was time for me to leave the castle in the sky and return to reality. I cast a last, longing glance at the floor-to-ceiling windows and the skyline beyond, and turned toward the door.

CHAPTER FOURTEEN

Back in Hillwood, everything looked the same. Including the office.

The CSI team had left a liberal sprinkling of fingerprint power on every flat surface, and the bright light of day exposed every tiny detail of destruction I had missed last night.

I stood in the doorway with my hands on my hips, surveying the terrain and realizing that it would take me the rest of the day just to clean this one room up. Meanwhile, the sun was shining outside and someone was trying to frame me for murder.

It didn't seem like a good use of my time.

But maybe I didn't have to.

I fished the phone out of my purse and dialed Detective Mendoza's number.

"Mrs. Kelly." He didn't sound happy to hear from me.

"Good morning, Detective," I said brightly.

"So far," Mendoza answered. My eyes narrowed. I hadn't even gotten around to asking what I wanted to ask yet, and he was already being insulting.

My feelings must have conveyed themselves down the line, because he added, more conciliatory, "What can I do for you, Mrs. Kelly?"

"I had a quick question," I said.

"Just one?"

I pursed my lips, but didn't comment, even though I wanted to. "For the moment. Although the first answer might lead to more questions."

Mendoza muttered something, and then raised his voice. "What do you want to know?"

"I was wondering whether your CSI team made a list of the paperwork they came across in David's office last night. Or doesn't their job extend to that?"

Mendoza admitted, somewhat reluctantly, that it did.

"So if something was here, it would be on the list?"

"Yes, Mrs. Kelly," Mendoza said patiently. "What are you looking for?"

I told him.

His voice rose. "Your husband's will?"

"I know his lawyer has a copy. But Anton Hess isn't going to share it with me. Especially on a Saturday. And I'm sure David must have had a copy, but it isn't in the new apartment. And it's going to take me all day to go through this mess. So I thought, if your crew had made a list of what they found, maybe I could just ask whether they'd come across it, so at least I won't waste my time looking for something that isn't here."

I smiled optimistically.

"Hold on," Mendoza said, his voice resigned. The next thing I heard was a click, and then nothing.

Several minutes went by. Long enough that I started to wonder whether he'd ever come back. Maybe he just planned to let me sit on hold until I got tired of waiting and hung up. It would be an easy way to get rid of me. At least for the time being. I'd be back, of course, but at least he wouldn't have to deal with me right now.

But then the phone clicked again. "Mrs. Kelly?"

"Still here," I said.

"There was no will in your husband's office last night."

Huh. "Thank you."

"Did he have a safety deposit box?"

"If he did, I won't be able to access it today. The banks are closed."

Mendoza didn't respond to that.

"I'll check on Monday."

And in the meantime, I'd use the keychain to make a trip to the Hollingsworth & Kelly office. Just in case David had put his will in the safe there. Today would be a perfect day to look around, anyway, since nobody would be working. Not even Farley put in time at the office on Saturdays. And since he'd fired Rachel, the place would be empty.

"Since I've got you..." I said, and then bit my tongue, a second too late. "What I meant to ask is, did your crew find any fingerprints in the office last night?"

"Lots," Mendoza said. He sounded gleeful.

"Mine, David's..."

"We don't know yet. There hasn't been time to process them all. And we don't have anyone's fingerprints to match them against."

"I left a glass with mine on the counter," I said helpfully.

"They told me." He sounded like he might be thinking about laughing. Or like he might actually be laughing, but doing a halfway decent job of hiding it. "Thank you."

"Hunh," I said. "What about the knife? Did you check that for fingerprints?"

"Yes. Yours weren't on it."

"I know that," I said, irritated. "I never touched the knife. How could my fingerprints be on it?"

"They couldn't."

"Right. Were someone else's?"

"No," Mendoza said, still sounding like he was having a hard time not laughing. "It was wiped clean."

"Figures."

"You could have wiped it clean as easily as anyone else."

I rolled my eyes. "I didn't."

He didn't respond to that. "Anything else, Mrs. Kelly?"

"No," I said. "Have a nice day, Detective. Enjoy spending time with your wife and kid."

I hung up before he could answer. I hadn't even lowered the phone when it rang again. "For your information," Mendoza told me, "I'm working today. So watch your back."

This time he hung up without waiting for me to answer. And since I didn't want to lower myself to his level, I didn't call back. Although I did stick my tongue out at the phone for a second, before putting it back on the base and heading out the door.

The drive to Music Row was uneventful. Traffic was light, except for the stretch past the Green Hills Mall, which is always crazy, no matter the day or time. I pulled into the empty parking lot behind the Hollingsworth & Kelly office a few minutes before noon and cut the engine.

Mine was the only car in the lot. Farley and Martha were probably hanging out at home, or enjoying a brisk game of golf, or maybe a museum. And of course Rachel was somewhere, doing whatever it was Rachel did. Polishing up her résumé, most likely.

I walked into her office first. It's in front of David's, since Rachel's job was to make his job easier.

Now it was empty. All the things that had given the place personality were gone. The bobble-head football player on the desk, the family photos on the console, the cat-faced mug with pens and pencils. The pens and pencils were there, jumbled in the desk drawer, but anything that Rachel had brought into the place was gone.

It was weird.

And not just because it was empty; because I didn't understand.

OK, so it was David who had hired Rachel. He'd felt he needed an assistant, and he'd gone out and found one. And now that David was gone, Rachel's job was, to a degree, obsolete. Farley certainly wasn't going to be doing it.

But he'd need someone to help him with things, wouldn't he? Someone to answer the phones, if nothing else. And someone to bring in new clients. Rachel hadn't been doing that, but as David had discovered, it took two people to keep things running. One person couldn't do both the administrative work and schmooze the clients.

So what was Farley going to do, all on his own? And why hadn't he kept Rachel around at least long enough to get things back on track after David's passing? I had to believe that David's death would have an impact on the clients. Some of them must be considering, right about now, whether to find a different financial team.

And what was Rachel going to do now? David had taken a chance on her at forty-plus. But was anyone else going to take a chance at her at almost fifty? And what if no one did? That severance package of Farley's wouldn't last forever.

But it wasn't any of my concern, and more importantly, there was nothing I could do about it. David's share of the business wouldn't come to me, or to any of his children. It went to Farley. So Farley could do whatever he wanted to keep things running. Or run the business into the ground, if he so chose. There was nothing anyone else could do about it. And I wasn't in a position to offer Rachel other work. Unless she wanted to come clean my house once a week, but that would be an insulting offer, and besides, who knew if I could afford to hire someone? I might have to learn to vacuum my own floors soon.

I left my contemplation of what had been Rachel's office, and pushed open the door to David's.

And stopped in the doorway, struck by emotions.

Here, everything looked the same. It even smelled like him, and although I'm not a fan of Nautica, I inhaled deeply. When my eyes filled with tears, I didn't try to fight them. We'd spent eighteen years together. Eighteen—for the most part—good years. A lot of affection and laughter, some fighting, some makeup sex, and a whole lot of breakfasts and dinners and conversations and TV shows. And now he was gone. The smell was the only thing left, and soon that would be gone, as well. And while I didn't mourn the man who had cheated on me, and left me, and tricked me into filing for divorce first, and tried to hide assets from me so I would get as little as possible in the divorce settlement—I did mourn the husband he'd been for the seventeen years prior to that.

I don't know how long I might have stood there, sniffing, if it hadn't been for the sound of a key in the front door. Then the scrape of the handle turning, and a change in air pressure as the door opened.

I figured it was either Rachel or Farley. Nobody else had keys, as far as I knew. Which was why, when I heard a thud, followed by a very unladylike curse in a breathy, female voice, I arched my brows and turned in that direction.

The newcomer was someone I had never seen in my life before. Younger than Jacquie, with a cloud of sunny, blond hair and big, China-blue eyes. An extremely nubile little body was decked out in faded jeans and red-and-white gingham shirt tied between her breasts. She was even wearing cowboy boots. It was like watching Ellie Mae Clampett in the flesh.

The very, very young flesh.

Happily, I seemed to have startled her as much as

she'd startled me.

"Oh!" For a second, it looked like she might be about to drop the cardboard box she was carrying. It slipped an inch or two before she firmed her grip on it.

"Hello." I smiled. Tightly, and with no teeth.

There was a pause. When she didn't speak, I added, pointedly, "I'm Regina Kelly."

"Oh." This time she flushed, from the cleavage to the roots of her hair. She juggled the box so she could reach out a hand to shake. "Michele Weber. But you can call me Shelby!"

Or not. "Nice to meet you," I said. And waited. She still hadn't explained what she was doing here.

She shifted her weight from one foot to the other. "I'm Mr. Hollingsworth's new assistant."

Ah. Well, that explained Rachel, at any rate.

"Congratulations," I said. "I'm just here to pick up some of David's personal effects."

She nodded. "Farley..." She shot a guilty look at his office door. "I heard about your husband's accident. I'm sorry for your loss."

She was well brought-up, if nothing else. "Thank you."

There was another beat.

"If you're looking for Rachel's office," I said, "it's through there." I gestured to the door. "I'll just go back into David's office and see what I can dig up."

Shelby nodded. I waited a second to see whether she'd say anything else, and when she didn't, I headed back in the direction I'd come.

This time I didn't stop in the doorway to smell the

Nautica. The scent had mostly dissipated anyway, in the couple of minutes the door had stood open. Or maybe my nose had gotten used to it. Instead, I headed directly for the safe in the corner of the room, as I dug David's keychain out of my pocket. I could hear Shelby moving around in what used to be Rachel's office. Getting ready to start work on Monday, I guess. Maybe Farley had informed her that he wouldn't be paying her to get settled in; she'd have to show up Monday morning ready to work. Maybe that's why she was moving her stuff in today.

And then I stopped thinking about it when the door to the safe opened.

Five minutes later, I closed it again, frustrated. The safe had yielded nothing of interest. Certainly no copy of David's will. There'd been the original documents David had used to set up the accounts I had found statements for in the penthouse, as well as the original documents for the accounts we held together, but I already knew about those. There'd been a couple of life insurance policies: one each for Krystal and Kenny, with David as the beneficiary, now moot. One on me, with David as beneficiary; also moot. One on him, with me as the beneficiary—and I had kept that one out, so I could notify the insurance company on Monday that he'd passed away.

He'd also had an insurance policy on Farley. For business purposes, I guess. Farley might have had one on David, as well—for business purposes—but if so, it wasn't in David's safe. And if he'd ever had one on his first wife, it wasn't here.

I locked the safe and straightened to look around.

There were filing cabinets alone one wall, full of business files, I assumed. But it wasn't likely that David's will would be there. Why would it be, when he had a safe he could keep it in?

I opened a drawer at random anyway, just so I could say I did, and saw what I'd expected to see: a row of manila folders arranged in alphabetical order by last name. Client files.

And as such, none of my business. I closed the drawer again, just as I heard a door open in the outer office. A second later, there was Farley's voice. "Shelby?"

If Shelby answered—with anything but a smile—I didn't hear it. And I didn't hear Farley say anything else, either; not even a murmur of voices. But after a moment I heard his footsteps come across the floor, and then he appeared in the doorway.

"Gina?"

I pushed the file drawer shut with a finger. "Hi."

Farley looked at it, before turning his attention to me. "What's going on?"

"Nothing." I walked toward the desk, where I'd left my purse. "I was just looking for something in David's things."

"What?"

Not that it was any of his concern, but— "David's will."

He blinked. Maybe he'd expected me to say I was looking for something to do with the business. And of course I wasn't. His and David's business holdings were none of my concern.

"It isn't here," Farley said.

No, it wasn't. "I'll check the safety deposit box at the bank on Monday."

He nodded. "What's that?"

He was looking at the papers in my hand.

"Insurance policy," I told him, as I approached the door.

He made no move to step out of the doorway. Instead, his brows drew together. "Let me see that."

"It's mine," I said, although I held it up and pointed. "See? My name. Yours is still in the safe."

"Mine?"

"David had an insurance policy on you, too. One on me, one on you, one on each of his kids. And this one, which has me as the beneficiary. I have to call the insurance company on Monday."

Farley didn't react for a second, then he moved out of the doorway. "There's a lot to remember when someone dies."

Yes, indeed. I glanced around the office. "Most of what's here looks like it's business related. But if you come across anything personal, and you want me to come pick it up, you know where to find me."

Farley nodded.

"I think there are copies of everything in his office at home, too. What do you want me to do with those?"

"Have a bonfire," Farley said.

I arched my brows—as a suggestion, it seemed a little out of character—and he added, "If the originals are here, I don't need the copies. Shred them or burn them. Or if you want, you can box them up and I'll come pick them up and shred them myself."

"That won't be necessary." I'd just use them for kindling in the fireplace this winter, if that's what he wanted. By then, I might not be able to afford firewood. "I guess the same thing goes for the files in the penthouse?"

Farley muttered something. I waited. "Yes," he said. "Please."

"No problem. I'll take care of it. I'm sure you have plenty to do to get Shelby up to speed."

I waited for him to say something—something to explain why he'd fired Rachel, who had the experience and who was familiar with the ins and outs of the business—in favor of this fresh-out-of-high-school eighteen-year-old who would probably give his wife conniptions... but he didn't.

"Let me walk you out," he said instead.

"Thank you." Nice of him, but completely unnecessary. I knew my way, and it wasn't like I could get lost.

"My pleasure." He put a hand at the small of my back. Again, nice and polite. I don't know why I felt like he was pushing me toward the exit, because he really wasn't. I was moving under my own steam. I just felt maneuvered.

It wasn't until I was outside in the parking lot, with the door securely latched behind me, that I realized why Farley might have wanted to get rid of me.

Duh.

I'd been holding Farley up as the ideal of masculine fidelity—faithful to Martha through thick and thin, while David had been sticking it to Jacquie and anyone else who'd have him—and all along Farley had been planning to hire a younger woman to take Rachel's place. A younger woman he was probably trying to talk out of her jeans right now.

Duh.

I turned the key in the ignition with a little more force than necessary, disgusted with David and Farley and the entire male half of the human race.

CHAPTER FIFTEEN

Now that I knew I could just get rid of David's business papers, that I didn't have to sort them and get them back into the correct folders, it didn't even take two hours to put the office to rights.

I ate some leftovers when I got back to the house—the CSI crew had grazed their way through a lot of what was in the fridge, but there was enough left for lunch—and then I went to work. All of David's business papers went directly into the shredder, and then into a half dozen small lawn-and-leaf bags I found in the garage.

When they were full, I wrestled them, one by one, out to the trash can and tossed them in. After that, the rest of the cleanup was a breeze. All the pens and pencils went back into the desk, along with all the paperclips and rubber bands. I had to sort the various bank statements and bills into piles and stuff them back into the filing cabinets, but there weren't enough of them that it took forever. I might not have been as precise as perhaps I should have been, either, since I wanted to get the job done. So no chronological order from latest to first or vice versa. But when I was done, everything looked pretty much like normal, other than the streaks of gray fingerprint powder everywhere.

The first thing I did, was pull out the vacuum, to suck up as much of it as I could. That turned out to be a double-edged sword, as the vacuum picked some of the powder up, but swirled more up into the air. I sneezed.

After I'd gotten rid of as much of the dry stuff as I could, there was still plenty left, on all the flat surfaces. The window sills, the top of the desk, the filing cabinets. I looked around helplessly, and then reached for my phone.

"Mendoza," Mendoza said. He must be in the middle of something, to sound so brusque. Either that, or he was tired of hearing from me.

Just in case he was in the middle of something, I'd better be brisk, too, and not indulge in pointless chatter. "What do you use to clean fingerprint powder?"

There was a beat. "You're calling me for cleaning advice?"

"Your CSI crew left fingerprint powder all over my office," I said. "Not that I'm not grateful for everything they did. But I have to clean it up. And it doesn't vacuum well. It's making me sneeze. And some of it has stained the carpet."

Mendoza sighed. "Dishwashing liquid."

"That's it?"

"And water."

Dishwashing liquid and water. Who knew?

"Thank you," I said.

"You're welcome, Mrs. Kelly."

I waited, but he didn't hang up.

"Farley has hired a new administrative assistant," I told him. "He fired Rachel. It was her last day yesterday. Today, when I got to the office, a new assistant was getting organized. Blond, beautiful, and dumb as a post. Not a day over twenty." The kind of woman I had expected Rachel to be, back when David hired her.

Mendoza made a noise. I'm not sure whether it was amusement or cynicism.

"Do all men cheat?" I said, exasperated.

I hadn't expected an answer. I hadn't asked the question thinking I'd get one. It was more of a rhetorical question, or a complaint.

Imagine my surprise.

"Yes," Mendoza said.

Great.

And because I felt stupid, I didn't think before I spoke. "Does your wife know?"

There was another moment of silence, long enough for me to realize I'd gone way beyond personal and into pretty damned rude.

"I'm sorry—" I began, just as Mendoza said, "Yes. That's why we're divorced."

This time the pause was all mine.

I was feeling a bit conflicted. Embarrassed, because I'd asked totally inappropriate questions and probably offended him. But also a bit relieved, because... well, because he wasn't married. So maybe I wouldn't go to hell for lusting.

Of course, he was still too young. Although he was well over legal age, so it wasn't like I was having inappropriate thoughts about a teenager.

"I'm sorry," I said again when I'd gotten my breath back. "It's none of my business. I was very rude. I apologize."

This time I'm sure I heard amusement. "Don't worry about it."

"I'll just go away now." And clean my office. As penance.

He didn't tell me not to. "Have a good evening, Mrs. Kelly."

"Thank you, Detective Mendoza," I answered. "You, too."

After I'd hung up, I thunked my forehead against the tabletop a couple of times for good measure, and had to go to the bathroom to wash the fingerprint powder off my skin before I mixed up the solution of dishwashing liquid and water I hoped would clean up the rest of the mess.

I had hoped—really, I had—that this would be my last encounter with Detective Mendoza for the day. Usually, I enjoyed a chance to look at him, or even talking to him, but after wedging my foot so firmly into my mouth earlier, I just wanted to avoid the man for a while.

So of course something happened that necessitated another call to the MNPD.

It was late afternoon, after five, when my phone rang. The number was not familiar, nor was the voice that greeted me. "Mrs. Kelly?"

"This is she."

"This is Zachary Brennan."

Who?

"I'm the doorman at the Apex, where your husband's

penthouse is."

"Of course," I said smoothly. "I'm sorry. What can I do for you, Zachary?"

"Well," Zachary—whose voice I now sort of recognized—said, "are you upstairs right now, Mrs. Kelly?"

"No," I said. "I'm in Hillwood."

"Is it possible someone else could be upstairs?"

No one should be upstairs. Unless David had given a key to someone. Like Jacquie.

Although, even if he had, she had no business there now that he was gone.

"It's possible," I allowed. "Why do you ask?"

"Because the door's cracked open," Zachary said. "One of the other penthouse floor tenants informed me. I went upstairs and knocked and called out to see if anyone would answer, but no one did, and I didn't want to go inside without permission..."

He trailed off.

"I'll be right there," I said. "Or not *right* there—it'll take about thirty minutes—but I'm on my way. Don't let anyone into the place."

"No, Mrs. Kelly," Zachary said.

"And don't go inside yourself." Just in case.

"No, Mrs. Kelly," Zachary said.

"I'm on my way."

"Yes, Mrs. Kelly," Zachary said. "Should I call the police?"

I hesitated. I should probably put in a call to Mendoza, but I didn't want to. I had already made a fool of myself in front of him, or on the phone with him, once today, and if he got there and everything looked normal, I'd look like even more of an idiot. Maybe no one had been inside at all. Maybe the door just hadn't latched completely behind me when I left this morning.

OK, so I really didn't think so. They were strong, sturdy, heavy doors. I'd be more worried about locking myself out than about the door not latching. But it was possible. And until I knew more, I didn't want to jump the gun.

"No," I said, eventually. "Let's take a look first. There's no point in involving them if nothing's wrong."

"Yes, Mrs. Kelly," Zachary said.

He was waiting for me in the lobby when I burst through the door, still in the same uniform of black pants and red jacket. He looked a bit like a bellhop from an old-fashioned movie. And although he appeared to be around fourteen, he probably wasn't. Considering how many hours he worked, he had to be of legal age. There are laws against child labor.

"How old are you?" I wanted to know.

He swallowed. "Twenty."

"Why aren't you in college?"

"I'm waiting to apply to the police academy when I turn twenty-one," Zachary said.

"You could be getting an education while you're waiting. Study criminal justice, or something."

"I'm sick of school," Zachary said. "I sucked at it."

OK, then. "Do you want to come upstairs, or do you have to stay here?"

"I'd like to come upstairs," Zachary said. "Just in case

you need help."

If any of us needed help, I'd put my money on me helping Zachary rather than vice versa—he was shorter than me by an inch or two, and we probably weighed about the same—but if he wanted to tag along to protect me, I wasn't going to stop him. It was sweet, and probably made him feel manly.

So we took the elevator up to the top floor and walked over to the door. It was open about a foot.

"Did it look like this when you saw it?" I asked.

Zachary shook his head. "It was open just a few inches. The door mat was caught in the gap. I pushed on it and called out to see if anyone was inside."

"I guess the neighbor across the hall was the one who notified you?"

The other two penthouse apartments were in the other direction, on the far side of the elevator banks.

Zachary nodded.

"And I guess he didn't see or hear anything?"

"He was coming home," Zachary said. "And he noticed the door being open."

So whoever had been here, was already gone by then.

I squared my shoulders. "Let's do this."

Zachary squared his, as well. I gave the door a push. It opened far enough to let us through if we sucked in our stomachs and slithered sideways.

I had been prepared for destruction. When there wasn't much destruction to be found, it was both a relief and, in a funny way, a letdown.

The place was messy, sure. It looked a lot like David's office had, before I started cleaning. Stuff everywhere. But there had been less stuff here to begin with, so the mess was less. In the kitchen, the drawer with the bank statements and bills had been upended on the floor, so there were papers everywhere, and a couple of the utensil drawers had been emptied, too—God knows why. So there was a jumble of credit card statements and silverware, electric bills and spatulas, scattered across the floor. The pillows had been taken off the sofa and tossed on the floor, but that was it for the destruction in the living room. And in the bedroom, the old files David had kept there, boxed up in the closet, were spread across the floor along with the entirety of David's wardrobe. Shirts, pants, and jackets had been yanked off their hangers and tossed to the ground. Sometimes, the hangers were still in place. Sprinkled across the top of everything was David's socks and underwear.

I sighed. "I'd better call the police."

Zachary nodded, his eyes big. "I'll go downstairs and wait."

I turned away from the mess. "I'll come with you. There's no point in hanging around here." And Mendoza would probably tell me I had compromised his crime scene, even if I didn't touch anything.

I made the call directly to the police hotline, and asked them to notify Mendoza. That way I could put off having to talk to him a bit longer. If I got lucky, maybe he'd decide it wasn't worth his time stopping by to check out a common, garden-variety burglary. Maybe a fresh homicide had landed in his lap, that took precedence over David's.

It was a horrible thing to wish for, and I felt a bit

guilty for hoping, but luck would be a fine thing.

Of course, I wasn't that lucky. He walked into the lobby twenty minutes later.

By then, Zachary and I were chatting like old friends, and Mendoza's brows rose as he looked from one to the other of us. "Convention?"

"Huh?... Oh." It took another moment for me to put two and two together and understand what he was talking about.

Then it dawned. Redheads aren't very common, and here were two of us, heads together, chatting up a storm. Zachary was more of a strawberry blond, really, but close enough.

"This is Zachary Brennan," I said. "Zachary, this is Detective Jaime Mendoza."

"Nice to meet you, Detective," Zachary said. His cheeks were flushed with excitement at finding himself face to face with a real, honest-to-goodness homicide detective.

Mendoza nodded, but turned to me. "I thought I told you to stay out of trouble."

I shook my head. "You can't pin this on me. I was at home, minding my own business, when Zachary called. And I waited to bother you until I made sure there was something to bother you with."

Mendoza looked unconvinced.

"Believe it or not, Detective, seeing you is not the high point of my day. And I'm not making up excuses to make it happen."

He grinned at that, dimples and all. My toes curled.

"So what've we got?" he asked.

I reeled in my rampant hormones. "Someone went through David's penthouse. There are papers and kitchen utensils and clothes all over the floor."

"You discovered it?" Mendoza glanced at Zachary, who shook his head.

"The neighbor across the hall did. He called me, and I called Mrs. Kelly."

"And I called you," I said.

Mendoza nodded. He glanced around the lobby. "This place have security cameras?"

"On the secondary doors," Zachary said. "Not on this one."

"Someone's supposed to be here 24/7?"

"Six AM to midnight. The sliding doors are locked through the night. Only the secondary doors are open. Garage and side entrance."

"And those have cameras?"

Zachary nodded. "Motion activated. They come on when the door opens."

"And the rest of the time someone's here?"

Zachary shrugged. "We come and go, you know? I was upstairs for ten minutes with Mrs. Kelly just now. And for five minutes earlier, when I first heard about the open door. And I'm always outside hailing cabs or helping to carry packages or something."

"So someone could get inside and upstairs without being seen? As long as he—or she—timed it to when your desk was empty?"

Zachary nodded. "You want I should pull the feed from the secondary cameras?"

Mendoza hesitated. "Does someone have to have a

key to get through those doors?"

Zachary nodded.

"Then no. Whoever we see, will belong here. Any cameras on the front?"

Zachary shook his head.

"Give it some thought," Mendoza said. "See if you can remember the people who went in and out this afternoon. And whether there was anyone who didn't belong."

Zachary nodded, already groping for pen and paper.

"When I come back downstairs, we'll see what you've got."

"Yessir." Zachary flushed excitedly.

"Nice kid," Mendoza told me when we were in the elevator on our way back upstairs.

"I guess." He wasn't mine, so I couldn't take credit. "He told me he's waiting to turn twenty-one so he can apply to the police academy."

His brows arched. "How old is he?"

"Twenty," I said.

"Why isn't he in college?"

"He said he was sick of school."

"Hmmph," Mendoza said.

I hid a smile. "I'm really sorry I had to bother you again today. I was hoping I wouldn't have to."

"You're not bothering me," Mendoza said. And then ruined it by adding, "This is my job."

"But I was rude to you earlier, and I imagine you would have preferred not to have to deal with me again for a while."

That gained me another grin. My stomach swooped.

"Believe me, Mrs. Kelly, if your brand of rudeness was the worst thing I had to deal with on a daily basis, I'd consider myself very lucky."

Well, yes. Compared to dead bodies and blood, guts, and gore, my putting my foot in my mouth probably didn't rank very high. Still, I felt bad.

"I really am sorry, though."

"Don't be. I was the one who started it." When the elevator came to a stop and the doors opened, he gestured me out. "After you."

I wanted to keep arguing, to make sure he wasn't still angry, but that would make him angry, so I didn't. When we got to the door to David's penthouse, he glanced at me. "It's empty?"

"As far as I know," I said. "I didn't see anyone."

"Stay here."

Why, if I had already been inside?

But mine was not to argue. I nodded meekly and waited beside the door until he came back, holstering his gun in a harness under his arm. "C'mon in."

I thought about saying something snarky, but bit my tongue. "Thank you."

"You know, Mrs. Kelly," he told me as we walked back into the penthouse, "you shouldn't have gone inside. You should have called me and waited."

"I told you. I didn't want to call until I knew there was something to call about. If the place looked pristine, you would have been angry."

"I would have been angrier if someone had shot you and you'd bled to death on the floor while I made my way here," Mendoza said.

A chill crept down my spine, like a trickle of ice water. That possibility hadn't even crossed my mind.

"Whoa." He reached out and grabbed my elbow. I guess I'd turned pale.

I looked up at him, sort of blindly. Not seeing him so much as the horrible possibilities. "Do you think whoever did this was still here when Zachary came upstairs earlier?"

"Might have been," Mendoza said.

Good thing Zachary hadn't gone inside, then. Or he might not be sitting downstairs making his list of tenants right now.

"But once he knew Zachary had noticed the open door, he would have left. So we weren't in any danger."

"Unless he wanted to shoot you."

Mendoza waited a second to let that one sink in. "So tell me about this." He gestured to the mess with his free hand. He must have realized he was still holding on to my arm with the other, because he let go.

I looked around at the kitchen floor. "I'm not sure what to say. I don't understand why anyone would do something like this."

"There are a couple of reasons someone might," Mendoza said and stuffed his hands in his pockets. "Someone wanted to give you a mess to clean up. Or someone was looking for something."

"The same something someone was looking for in David's office in Hillwood yesterday?"

"Seems logical," Mendoza said.

"Wouldn't it be easier to make everything look pristine, like no one had even been here?"

"Sure. But that's not always possible."

"Yesterday, maybe not. I imagine time was of the essence when this person, whoever he was, went through the office. Someone could have walked in at any time and caught him or her in the act."

Mendoza nodded.

"But the penthouse was empty all day. I left this morning, and I haven't been back. There was no need to hurry. And I don't think there was really a need to empty out the silverware drawers, either. I don't think whatever he was looking for, was there."

Mendoza shook his head. "When people make a mess like this, it's usually because they're angry, and throwing things around relieves their feelings."

Like a child with a temper tantrum. I remembered Kenny throwing his crayons at the walls as a child, if he didn't get what he wanted.

Not that I was trying to pin this on Kenny. Although he was as likely a suspect as anyone else at this point.

"I don't think that's the case this time," Mendoza added.

I stopped thinking about my stepson. "Why?"

"The mess is too orderly." He gestured around the kitchen. "There's plenty of glass here. Someone who was angry would start with that. It's very satisfying, watching glass break. Makes more of a mess that someone has to clean up, too."

True.

"Not to mention the chance that someone could cut themselves."

Yes, indeed. That was probably incentive to someone

who was angry, as well.

"The sofa pillows are on the floor," Mendoza continued, moving from kitchen to living room, "but they're intact. Someone who was really pissed, would probably go at them with a knife." He nodded at a block that was still sitting pristinely on the kitchen counter, full of cutting instruments of varying sizes.

I nodded, and looked around at the mess with new eyes. Now that he'd pointed it out, it all made sense. "So what made someone do this, then? If it wasn't necessity, and it wasn't anger?"

"The hope that you wouldn't notice anything missing if the mess was big enough," Mendoza said.

Ah. Yes, that made sense, too. "I guess, if he hadn't found it, the mess would have been bigger."

"Like your office at home," Mendoza nodded.

I glanced around. "Well, then it wasn't David's will he was looking for. Because I already looked for that, and it wasn't here."

Mendoza nodded. "I've read the will."

Really?

"Mr. Hess was kind enough to give me a copy."

I smiled. "I don't imagine you gave him much choice."

"Not much," Mendoza agreed. "It's standard procedure in a homicide investigation to determine who benefits."

Of course. "And do Kenny and Daniel?"

"It's hard to determine what might be worth murder to someone else," Mendoza said, "but between them, they inherit enough to get their business off the ground."

"So they might have killed David."

"Might have," Mendoza nodded.

"Are you going to check their alibis for this afternoon? And ask them whether they tossed the office yesterday?"

"As soon as I leave here," Mendoza said. "Are you going back home?"

I nodded. "I've cleaned up one mess today. I'm not cleaning up this one."

"I'll send a team over," Mendoza told me. "See if they find anything different here than they found in your house."

"Do I have to wait for them?"

He shook his head. "Zachary can let them in."

Good. I was feeling wiped out. All I wanted to do, was get home to my house in the woods and curl up on the sofa with a glass of wine and a movie and forget everything that had happened.

CHAPTER SIXTEEN

I was walking through a desert. The air was so hot it hurt to pull it into my lungs, and I could hear my hair crackling as the moisture was drawn out of it. Or maybe that was my skin crackling as it dried and pulled closer to my bones. If I didn't get out of here soon, I'd burn to a crisp. And no one would miss me, because I had no one in my life to mourn my passing. No husband, no children, no mother or father...

I would have traded my soul for a sip of water, but there was none to be had. Just sand dunes as far as I could see, and the burning heat of the sun, searing my eyeballs. I didn't even have tears to cry for my sad situation. And my chest hurt, like a heavy weight was pressing down on it. I tried to cough, but that hurt, too—

And then a spasm of hacking brought me upright and awake, into a reality that was hardly better than the dream.

A reality that was worse than the dream, because it *was* reality.

The house was on fire. I could feel the heat all around

me, and hear the crackling of the flames and the groaning of timbers. Smoke seeped under the bedroom door and rose, wafting toward me. My chest hurt from trying to breathe the air, and another spasm of coughing bent me nearly double on the edge of the bed.

Move!

I had to, or I was going to die right where I was, in the bed I had shared with David.

Clothes.

I peered through the smoke and gloom for something to wear. Something more than this slinky satin and lace nightgown. Why hadn't I put on something more practical when I went to bed last night? It wasn't like I had anyone to dress sexy for.

If I survived this, I'd start sleeping in yoga pants and T-shirts.

No time.

No. I'd have to get out the way I was, or there was a chance, a very good chance, I wouldn't get out at all.

Sometime, I had heard that the air was cleaner closer to the ground. So I rolled off the bed and crept, on hands and knees, across the floor to the door, stopping every so often to hack up a lung. The floor was warm, almost as if there were heating cables under it, and the door was hot enough to burn my palm when I touched it. I knew better than to open it. Something about funnels and flames. Keep things closed.

There was only one thing for it, then. I'd have to go out a window.

A second-story window.

I crept back toward the bed, across the desert-like

expanse of carpet, cursing David for insisting on this twenty-by-twenty-five master bedroom with a vaulted ceiling. Why couldn't he have been satisfied with a nice, tight, ten-by-twelve box, instead?

Beyond the door, I could hear the flames crackle. The floor felt hotter than it had been just a minute ago, too. That might have been my imagination. On the other hand, it might be that the flames from downstairs were ready to burst through and would devour the second story any moment now.

I reached up and grabbed a corner of the goose-down comforter on my way past, and dragged it with me as I crawled. When I got to the nearest window, I wrapped it around myself before I staggered to my feet.

The air was so much worse at five-and-a-half feet than a foot off the floor. I knew I wouldn't have much time to make my break for it—literally—before the smoke knocked me out. I was lucky I was still breathing. So I made sure I was clutching the comforter tightly, but I didn't bother to take a deep breath—it would only make me cough—before I threw myself at the window.

It shattered into a thousand pieces, some of which sliced into the comforter and into the top of my head as I tumbled past the jagged shards, headed for the ground and the holly bushes below.

It wasn't a very long trip, and my life did not flash before my eyes, so I knew I wasn't dying. I did know the landing would be unpleasant, if not as unpleasant as it could have been if the vegetation hadn't been there.

The thing about holly bushes is that they're nice and dense, and they have leaves all year around. They broke my fall very nicely. Or as nicely as could be expected, when I'd jumped out of a second-story window.

The other thing about holly bushes, of course, is that their leaves are hard and pointy. They cut me almost as badly as the glass. And although landing in the bushes sure beat landing on the hard ground, the impact still knocked the wind out of me. I couldn't do anything for several seconds but lie there and try to catch my breath.

It was the flames bursting out of the second story window above me—the window where I'd been standing less than a minute ago—that roused me. I rolled out of the bushes and onto the lawn, trying to hold on to the comforter, just as the first fire engine turned into the driveway and came screaming up to the house. It was followed by two more, lights flashing, and then an ambulance. A black-and-white police car brought up the rear.

The next few minutes are confused. The fire trucks slid to a stop, one after the other into the driveway, and what looked like an army of firemen unwound hoses and began to shoot sprays of water at the house. Meanwhile, the paramedics descended on me. "Ma'am? Are you all right?"

"Do I look all right?" I wanted to know, standing there in my bare feet, with a pale blue goose-down comforter wrapped around me, and blood trickling down my face from a dozen tiny cuts.

They cooed and cajoled and got me over to the ambulance, where they put an oxygen mask over my nose and mouth while they slathered salve on my scorched knees and palms, and cream on the cuts on my head. After everything was bandaged and I'd had enough air, they made me drink water, because they said I was dehydrated.

"Is there anyone you want us to call for you?" one of them asked.

My cell phone was inside the house. Left to charge on the kitchen counter. I hadn't thought about that.

I shook my head. "Not yet." My voice was hoarse, even after the water and oxygen, and talking hurt. "I want to see how things go first."

And anyway, I didn't know who to call. I had no family of my own. Krystal and Kenny wouldn't lift a finger to help me, nor, I assumed, would their mother. Farley and Martha? Rachel? Diana?

The paramedics exchanged a glance, but didn't argue with me. "Nobody else was in the house with you? Any pets?"

No, no pets. I didn't even have a dog to keep me company. Or a cat. It's very sad, to be so alone.

The tears trickling down my cheeks stung my scorched skin. The paramedics handed me a box of tissues and another bottle of water. But at least I could cry, which was something to be grateful for.

I'd been sitting there ten minutes or so when another car took the turn into the driveway with a spurt of gravel and a shriek of tires. It jumped the border onto the grass and came to a quivering stop with a squeal of brakes. The driver's side door flew open and a man tumbled out. It took me a few moments, between the dark and the flashing lights and the tears in my eyes, to recognize Detective Mendoza.

In justice to myself—or to him—he didn't look like himself. Or at least he didn't look like the man I was used to seeing.

Gone was the expensive designer suit and the crisp shirt and tie. Gone was the carefully styled hair and the take-charge demeanor. The man who jumped out of the car was dressed in faded jeans, running shoes, and a sweatshirt with the MNPD logo on the chest. His hair was standing up, like he'd either come straight from bed and hadn't bothered to smooth it, or like he'd run his fingers through it repeatedly as he drove. Maybe both. And he looked a little wild-eyed as he took in the scene with the milling firemen, the spurting water, the other cops, and the flashing lights. There was so much activity on my front lawn, I was surprised not to see a few of the neighbors coming out of their houses to join in.

Mendoza looked around, and I could see when he spotted me sitting in the back of the ambulance. His posture softened for a second, eased, before he squared his shoulders again and marched toward me, his sneakers squishing across the now-soggy ground.

"Mrs. Kelly."

I raised my (third) water bottle in a toast, and wrapped the comforter more securely around myself. "Detective."

"You all right?"

"As all right as I can expect to be," I said. "Cuts and bruises. And apparently I'm dehydrated."

He nodded. "Where did you get the cuts and bruises?"

"When I jumped out the window," I said.

He stared at me. "Come again?"

I gestured to the window. It was visible from here, and a fireman was directing the hose directly into it. By now, the flames were mostly gone; the firemen were just making sure the fire was out.

"You jumped out a *second-story* window?!"

"What was I supposed to do?" I asked. "The first floor was on fire. I couldn't go that way."

"So you jumped out a second-story window."

"It was that or fry."

He didn't look mollified, so I added, "I was as careful as I could be. I wrapped myself in the comforter before I jumped through the glass. And I aimed for the bushes."

The bushes that now looked distinctly bedraggled.

It was hard to see in the dark and with the blue flickering coming and going over his face, but I think he turned a shade paler. His voice was half choked. "You jumped through the glass."

He didn't seem to understand what I was saying.

"I think you had to be there," I said. "I did the best I could, Detective. It was that, or dying of smoke inhalation. Or worse. And I got out. I didn't break any bones. I have some cuts and bruises, but that's all. I think I did well."

He didn't respond, but a muscle in his jaw was working. Eventually he asked, "What happened?"

"I have no idea," I said. "I was sleeping. And when I woke up, the house was on fire."

"Did you leave the stove on? Candles burning? Dryer running? Do you smoke in bed?"

"I don't smoke at all," I said. If I smoked, he would be able to tell. It affects the way you look. My teeth were white and my skin was clear and I didn't have those little lines around my lips you get from pursing your lips to suck on cigarettes. "And I didn't do anything else, either. I didn't wash clothes last night. I didn't cook. And I didn't leave candles burning."

"What did you do after you got home?"

"Watched TV and drank wine," I said.

He opened his mouth, and I added, "No, I wasn't drunk. I didn't turn on the stove and forget about it. Or turn on and forget anything else, either."

For a second, a funny expression crossed his face. Then it was gone. "Excuse me," he said politely.

"Of course." I waved him off and lifted my water bottle as he walked across the lawn toward the cluster of firemen and patrol officers. They talked for a few minutes, and then Mendoza went to inspect the house. I could see him peering through the French doors into the family room, but he didn't go inside. Then he went over to the holly bushes and looked at them for a moment, before tilting his head back to look up at my bedroom window.

Eventually he came back across the lawn. "Do you have somewhere to stay?"

"David's penthouse," I said. "If my purse is still intact with the key in it."

"If it isn't, I'll pick the lock," Mendoza said grimly. "Where would the purse be?"

I told him it would be right inside the front door. Since the fire seemed to be localized more toward the back of the house, it might have escaped immolation. That would be nice. I'd have to arrange for a new cell phone tomorrow—I could tell from here that the kitchen and family room were a total loss—but if I didn't have to spend several days replacing my driver's license and all my credit and debit cards, I'd consider it a win.

"Wait here." He turned toward the house.

"No problem." Where was I going to go? I wasn't even wearing shoes.

He came back a few minutes later with my bag over his shoulder, and with a trench coat he must have found in the coat closet over his arm. He'd even snagged a pair of boots. It wasn't quite boot-weather yet—fall had just arrived; the leaves weren't even yellow, let alone orange or red—but beggars can't be choosers. It was footwear, and better than nothing. I stuck my dirty, naked feet into them, happy to have something between me and the ground.

Then I stood up, and hesitated.

"Need help?" Mendoza inquired, reaching out an arm to steady me.

"No. Thank you." I was perfectly capable of standing up straight, and of dropping the comforter and revealing myself, in all my slinky satin-and-lace glory. I just wasn't sure I ought to.

His lips twitched. "You want me to turn my back?"

"It's not just you," I said. "It's the two dozen other guys. You can't make them all turn their backs."

"I could if I wanted to."

He probably could. That was ridiculous, though. I was forty years old. Not exactly a blushing virgin. I wore less than this at the pool. And although I was a few years past my prime, I knew I had nothing to be ashamed of. I worked hard at keeping my figure. And I'd looked at myself in the mirror tonight, after I put on the nightgown. I'd looked just fine. I probably looked a little more bedraggled now, soot-streaked and scratched, but that couldn't be helped.

I dropped the comforter and reached for the trench coat.

"Damn," Mendoza said. I had to tug before he'd relinquish it.

"Sorry." I shoved my arm into one of the sleeves.

He shook his head. "Don't be. You just made my weekend."

"Really?" I wiggled my other arm into the other sleeve. "That's all it takes? A woman in a nightgown?"

"More often, a woman out of a nightgown, but I'll take what I can get."

I would have been happy to give him more, but this wasn't the time to mention it. And besides, he was probably just joking, anyway. Trying to make me feel better, after almost being burned alive.

"C'mon." He crooked his elbow. "I'll drive you downtown."

"Thank you." I stuck my hand through it. The ground was wet and difficult to navigate, and the boots had heels. I was happy for the support, even though he treated me like I was his aged grandmother. He even held the car door open for me and kept his hand under my elbow until I'd gotten in.

"I'm fine," I told him once he was inside, and we were making our slow way down the driveway, navigating around the various fire trucks and police cars parked every which way.

He shot me a look. "You must have been scared."

I had my mouth open to say no, I had been too focused on survival, on what I had to do to get out of the house with my skin intact, to think much about the fear... but then I couldn't get the words out past the lump in my throat. Instead, I concentrated on blinking away the tears in my eyes.

"I wasn't sure I'd make it out," I admitted when I could talk again. "There was a lot of smoke, and the flames were really close. It's a good thing I woke up when I did. If I'd slept longer, I'm not sure I would have woken up at all."

Mendoza nodded, and his hands tightened on the steering wheel. "What do you think happened?"

"I don't know," I said. "Some sort of spontaneous combustion? I heard of a yucca plant once, that burst into flames while the family was away on vacation. From lack of water."

Mendoza's lips compressed. It was probably laughter. "Did you have a yucca plant you'd forgotten to water?"

I shook my head.

"Then I don't think that's it."

He glanced at me. "The fire chief told me the fire looked like it started in the family room. Are you sure you turned off the fireplace before you went up to bed?"

"I didn't use the fireplace," I said. "I..."

When I didn't continue, he shot me another look. "What?"

"Nothing. Just that I thought about using the fireplace. Earlier yesterday. Because of Farley."

Mendoza's brows drew together. "Mr.

Hollingsworth? What about him?"

"I shredded a bunch of David's old files yesterday afternoon," I explained. "Farley said he didn't need them, that they were just extra copies of the files in the office on Music Row, and that I should have a bonfire and burn them all."

"Mr. Hollingsworth said that?"

I nodded. "When I saw him yesterday afternoon. When he was getting his new assistant situated in the office."

"He told you to burn the files."

"Or shred them. Anything I wanted to do, since they weren't needed. But it was too hot for a fire, so I just stuffed the shreds in a bunch of garbage bags and put them in the trash."

"Interesting," Mendoza said.

I shrugged. "I didn't use the fireplace, so it doesn't really matter. The fire couldn't have started there, if I didn't use it."

Mendoza nodded, but didn't speak. I left him to his thoughts as we drove down Charlotte Avenue, past the Body Shop where Nick worked, and toward the bulk of the Apex building in the Gulch.

It didn't take long to get there. There was very little traffic, and all the lights were blinking yellow now in the middle of the night. The one time we encountered a red light, Mendoza flicked on his own lights and siren long enough to allow us to zoom right through, and then he flicked them off again as soon as we were on the other side.

"Convenient," I said.

He shrugged. "It comes in handy sometimes."

Outside the Apex, he pulled up to the side entrance and parked, illegally, in a loading zone. "I'll walk you up."

"I can manage," I began, although I didn't say it with much conviction. Reaction was starting to set in. The adrenaline rush from earlier was fading, and the pain of the various cuts and bruises was catching up to me, along with a seriously sore throat. I was shaking, and my teeth were chattering.

""I'm sure you can." Mendoza took my elbow. "But you don't have to. Give me your key."

I gave him the whole purse, since my hands were shaking too much to get the keychain out. He unlocked the door and we went in. Through the side door, into the elevator, and up to the top floor.

"It's still a mess," Mendoza said apologetically as he steered me down the hallway toward David's door. "But the crime scene crew is finished. I'll get someone over here to help you clean up tomorrow."

"Don't worry about it," I answered.

He glanced at me, and I added, "I don't even want to think about it right now. All I want to do, is get warm."

He nodded. "Are you sure there isn't anyone I can call to come stay with you?"

"I'm sure." If Mendoza himself had felt inclined to keep me company, I wouldn't have said no, although I was too tired to want to do anything but sleep. But he didn't offer.

"I'll be in touch tomorrow," he told me, as he pushed the door into the apartment open. "Lock this when you get inside."

"Of course."

"Sleep well."

"I'll do my best," I said, although I thought it quite likely I might have nightmares. "Thank you for coming out to the house. You didn't have to do that. The firemen had it under control."

"It's my case," Mendoza said.

"Nobody died." So technically, it was no case at all. Not for a homicide detective.

"It was your husband's house, and he's my victim, so it's my case."

At least he didn't say, 'it was your house, and you're my suspect,' making it his case. "Well, I appreciate it. And thank you for the ride. And for getting my purse and boots and coat."

"My pleasure," Mendoza said. "It isn't every day a woman strips to her nightgown in front of me."

"I can't imagine why." I heard the words come out of my mouth, but I swear I hadn't planned to say them. I shook my head. "Sorry. Stupid tired. I should go inside."

"Probably a good idea," Mendoza agreed blandly. "Sleep well, Mrs. Kelly."

"You too, Detective."

"I doubt I'll get back to bed," Mendoza said. "I'll give you a call in the morning."

I nodded. And then I waited for him to go back inside the elevator before I closed and locked the door, kicked off the boots, and staggered down the hallway and into David's bedroom. I waded through a sea of clothes and papers until I could crawl under the covers of the king sized bed and find oblivion. The question of whether he'd ever screwed Jacquie in this bed didn't even cross my mind. If it had, I don't think I would have cared.

CHAPTER SEVENTEEN

I slept late. And when I woke up I was uncomfortable. My throat hurt, and all the little scratches, from glass and holly leaves, were itching like crazy. My knees and palms were blistered from crawling across the hot floor, and my face was burnished, like I was sporting a tan. It clashed with my new hair.

And of course I realized, once I got up, that my wardrobe consisted of a nightgown, a trench coat, and a pair of boots. I didn't even have underwear or a toothbrush to my name.

The latter was easily fixed. I used David's. After sharing a house and bed with him for eighteen years, I figured it was OK to use the man's toothbrush. Besides, it wasn't like he'd ever know.

The underwear was a bit more difficult. I ended up borrowing a pair of black silk boxers, which looked more like shorts on me. They made quite the statement with the knee-high leather boots.

But of course there was no bra to be had. And at forty, I'm just not as perky as I used to be, if you know what I mean.

I ended up in one of David's undershirts, which did what it could to keep things in place. It wasn't what I'd call high fashion, but I was more or less decently covered. Or so I thought, until Zachary called up from downstairs to tell me that Detective Mendoza was here to see me. I told him to send the detective up, and when I opened the door—barefoot and dressed in boxer shorts and a wifebeater shirt—Mendoza's eyes bugged out of his skull.

"Sorry." I took a step backward, and then another. "Excuse me."

I scurried off into the bedroom, leaving him to enter and close the door behind him on his own. When I came back out, I was wearing one of David's shirts, which covered me from shoulders to mid-thigh.

From Mendoza's expression, this wasn't a huge improvement.

"I don't have any clothes," I said defensively.

He cleared his throat and made what looked like a very concerted effort to pull his eyes back into the sockets. He ended up looking at the tips of his shoes.

Gone were the jeans and running shoes from the middle of the night. He was back into the nice business suit and tie this morning. The shoes were black with squared-off toes, and he used one of them to scuff the fluffy carpet. "I'm here to drive you back to your house. You can get your car and go to the mall."

Wonderful. "Does that mean none of my clothes survived?"

"I don't know," Mendoza said. "I haven't been back there this morning. The fire chief is meeting us in thirty minutes."

We'd better get a move on, then. "I've spent the morning cleaning up the mess our burglar left," I told Mendoza as I bent to zip up the boots. He made a weird choking sound, but when I straightened and turned, he was looking at the ceiling light.

When Mendoza didn't respond, I added, "If anything's missing, I have no idea what it is. I took some of the bank statements with me earlier this week. I didn't notice anything else being gone from the drawer in the kitchen, although of course I could have overlooked something. As for the bedroom, it's not like anyone would steal David's clothes. And the business files, again, are just copies. The originals are in the office. So stealing the copies wouldn't help anyone."

Mendoza nodded.

"Maybe there was something here that meant something to someone, and I just didn't realize it." I looked around.

"No safe on the premises?" Mendoza asked.

I shook my head. "David had a safe at the office. He could leave anything valuable there. There was no need for a safe at the house or here. He spent half his time at the office, anyway."

Mendoza nodded. "Ready to go?"

"Yes." I wrapped the trench coat around me and tightened the belt. As I caught a glimpse of myself in the mirror, I realized that all I needed to look like Mata Hari, was a pair of big sunglasses.

"I look like a spy," I told Mendoza, grinning.

He grinned back. "Or a wife—"

And then he stopped, and blushed.

Or a wife going to surprise her husband, in a trench coat and heels with nothing underneath.

Except my husband was dead, and I had no one to surprise.

"Sorry."

The tops of his cheekbones were still hot.

"Don't worry about it," I said, my voice steady. "I'm fine. It probably makes it easier that we weren't living together the last couple of months of his life. He wasn't an everyday part of my life anymore."

Mendoza nodded and held the door for me. "Still, it was unprofessional of me."

I shrugged. "So you're human."

"Was there any doubt?" He pushed the button for the elevator. We could hear things start to whirr inside the shaft.

Luckily he didn't seem to want an answer. "Sleep well?" he asked, before I had thought of anything to say.

"Like the dead." Another not-so-appropriate remark. I winced. "Yes. I slept very well, thank you. Conked out as soon as I got into bed, and didn't stir until nine. I didn't even have bad dreams."

"Would you mind going through what happened again, now that you've had time to recover?"

The doors to the elevator opened, and he gestured me in.

"I'd be happy to," I said, watching him push the button for the lobby, "but I don't know what good it'll do. I told you everything last night."

"Humor me."

Of course. I went through everything again, from the moment I woke up coughing in the middle of the night, to the moment his car screeched into the driveway. In every particular, it was the same story I had told him last night. Because it was all I knew to tell him.

Halfway through the reiteration, we arrived in the lobby, and Mendoza squired me out of the elevator and toward the doors. Zachary jumped up from behind the desk. "Mrs. Kelly! Are you all right? The detective told me what happened!"

"I'm fine," I said, with my most brilliant smile, "thank you for asking."

He flushed all the way to the roots of his hair. He even stammered. "Is there anything I can do?"

I couldn't think of anything, and told him so. "I'll probably see you later, though. I expect I'll be staying here a while."

Mendoza nodded, so obviously he agreed. "Do me a favor," he told Zachary. "Pull those security tapes from the secondary doors and start going through them. I doubt you'll see anything, but it has to be done. After last night, we can't afford not to look at every angle."

Zachary nodded. "Right away."

Mendoza didn't say anything while we were inside the lobby, but once we were outside on the sidewalk, he said, "He's got a crush on you."

I shook my head. "He can't possibly. He knows I'm forty. I'm probably older than his mother."

"You don't look forty," Mendoza said.

Maybe not. Although I wouldn't be too sure, especially this morning. However— "I don't look twenty, either." And that's what I'd have to be, to be anything like suitable for Zachary.

"You don't have to look twenty. A lot of young men like older women. Haven't you ever watched *The Graduate*?"

"Yes." I shuddered. "Please don't mention it in the same breath as Zachary." *And for God's sake, don't call me 'older.'*

Mendoza smirked, but abandoned the subject. "So you're sure you didn't leave any candles burning last night? Or leave the stove on? Turn the stove off but leave an oven mitt inside?"

"That would be crazy," I said. "Do people do that? No, I didn't leave anything running or burning. I didn't use anything that ran or burned."

"Hair dryer? Curling iron?" He was starting to sound a bit desperate.

"Why would I curl my hair before going to bed?" I asked. "No. I didn't take a shower, and I didn't dry my hair. I didn't curl it. I didn't cook anything. There were still leftovers in the fridge. I ate them cold. I had wine, so I didn't use the microwave or coffee maker. I didn't wash and dry clothes. The cell phone was plugged in and charging in the kitchen. Other than that—and things like the TV and refrigerator; things that are always plugged in—nothing else was on."

Mendoza grunted. We had reached the gray sedan he drove, and he stopped to open the door for me before walking around the car to get in himself.

I waited until we were moving and had made the turn onto Charlotte Avenue before I opened my mouth again. "Krystal's boyfriend was out behind the house sometime on Friday afternoon, smoking pot. I don't suppose it's possible that one of his joints was lying around smoldering for that long?"

Mendoza glanced at me. "I wouldn't think so, but we can ask."

I nodded.

"I would say that it would either burn itself out or catch fire much sooner, if that was the case. Not more than twenty-four hours later. Especially since Friday was a wet sort of day."

That's what I'd say, too, but I was grasping at straws here.

"Maybe the cell phone really did explode," I said. "I think I've heard of that happening."

Mendoza grunted.

"It makes as much sense as anything else," I insisted. "Because I know I didn't leave anything running."

Mendoza shrugged. "The fire chief will tell us," he said.

WHEN WE GOT to the house, the chief was already there, and poking around in the debris with a stick.

There was a lot of debris. In the harsh light of day—the weather was nice, with crisp, blue skies and sunshine—everything looked a lot worse than it had under the merciful cover of darkness.

From the front, things didn't look too bad. The fire station is only about a mile away, so the first fire truck had gotten here in time to save the front half of the house. As we turned off the main road and headed up the driveway,

I told myself that this really wasn't that bad at all.

And then we got a little closer, and I saw that the damage was mostly localized toward the rear, and it was hideous.

All the windows on the second floor were blown out, not just the one I had burst through to save myself. The ground was littered with shards of glass. The cream-colored walls were smeared with soot, and the underside of the roof was charred. On the first floor, the French doors to the family room stood open, and black water stood in puddles and trickled in rivulets across the now-buckled hardwood floors. The Persian rug was a soggy mess. The painting above the fireplace—David's debutante mother in her younger days—had been reduced to a few shreds of canvas inside a charred frame. The ceiling timbers had turned into blackened beams, and the drywall had burned away. What was left of it, lay in charred flakes across the floor. And everything stank to high heaven.

I couldn't help the tears that gathered and overflowed. My bottom lip quivered as I tried to keep myself from breaking down completely.

"Don't cry," Mendoza said, a trace of panic in his voice. He put a careful arm around my shoulders. "It's just stuff. The most important thing in the house was you. And you got out."

I knew he was right. But this house had been my home for eighteen years. And seeing it like this—all of David's (and the designer's) meticulous beauty reduced to soot and ashes—hit me hard. I turned and leaned my forehead against the detective's broad shoulder. What I wanted to do was wrap my arms around his neck and have a good cry against the side of his neck, but that probably wouldn't go over well. So I took what he was willing to give—a careful embrace and awkward patting on the back—and controlled myself as best I could.

It can't have been very well, because as I kept sniffing, the patting became increasingly frantic. I could feel the relief permeate his body at the sound of a throat clearing behind us. Or behind me, rather.

I lifted my head and turned around, to face the fire chief. "Sorry."

It was tough to get a good look at his face due to a very impressive handlebar moustache that took up a lot of real estate, but he appeared to be acutely uncomfortable. About as uncomfortable as I imagined Mendoza might be. The detective had stopped patting me, but kept a steadying hand under my elbow. When I turned my head to glance up at him, he quirked his brows.

"Gunn," the fire chief grunted. It took me a second to realize this was his name, not a warning.

"This is Mrs. Kelly," Mendoza said. "The home owner."

Gunn nodded. "Gotta big mess here."

No kidding.

"It can be saved," I asked worriedly, "can't it?"

"Gotta ask a contractor that," Gunn said. "You're gonna need a new kitchen and a new bathroom upstairs. New fireplace, new family room. Lotta new windows."

"I'll call a contractor tomorrow morning," I said. "And get an estimate."

Gunn nodded. "Fire started in the back. First floor.

You sleeping upstairs?"

I nodded. "Right up there." I pointed to where the silk curtains were hanging in soggy ropes through the broken window.

We all peered up at it, and at the bedraggled holly bushes below. From here, it looked like a pretty far drop. I couldn't quite believe I had jumped out of a second story window last night, and was standing here now, able to tell the tale.

"Lucky you got out," Gunn told me. "The fire spread fast."

I had noticed that. "I'm just glad I woke up when I did."

Both men nodded. "Any idea what started the fire?" Mendoza asked. "Mrs. Kelly says she didn't leave anything on or burning, but..."

Gunn waved us both around the corner of the house, and pointed to a spot on the ground by the foundation, right next to the chimney. The earth was charred. "There."

Mendoza blinked at it. I did, too. "That's where the fire started?"

"How can you tell?" Mendoza asked.

"Been doing this thirty-five years," Gunn grunted. "Longer'n you've been alive. You gonna question my expertise?"

"Of course not." I smiled sweetly, and when Mendoza opened his mouth, I put the heel of my boot on his foot and pressed down. I don't think I hurt him—he was wearing a nice pair of leather shoes—but he winced. I added, still smiling at Gunn, "I'd just like a little more of an explanation. I assumed the cell phone exploded, or..."

"The yucca plant," Mendoza muttered.

Gunn looked from one to the other of us. "Wasn't no plant. And no phone, neither. This was arson, plain and simple."

There was a moment of silence. A rather long moment.

"You're kidding," I said, at the same time as Mendoza said, "Arson? Are you sure?"

Gunn pulled himself up to his full height—about an inch shorter than me, but a lot bigger around—and before he could cite his vast experience once again, Mendoza added quickly, "I'm not questioning your conclusions, Chief. I'm just surprised. How do you know? Specifically?"

"Burn pattern," Gunn said, and went into a highly technical explanation of which I only understood about half. I won't bore you with it, especially since it would be incomplete anyway.

By now Mendoza was scribbling notes in his little book. "What did you say the accelerant was?"

Gunn repeated the same multi-syllabic name. "Gasoline," he added.

"The kind you put in a car?"

Both men turned to me. Mendoza's eyebrows had crept halfway up his forehead. Gunn's expression was mostly hidden behind the handlebar, but I could tell what he was thinking.

"Yes," Mendoza said. "The kind you put in a car."

"Thank you."

Nick would have access to gasoline. More than likely, it was sitting around his place of business.

Then again, anyone can go to the nearest gas station with a can and fill it up, so that didn't necessarily mean anything. Everyone I knew owned a car. Some people owned several. No one would have thought anything of it if someone showed up with a gas can they wanted to fill. Even someone like Jacquie or Martha Hollingsworth.

Not that I suspected either of them of torching my house.

Or at least I didn't suspect Martha. That would be ridiculous.

Jacquie...

Well, if Jacquie hadn't cut David's brake lines—and she probably hadn't—but she thought I had—and judging from her performance at the funeral, it seemed like she did—she might resent me for killing her cash cow. She might have reasoned that if she couldn't get her hands on David's house and David's money, I didn't deserve to keep them, either.

It was a bit kooky, true. But then her outburst at the funeral hadn't been exactly sane.

I glanced at Mendoza. He was deep in conversation with Gunn, so I made a mental note to run the idea past him later. Then I went back to thinking about it.

If Jacquie wanted to burn me out of David's house, she wouldn't dirty her own hands with gasoline and matches. I could no more see her creeping around my house in the dead of night, than I could see Martha doing it.

But I could see Nick wanting to please Jacquie.

I could imagine Nick breaking into the penthouse, too. What I couldn't imagine, was why. I'd been over that penthouse from top to bottom. There was nothing there that could possibly interest either of them. Jacquie and Nick wouldn't care about David's hidden bank accounts, or about David's old client files.

Had she left something there she wanted back? Something stupid, that it wouldn't even cross my mind to notice? Had she bought him a gift—expensive black boxer shorts, like the pair I was wearing—and now that he was dead, Nick wanted them?

It made as much sense as anything else. Not a whole lot, in other words.

"Thank you for your time," Mendoza said behind me. "Can you make sure I get a copy of that report?"

Gunn grunted something to the effect that he would, and headed for his car. Mendoza turned to me.

CHAPTER EIGHTEEN

"Who called the fire department?" I asked before he could say anything. "I didn't."

I'd been too busy saving my skin. And besides, my phone had been downstairs in the kitchen, in the thick of the flames.

"One of the neighbors," Mendoza told me. "Mr. Owen Harrison."

I knew who Mr. Harrison was, but I didn't really know him. He lived directly across the street, an eighth of a mile away. I'd seen him come and go a few times, but he'd only been living there a couple of years, and he stayed busy, so we hadn't been formally introduced.

"I don't suppose you've talked to him?"

Mendoza shook his head.

"Do you think he might have seen something? The fire spread very fast, so he might have been awake when it started."

"It's possible," Mendoza said. "We can knock on his door and ask."

"Could we?" With any luck, maybe Owen Harrison

had seen a dark pickup speed away from the house just as the flames took hold, but he'd forgotten all about it in the excitement of having to call 911 and then watching what was going on across the street.

"Why not?" Mendoza said philosophically. "Get in the car. You have big properties around here."

I got in, and he drove down the driveway, a few yards down the street, and then into Mr. Harrison's driveway on the other side.

A minute later we were knocking on Mr. Harrison's door. A minute after that, Harrison answered.

He was a small, spare man, David's age or maybe a few years younger. Thinning hair, and dressed in faded jeans and Tennessee Vols sweater. From within the house, we could hear the sound of a TV, or maybe a radio.

"Yes?" He looked from one to the other of us.

"Mr. Harrison?" Mendoza hauled out his badge. "Jaime Mendoza, Metro Nashville PD."

I got a flashback to him standing on my doorstep, doing and saying the same thing. Six days ago now.

It felt like a lifetime.

"Regina Beaufort Kelly," I added when Harrison turned his attention to me. "From across the street."

His face changed. "The fire."

We both nodded.

"You made the 911 call," Mendoza said. "We thought maybe you'd noticed something. Anything. Someone moving around outside, a car driving away..."

Harrison shook his head. "I'm afraid not. I had to get up to use the bathroom. It's in the front of the house. I happened to look out the window and saw the glow of the flames. So I made the call."

Mendoza nodded. "Were you already awake, or did something happen to wake you?"

Harrison's eyes, pale blue, turned distant. "I was asleep," he said. "I don't know what woke me. Or if anything did. But I was awake. So I went to the bathroom. And I saw the flames."

"But you didn't see anything else? Like, maybe, a dark pickup truck driving away?"

Mendoza frowned at me. "No leading the witness, Mrs. Kelly."

"Sorry." I smiled apologetically.

"No," Mr. Harrison said. "No dark pickup truck last night. I saw a small, light-colored car go by just after the fire trucks pulled in, but no trucks."

"Were you able to get a make and model?" Mendoza had pulled his notebook out.

"I'm a football field's distance from the road, Detective," Mr. Harrison answered. "No. All I know is that it was fairly close to the ground—not a truck or an SUV—and the color was light."

Mendoza nodded. "Did it slow down as it went by?"

"Yes," Harrison said, "but there was a fire going on. I'm sure the driver was curious."

Mendoza closed his notebook with a little snap. "Thank you for your time, sir. If you think of anything else, would you give me a call?" He extended a card.

"Of course." Harrison took and pocketed it before turning to me. "My condolences on the loss of your husband, Mrs. Kelly."

"Thank you," I said.

"And on the loss of your home. I trust it was insured?"

"I'm sure it was," I said. This was the first time I had thought about that, at least today. I lived there, but it was David's house.

But David had had life insurance policies on me, on his business partner, and on both his kids, so he'd probably had insurance on his house as well. Someone else I'd have to contact tomorrow, along with the contractor and the life insurance company.

"I don't mean to pry," Mr. Harrison said, "but has there been a determination made as to the cause of the fire?"

Mendoza nodded. "We just finished talking to the fire chief. Apparently it was arson."

"Ah." Harrison didn't say anything else, but his silence spoke volumes.

"That's why we were wondering whether you'd seen anyone drive away in the middle of the night," I said.

Harrison shook his head. "No, Mrs. Kelly. I'm afraid not. Not a soul."

There was a pause.

"What do you do, Mr. Harrison?" Mendoza asked. "For a living?"

"Claims adjuster," Harrison said.

Of course. I could see Mendoza's lips quirk, but he didn't speak. Just wished Harrison a pleasant afternoon and nudged me out of there.

"He thought I tried to burn my house down!" I said indignantly when we were back in Mendoza's car and on our way up the curving driveway.

He wasn't trying to hold back the grin anymore. "Yep."

"The fire chief didn't think that, did he?"

"If he did," Mendoza said, "he didn't say so."

After a second he added, "Although he did mention a couple of times how lucky it was that you were able to make it out alive."

Almost as if I'd known that the fire was going to start. Right.

"If I'd set fire to my own house," I said, "I would have made sure to put on pajamas before I jumped out the window."

"That nightgown was very effective, though."

I squinted at him. His voice sounded uneven, although his face was solemn. There was, perhaps, a slight curve to the lips.

"Are you laughing?" I asked suspiciously.

He glanced at me. And while his face may not have been laughing, his eyes were. "Not at all."

"Liar," I said.

"It was a very nice nightgown. I would have liked it even better if I hadn't known you'd probably bought it for your husband."

Since he was right—I had bought it for David—there wasn't much I could say to that.

"I need to go back up to the house," I said instead. "I didn't get a chance to check and see whether any of my clothes survived."

"And won't get to now." He turned in the other direction instead.

"Hey!"

He shot me a look. "Did you see the underside of your bedroom floor? I'm not letting you walk up to the second story of that house."

"I survived the window," I said.

"You survived jumping into the bushes. If the floor gave way, it would dump you into a pile of debris." He shook his head. "No. When you meet the contractor tomorrow, you can check your closet then."

"So what do I do in the meantime?" I wanted to know. "I can't spend the rest of the day in David's silk boxers and this trench coat."

Mendoza sent me a look.

"Are you coming shopping with me?"

He shuddered. "No."

"Then what am I supposed to do? You didn't even let me get my car!"

"There's a Walmart just up Charlotte Avenue. We can stop there."

"At Walmart?"

He shot me another look. "Too good for Walmart?"

"No!" I said, stung, in spite of the fact that I hadn't been inside a Walmart in the time David and I had been married.

Perhaps it was time I got used to shopping like the rest of the world did.

I have to say, the Walmart experience did not make me want to repeat it, though. There were a lot of people in the store, and a lot of pushing and shoving. The dressing rooms were tiny and the light garish. And they didn't sell anything I would normally consider putting on my body, apart from the active wear. I grabbed a couple of pairs of yoga pants and tops, a package of cotton underwear, and two sports bras.

The first thing I was going to do once I got my car back, was make a trip to Victoria's Secret. Not that I had anyone to wear Victoria's Secret for anymore, other than my own self, but sexy underwear makes a woman feel good. The cotton stuff with small sprigs of flowers made me feel like I were twelve.

I hesitated in front of the jeans.

"Problem?" Mendoza inquired. He'd been trailing behind me, trying to keep a straight face as I turned my nose up at the offerings.

I glanced at him over my shoulder. "David didn't like me to wear jeans. He said they weren't ladylike."

"I bet you wore jeans when he met you," Mendoza said.

"I was twenty-two then." And a few years after that I stopped, because jeans weren't appropriate for David Kelly's wife.

"Jacquie wears jeans," Mendoza said.

Low blow. I narrowed my eyes at him. "She's twenty-five. I'm forty."

"You don't look forty," Mendoza said. "And you'd look good in a pair of jeans."

He was probably just saying that to make me feel better about being forty while Jacquie was twenty-five. Nonetheless, I bought a pair of jeans. Tight ones. And if I looked ridiculous, then I'd just not think about that. Although compared to some of the people around me—who went shopping in sleep-pants and slippers and with rollers in their hair—I probably didn't look too bad. Even in my trench coat and boots.

We ended up walking out with several plastic bags. I bought a new pair of sneakers, too, so I could go to the gym in my new yoga pants—so I could make sure I'd continue to fit into my new jeans—and a couple of T-shirts in various colors. It was all a bit on the juvenile side, but the selection would see me through the next couple of days, at least, until I could assess the damage to my closet at home. If I needed to replace my entire wardrobe, a trip to the Green Hills Mall would be in order. No way was I buying a whole new wardrobe at Walmart. Not unless the judge left me destitute and I had no other choice. The one thing I will say for it, is that it was cheap.

We were getting in the car when Mendoza's phone buzzed. He answered it, his voice businesslike. "Mendoza. Yes. Yes. Right now. Yes. We'll see you then."

"We?" I said after he'd gotten behind the wheel and was reversing out of the parking space. There was a camouflage-painted pickup truck rumbling behind us, waiting for a ten year old Camaro belching exhaust to get out of the way. When they both had moved on, Mendoza finished backing up and then turned to me.

"That was Zach."

At the Apex? "Is everything all right?"

"Fine," Mendoza said. "He's spent the time since we left going through the security tapes. He has found a suspect he wants us to look at."

"Nick," I said.

Mendoza glanced at me. "Nick Costanza?"

I nodded. "I just thought of this while we were out at the house. Listen—"

I proceeded to outline my theory of Jacquie being the mastermind—or at least the instigating factor—in the last few happenings, while Nick was her muscle. "I don't think she had anything to do with killing David. She had no reason to. Nick might have done that on his own. But if she believes I killed him, she could have decided to torch my house. And she wouldn't want to dirty her own hands. She'd send Nick to do it."

"Maybe," Mendoza said.

"What do you mean, 'maybe?' It makes perfect sense."

"Maybe," Mendoza repeated. "Your neighbor didn't see Nick's truck last night."

"He didn't see anyone at all last night," I said. "He thinks I did it."

"He saw a small, light-colored car."

"But that could have been someone driving by. It needn't be anyone with any connection to the fire. If I were out driving around at 3 AM—" And OK, that was a bit unlikely, especially in our quiet, upscale neighborhood, "and I saw a bunch of flashing lights, I'd slow down to take a look."

Mendoza shrugged. "Who do you know who drives light-colored sedans?"

"Rachel," I said. "She has a white Toyota. Farley has a white BMW. Shelby, Farley's new..." I hesitated over the word 'mistress' and ended up saying, "assistant has a pale blue Volvo. Heidi Newsome has a tan Mercedes. Diana has a white Mercedes."

"Diana Morton?"

I nodded.

"I don't think Diana burned your house down," Mendoza said.

I didn't, either. I didn't think any of the people I mentioned had burned my house down. "You asked who I knew who drives light-colored sedans."

"I assumed you'd edit out the people who can't possibly be involved," Mendoza said. "What about your husband's family? What do they drive?"

"I don't know about Kenny. Krystal has a black BMW. Daniel has the truck. Sandra must be driving something, but I don't know what. Other than funerals, I haven't seen her in years. Martha Hollingsworth has a dark blue Cadillac. Gwendolyn Oliver has a burgundy SUV. Her husband has a Porsche, like David's. He's probably thinking of cheating, too."

"Not everyone cheats," Mendoza said.

"That isn't what you said yesterday."

He opened his mouth, and I held up a hand. "Never mind. I'm sorry. I don't want to start that conversation again. Did Zachary say anything more?"

"No," Mendoza said.

"That's too bad."

"We're five minutes away," Mendoza said. "You can wait."

I daresay I could. It was annoying that he could be so calm about it, though.

"This is like an everyday thing for you," I said, "isn't it?"

He glanced at me. "Going to Walmart to buy women's clothes? Not at all."

I rolled my eyes. "The fire, and the break-in, and

David's accident."

He quirked a brow in my direction. "You know what I do for a living, right?"

"Police," I said.

"Homicide detective. So yeah, I deal with a lot of dead bodies. Some burglaries, because sometimes people get dead when they try to break into someone else's house. And sometimes I deal with fires, because people sometimes end up dead in fires, even if you didn't."

Right.

"So yeah, I've seen it all before." But then his voice turned serious. "I don't want you to think that this is all just another day on the job, though. Ho-hum, another dead body. Each case is important. Each victim deserves justice and each family deserves closure. I work hard to close my cases and make sure the guilty party goes to jail."

Good to know.

"Do you know who killed David?"

He looked at me.

"Do you think you know, but you can't arrest that person, because you can't prove it?"

"I have an idea," Mendoza said. "But no, I don't have the proof for an arrest warrant yet."

"Who?"

He shook his head. "I'm not going to tell you that."

"It isn't me, is it? Are you suddenly going to turn around and arrest me?"

That got me an almost-smile. "It's not you. At the moment, I'm working on the assumption that if you cut your husband's brake lines, you wouldn't be stupid enough to leave the knife in your garage during his funeral, where anyone could stumble over it."

"Thank you," I said sincerely.

He shrugged. "If I discover differently, I'll arrest you in a heartbeat. But you're not top of my list right now."

"And you're not going to tell me who is?"

He shook his head.

"Don't you think I ought to be warned? Someone tried to burn me to a crisp last night. What if it happens again?"

"Let's go see what Zachary's got," Mendoza said. "If it is what I think it is, then we'll know."

"Fine," I said. "But I bet you it's Nick."

Mendoza glanced at me, but didn't take the bet.

CHAPTER NINETEEN

It wasn't Nick.

"Holy crap," I said, staring at Zachary's monitor. "That can't be right."

Mendoza looked at me. "It's him, isn't it?"

I nodded. "Yes, of course it is. But..."

Mendoza turned to Zachary. "What makes you think this is our guy?"

"The timing's right," Zachary said, pointing to the red, digital numbers in the corner of the screen. A few minutes after three-thirty on Saturday. Time enough to go upstairs, ransack the apartment, and then vamoose before Zachary got the call from the neighbor about the open door, and headed upstairs. "He looks nervous."

Yes, he did. His face had a furtive expression as he came through the door from the garage to the back hallway and the service elevator.

"Where would he get a key?"

"David might have had a spare at the office," I said.

Zachary nodded. "All the tenants get two. Even when there's only one of them."

So unless David had given his spare to Jacquie, or left it in the kitchen drawer upstairs, he would have probably left it in the safe at the office. It was the logical place for it. Somewhere he could get at it if he lost his other set.

"Anyway," Zachary added, "I've seen him before. With Mr. Kelly."

No doubt. David must have taken his best friend and business partner down here not just once but several times, to show off his new place. He had probably showed the penthouse to Farley both before and after he bought it.

"I don't understand it," I said. "Farley had no reason to ransack David's condo. Or his office at home. All the files David had were copies. The originals are at the office. Where Farley could just look up whatever he wanted."

"I'll be sure to ask," Mendoza said, "when I talk to him." He nodded to Zachary. "Send a copy of that to my phone, would you?"

Zachary nodded and began to type. His fingers flew across the keyboard.

"With skills like that," I told him, "you could get a good job as an administrative assistant."

He glanced up while he kept typing. "I don't want to be an administrative assistant. I want to be a cop."

"While you wait to be a cop."

He shrugged. I turned to Mendoza. "Are you going over there now?"

He nodded.

"I want to come with you," I said.

He shook his head. "Can't."

"Of course I can. I don't have anywhere else to be."

"This is a police investigation," Mendoza said. "I can't

bring a civilian to a suspect interview."

"I don't want to listen to you talk to Farley. I want to be there for Martha."

Mendoza just looked at me.

"Listen," I said. "I've known her for eighteen years. She and Sandra were friends. When I first married David, she could have ignored my existence and left me to flounder on my own. Instead, she helped me become the kind of wife a man like David needed."

Mendoza muttered something.

"What?"

"I said, 'some favor.'"

Yes, well... "Be that as it may, if you're going to go over there and arrest her husband for breaking and entering, and vandalism, and God knows what else—"

"Murder," Mendoza said.

I swallowed, "—and murder, she's going to take it hard. And when she finds out about Shelby, she'll take it even harder. She'll need someone to stay with her. She'd probably prefer Sandra, but I can at least do what I can."

Mendoza hesitated.

"Please," I said. "I won't interfere. You won't even know I'm there. I'm just going to stay with Martha and leave Farley to you."

Mendoza sighed. "Fine. Do you want to take your bags upstairs?"

"No." If I did, he might decide to leave without me. I wouldn't put it past him. "You don't mind holding onto my bags until I get back, do you, Zachary?"

I accompanied the request with a smile.

"Not at all," Zachary said, turning pink. Mendoza

snorted, and Zachary blushed harder.

"I wish I could go with you," he said.

"Well, you can't. She shouldn't be, either." Mendoza scowled at me. "But you, at least, have a job. You can't leave. She can. And it'll be helpful, having someone there who can keep Mrs. Hollingsworth occupied while I talk to Mr. Hollingsworth."

I smiled. Zachary looked envious. "You'll come back and tell me what happened, right?"

"Of course," I reassured him. "As soon as we're finished, the detective will bring me back here, and I'll tell you everything."

Mendoza muttered something else. This time I didn't ask him to repeat it.

"C'mon, then," he told me. "Let's get this over with. Did you send that picture to my phone, kid?"

Zachary nodded. "Have fun," he said wistfully.

Mendoza shook his head, but didn't say anything, just pushed me back out the door and over to the car.

"You don't have to be mean to him," I told him when we were back inside and rolling down the road. "He's just a kid."

"He's a pain in the ass."

I must have looked surprised, because Mendoza took a deep breath and blew it out before shaking his head. "Sorry. He's a nice kid. He just thinks police work is like TV. And it isn't. Most of the time it's routine. Talking to people, writing reports, reading reports, poring over hours and hours of security footage..."

"He did just pore over hours and hours of security footage," I pointed out. "And it seemed like he enjoyed it, too."

Mendoza didn't respond to that. It might have been because he was concentrating on driving, but traffic wasn't very heavy, so I don't think so.

"I appreciate your letting me tag along," I added, making myself comfortable as we headed back out of downtown, along West End Avenue this time.

He glanced at me, a hint of amused malice on his face. "Maybe I'm just looking forward to seeing you take off your trench coat and sitting in Martha Hollingsworth's parlor in your late husband's boxer shorts and knee high boots."

Oops. "I didn't think about that," I said. I'd just shoved all the plastic bags with my new clothes at Zachary, not even considering the fact that I was hardly dressed to make a Sunday afternoon social call on anyone.

Mendoza chuckled. "Too late now. But you can stay in the car if you prefer."

"In your dreams," I said. If the price of going inside the Hollingsworths' house in Belle Meade was doing it in David's boxer shorts and tank top—braless—I'd do it.

Mendoza shrugged. "Suit yourself."

"Thank you," I said. "I will."

Farley and Martha lived in Belle Meade, in a two story French chalet that had been in Martha's family since it was built in the 1920s. She came from money, and married Farley when he was a young and struggling financial whiz kid. That was thirty years ago, and I've always thought their marriage was strong. Farley has always seemed to adore Martha. I was not looking forward to breaking the news about the burglary, and the murder, and especially Shelby.

It was Martha who answered the door, still in her Sunday best. They might not have been home very long. Sunday mornings were for the sermon at the Belle Meade Baptist Church, and lunch at the Pineapple Room at Cheekwood Botanical Gardens.

Her eyebrows rose when she saw Mendoza. "Detective. What's going on?"

And then she saw me, and the eyebrows crept up another quarter inch. "Gina. What are you doing here?"

"I'm here for you," I said.

Martha looked surprised. Mendoza gave me a quelling sort of look. "I'd like to have another conversation with your husband, Mrs. Hollingsworth."

"Now?" Martha said. "It's Sunday afternoon, Detective."

"I'm aware of that, ma'am. Unfortunately, this can't wait."

He was very polite to her. Much more polite than he was to me. I wasn't sure whether that was a good or a bad thing.

Martha sighed, a long-suffering sound redolent of the need to be gracious to those of lesser social standing—like policemen—even if they had no manners.

"Very well," she said and stepped back. "Come in if you must."

"Thank you, ma'am." Mendoza stepped aside and let me walk into the house first. His face was preternaturally solemn, but I could see the twinkle in his eyes. He wasn't any more impressed by Martha's lady-of-the-manor airs than I was.

"Farley's in his office," Martha said, turning on her heel. "If you'll follow me, I'll take you back to him."

"Thank you, ma'am." Mendoza followed, with a wink in my direction. I smiled back, before I headed into the parlor and took a seat on the crushed velvet loveseat circa 1932.

A minute passed, and then Martha's sensible two-inch heels came clicking back down the marble floor of the hallway.

"I've always loved your house," I told her when she came in through the door. "It's so beautiful."

"Thank you, dear." She looked around complacently before turning her attention back to me. "Can I get you anything?"

I thought about it. I hadn't had lunch, and it was getting on for that time of day. But I didn't want to impose, and besides, it didn't seem right to make her get me something to eat or drink when I'd come to be supportive while her husband was being arrested.

"I'm fine," I said.

She sat down across from me and reached for my hand, looking concerned. "Are you, really?"

"I really am. I got out of the house with minimal damage from the jump into the bushes, and before the smoke got too bad."

"Good," Martha said and let go of my hand with a last pat. She sat up. "Would you like to take your coat off?"

"I would," I said, "but I'm not wearing much underneath."

Martha frowned and glanced at the doorway. "Isn't it a little soon to get involved again, Gina? David's been in the ground just two days. And with a policeman?"

"Oh," I said, blushing. "No. I'm not involved with Mendoza." Who might as well have been a garbage-man, with the way her nostrils flared. "He had to take me back to the house so we could talk to the fire chief, and when he said he had to come here, I asked if I could tag along."

"Oh," Martha said, a tiny wrinkle between her brows.

"I wanted to be here for you."

"For me?" The brows rose. "Whatever do you mean, Gina?"

"I know this is going to be hard to believe," I said, leaning forward, "but apparently Farley had something to do with David's death."

Martha leaned back, away from me. Or away from what I was saying. "Don't be ridiculous, Gina."

"I'm not," I said. "He broke into David's penthouse yesterday afternoon, looking for something. Mendoza has a picture."

"A picture?"

"Photograph. Video footage of the door from the garage opening and Farley coming inside."

"I'm sure he had a logical reason for being there," Martha said.

I'm sure he did, too. "There was something in David's penthouse he wanted. Files, or something."

"Why would he want David's files?" Martha wanted to know. "There are copies of everything at the office."

"I'm not sure," I admitted. "I just know he was there."

Martha shook her head. "That's silly, Gina."

"I saw the footage," I said. "He came from the garage into the building and went into the service elevator. It was definitely Farley. And David's files were all over the bedroom floor."

"You're not making sense, Gina," Martha said kindly. "First you said Farley wanted David's files, and now you're saying he left them on the floor?"

"Some of them! There was something he wanted in the rest."

Martha shook her head. "The originals to all the files are at the Music Row office. And there are copies here. If you say Farley was there, I'm sure he was, but he had no reason to want David's files. He has plenty of files of his own."

"So maybe they're different files," I said, a bit desperately.

"Why would they be different, dear? There's no reason why there would be two sets of files."

"I don't know! Maybe... maybe he's been embezzling, or something!"

Martha's eyebrows rose. "Why would he embezzle from his own company, Gina? And don't you think David would have noticed if he did?"

Actually, no. David left the financial matters to Farley. Farley could have been skimming, and David wouldn't have had a clue. My late husband had been good at many things, but one thing he hadn't had, was a head for money.

"Don't you think *I* would have noticed?" Martha wanted to know.

That was a much better point. She probably would

have. Farley is smart, but so is she. She just happened to be born into a generation of Southern Belles who were still expected not to soil their hands with labor.

"He might have put it into a secret account," I said. "David did."

Martha didn't say anything to that, although her eyebrows spoke volumes.

"After he left me. Or before." Probably before. "He had an IRA I knew nothing about, and a savings account, and other things. It was how he paid for Jacquie so I wouldn't find out about her until he was ready to tell me."

"I'm sorry, dear," Martha said.

"Don't be. Be sorry for yourself instead."

"Why would I do that?" Martha asked.

"Because your husband is cheating on you."

Martha laughed. In someone else—someone less dignified—I would have called it a snigger. "You're talking about Farley?"

"Of course I'm talking about Farley! Who else would I be talking about?"

"Don't be ridiculous," Martha said. "Farley wouldn't cheat."

"I saw her. At the office. She's replacing Rachel."

"Who?"

"Farley's mistress! Shelby. She's barely twenty, and looks like a Playboy bunny!"

Martha kept shaking her head. "That's not possible, dear. Farley wouldn't cheat on me. And especially not with sweet, little Shelby."

I stared. "You know her?"

"Of course I know her, Gina. She has been helping

Farley for several months. Lovely girl."

We were either talking about two different people, or Martha was losing her eyesight or her sanity in her middle age.

And to top it off, she was sort of placating me. Patronizing. Mentally patting me on the head, like a child too immature to understand what was going on. It was beyond annoying.

"I'm sorry, Gina. I'm sure you mean well. But you must have misunderstood something. Farley would never have anything to do with Shelby. And as for breaking into David's apartment—"

"I don't know why he did that. I just know he did. Photographs don't lie."

"Sometimes they do," Martha said.

"Well, this one didn't. That's why Mendoza is here."

Martha glanced at the door. Farley's office was at the end of the hallway, too far away for us to be able to hear anything.

"I'm sorry," I said gently. "I know it's no fun to find out that your husband isn't who you think he is." Nobody knew that feeling better than me.

Martha looked conflicted for a second, and then she stiffened her spine. "I'm sure there's a logical explanation," she told me. "I'm sure you mean well, Gina."

I nodded.

"But you're wrong about this. You have to be."

She got to her feet and marched down the hallway toward the office. I watched her go, wondering whether I should go after her, or should just let Mendoza handle the situation. It was his job, and he was probably used to dealing with the distraught wives of the men he arrested.

On the other hand, I had offered to come with him to be useful. And it wasn't very useful of me to sit here and let him handle things in the office.

Then again, I didn't want to butt in on his interrogation. I had promised I wouldn't; that I'd only come along to be here for Martha.

Of course, now Martha was in the thick of it in the office...

Except she wasn't. In the time it took me to reason things out—no more than a minute—Martha disappeared into the office and closed the door gently behind her. There was silence for a few seconds—I strained my ears, but couldn't hear anything. Maybe there was a faint murmur of voices and some sort of thud or bump, or maybe there wasn't. Maybe I was imagining things. Then the door opened again. Martha came back into the hallway. "Thank you, Detective," she said over her shoulder.

She stopped for a second to adjust her sleeves, and then she came briskly down the hallway toward me. "Just as I thought," she told me as she entered the parlor. "There's a logical explanation."

"That's wonderful," I said, waiting for her to share it with me.

"The detective has requested a glass of water. Would you like one, as well? Or perhaps some sweet tea?"

If Mendoza thought it was OK to ask for refreshments, who was I to say no? "I'd love a glass of tea," I said.

Martha patted me on the shoulder. "You stay right where you are, Gina, dear. I'll be back in a jiffy."

Sure. I watched her disappear through the door to the kitchen and heard the clinking of glasses and the sound of cabinet doors and the refrigerator being opened and closed. After a minute, she came back in with a tall glass of iced tea in each hand.

"Here you are, dear." She handed me one and put the other on the table. "Let me just go give Farley and the detective their drinks, and I'll be right back."

"Of course," I said.

"You go right ahead and get started while you wait." She gave me a motherly sort of smile before heading back into the kitchen. A moment later she was on her way down the hallway with two more glasses: one clear for Mendoza, one whiskey brown for Farley, who must also have requested tea.

I sipped from my own glass and watched as she disappeared back into the office. This time she was gone several minutes before she came back out. And when she reached the parlor, she tossed back half the glass of iced tea in a single swallow.

"Everything all right?" I inquired. I'd been sipping mine more daintily, but I had managed to polish off half the glass, too. I was starting to feel more relaxed.

Martha smiled. "Yes, dear. Everything is fine."

"Would you like to tell me what's going on in there?" Because part of me couldn't wait to hear this logical explanation for why Farley had broken into David's apartment—or maybe not broken, exactly, since presumably he had a key—and tossed David's belongings around.

"Oh, they're just sitting and talking," Martha said breezily, taking another slug of her tea. "Don't be shy, Gina. Drink up."

I took another sip of tea. To be honest, it was a little too sweet, and I'd probably pay for it later, when the sugar rush wore off and left me hungry for more. "What are they saying?"

"Nothing that need concern you." She smiled. "How are you feeling, dear?"

"Fine," I said. "A little tired."

Martha nodded sympathetically. "And no wonder, with all the excitement you had last night. Would you like to lie down for a bit, perhaps? Until you feel better?"

I would. That actually sounded wonderful. But—

"I'd probably better not. Mendoza might be ready to go soon." I put the empty glass on the table and got to my feet. And found I had a bit of a hard time keeping my balance. Guess she was right and last night was catching up to me.

Martha peered up at me, looking concerned. "Are you sure you're all right, dear?"

"I'm fine," I said. "I'm just going to go down to the office and stick my head in the door and tell Monda... Mendoza we need to go soon."

I headed that way without waiting for her response. I could hear her putting her glass down and getting to her feet behind me, but my entire attention was focused on making my way down the hallway to the office door. The floor kept shifting under my feet, and the walls weren't entirely steady, either. Every once in a while, I had to put out a hand to steady myself against the wall. Behind me, I could hear the click-clack of Martha's measured footsteps.

Eventually, I reached the office door and put my hand on the knob. It took effort figuring out which way to turn it. When I leaned against the door, it didn't open, so I figured I must be doing it wrong. I rocked back on my heels instead.

By now Martha had reached me. "The door is locked, dear," she said kindly, and put an arm around my shoulders. "Let's just go and lie down. You can sleep it off."

That sounded great. However— "I wanna see Mond... Mend..."

Good Lord, I sounded like I was drunk!

"Jaime," I said firmly.

Martha sighed. "If you're sure, dear."

"I'm sure," I said.

Or at least I think I must have, because she knocked on the door. There was a response from inside, and Martha said, "It's us."

After a moment, there was the sound of locks and deadbolts being drawn back. Farley opened the door.

Unlike Martha, who hadn't a hair out of place, he looked distinctly disheveled. His glasses were askew, and so was his tie.

"Goodness," I said, "what happened to you?"

Or maybe I didn't. Maybe I just thought it. Farley didn't respond, anyway. Instead, he gave me a distinctly unfriendly look. "This is all your fault, you know."

No, it wasn't. It couldn't possibly be.

"You were supposed to be arrested for murder,"

Farley told me. "Not help the police investigate."

"What was I gonna do? Sit and do nothing?"

It came out garbled, but Farley understood what I was asking. "Not become Miss Marple," he responded angrily.

Miss Marple? Wasn't she, like, seventy-five?

I would have complained, but my tongue felt too big for my mouth, and I couldn't get it to cooperate in forming words.

"Come along, Gina," Martha said briskly. "Let's get you upstairs so you can lie down."

She took my arm. I tried to twitch out of her grasp, but my coordination was shot all to hell. "Don't wanna go upstairs. Wanna see Mond... Mend... Jaime."

"She wants to see Jaime," Farley's voice said, from far, far away.

"Then by all means, let her see the detective." Martha guided me over to a door in the side wall. She opened it and gave me a push. I stumbled forward, into darkness, and that's the last thing I remember.

CHAPTER TWENTY

When I woke up, it was later.

I'm not sure how much later. Could have been thirty minutes, could have been a day.

I was in a safe. Not a small one, like David had at the office. More like a vault. Seven by ten, maybe. Steel walls covered with shelves. Files. And Jaime Mendoza, gray as a ghost, leaning over me. He was slapping my cheek, over and over again. Not very hard, probably because he wasn't feeling that good himself. I tried to feel grateful, but it was hard.

"Ow," I said weakly.

He sat back. Or slumped, against the wall. "Good. You're alive."

"Was there any doubt?"

I could talk again. *Excellent.*

"You wouldn't wake up," Mendoza said.

"Never mind me." He looked awful. "What happened to you?"

"Martha hit me over the head with a trophy," Mendoza said.

A trophy? "You're kidding."

He shook his head, and must have thought better of it, because he winced. "I was sitting there, talking to Farley. She comes in, walks over to the console table, picks up a big, crystal trophy, walks back to me, and whacks me with it. I'm lucky she didn't bash my brains out."

"Let me see." I pushed off against the floor and managed to get to my knees. My head was still swimming, but at least I could speak and think mostly clearly.

Mendoza bent his head obediently, and I peered at the back of his head.

"Yep. Big bump here." I probed it, ignoring his yelp of pain. "I don't feel anything moving, so I don't think she cracked your skull. Do you see double?"

"No," Mendoza said. "She's an older woman. She probably didn't hit as hard as she thought she did."

Maybe not. Or maybe she'd only planned to knock him out instead of kill him.

"What are they going to do with us?"

"Dunno," Mendoza said. "They shoved me in here right away. I was still unconscious. I didn't hear them discuss it."

I hadn't, either.

He added, "What happened to you?"

"Something in the tea. Whatever it was, it knocked me out. Quickly." I glanced at his wrist, where that expensive Rolex was still strapped. "How long have we been here?"

"It's been a few hours. It's almost six o'clock."

"They're probably waiting for it to get dark before they take us out of here."

Mendoza nodded, carefully. "Probably planning to bury us somewhere, or pitch us in the river, or something."

He sounded remarkably calm about it.

"You don't sound very upset by the idea," I said. "Do you have a plan?"

He smiled. "No. But every day I strap on my gun, I know it could be my last."

"Speaking of your gun..."

"They took it," Mendoza said.

Of course they had. So now Martha and Farley had a gun, but we didn't. Wonderful.

I looked around the room. Files, and more files. "Is there anything in here we can attack them with when they come for us?"

"I haven't checked," Mendoza said, "but it looks like just paperwork."

It did. I suppose we might overwhelm them with files, and make a break for it while they batted them away, but it didn't seem like a very well thought-out plan.

"Anyway," Mendoza added, subsiding back against the wall, "they may not come for us."

I turned to look at him. "What do you mean, they may not come for us? I thought we agreed they were waiting for darkness to pitch us in the river."

"They could just leave us here a couple of days," Mendoza said. "Nobody's gonna come to our rescue. Nobody knows we're here. And the place is soundproof, so even if someone showed up, they wouldn't hear us call for help."

"We won't starve in a couple of days."

"No," Mendoza said, "but we'll run out of air long before that."

I stared at him, wide-eyed, and he added, "This room isn't just soundproof. It's sealed. No air in, no air out. When we run out, we die."

For a moment, a long moment, I was too appalled to speak. Then I got my voice to cooperate. "They wouldn't do that to us!"

Mendoza arched his brows.

"It's messy," I said. "They'd have to deal with two dead bodies. I don't think they'd want to do that."

"At this point," Mendoza told me, "I'm not sure what they'd do. I didn't think Mrs. Hollingsworth would hit me over the head with her husband's golf trophy, either."

Well, no. I hadn't seen that one coming, either. "They're not young, though. And neither of them is in particularly good shape. It would be much easier to wait until we both come to—like, now—and until it's dark, so none of the neighbors notice anything, and then tie us up and take us out to one of the cars and murder us somewhere else. Nothing to point to them."

Mendoza shrugged. He didn't argue, though, so I guess he saw my point.

"Do you have any idea what this is about?" I asked. "I'm a little confused, to be honest."

Mendoza grimaced. "I wasn't able to get a whole lot of information out of Farley before his wife whacked me with the crystal, but I think I've got most of it."

"Then please, elucidate me. All I know is that Martha says Farley wasn't cheating on her."

"I don't think he was," Mendoza said.

"So how do you explain Shelby? I realize you didn't meet her, but you can take my word for it: other than Jacquie, I've never seen anyone who looked more like a mistress."

Mendoza managed a smile, but it looked like it cost him. I really didn't like his color. He was much too pale, the usually golden skin having taken on a distinctly greenish cast.

"You're not going to throw up," I asked suspiciously, "are you?"

He closed his eyes. "Not if I can help it."

"But you're nauseous?"

"I think I might have a slight concussion," Mendoza admitted.

"I thought you said you weren't seeing double!"

"I'm not." After a second, he added, "Much."

"Great." I rolled my eyes. "I'm stuck in here with a man who needs medical attention."

"Don't worry about it," Mendoza said. "The air'll give out long before the concussion kills me."

Wonderful.

"So about Shelby..."

"Right." He made a visible effort to focus.

"If she isn't Farley's mistress, what is she? Clearly not an administrative assistant!"

"I don't think Mr. Hollingsworth is looking for an administrative assistant," Mendoza said. "If he was, he'd have kept Rachel."

True.

"So why not keep Rachel? She knows everything about the business. Why go to the trouble of firing her and finding someone else to answer the phones and look pretty?" Not that Rachel looked anywhere near as pretty as Shelby. Although that had never bothered David. I found it hard to believe that bothered Farley, who had always seemed like someone who valued brains over beauty.

"He wanted someone who didn't understand what was going on," Mendoza said. "Rachel knows too much about the business. Mr. Hollingsworth's been safely skimming for a while, and he felt safe for as long as Rachel only worked for your husband. But if she started handling the records for the whole business, she'd catch on to what he was doing."

That made sense. "Did he admit to skimming?"

Mendoza shook his head. "I've suspected it for a while. There were several people who benefitted financially from your husband's death."

"Me," I said.

He nodded. "His children got some money. His brother got some money. And Mr. Hollingsworth got the business. But you had the most pressing need for him to die. If he survived another day, the judge would make a decision about the estate, and you might lose everything."

Granted. "So how did that make you suspect Farley of embezzling?"

"I didn't think you'd done it," Mendoza said simply. "I've been wrong before. But you didn't strike me as a cunning murderess."

"Thank you." *I think.* "And Farley did?"

Mendoza shook his head. "Not particularly. He seemed sincerely sorry, and worried about what would happen to the business without his partner."

"That was probably genuine," I said. "I have no idea how Farley planned to keep the business alive on his own." Although, with what I now knew, maybe he hadn't.

"He was there at the restaurant that night," Mendoza said. "Johnny-on-the-spot. He did leave the table for a few minutes. Nobody can agree on exactly how long, but he would have had the opportunity to cut your husband's brake lines."

I nodded. "Why, though? Was he afraid that David had figured out that he was skimming? Because the David I knew wouldn't have had a clue. Math was not his strong suit. And if you tell me Jacquie is some kind of accounting whiz, I won't believe you."

"It's never a good idea to judge someone by the way they look," Mendoza told me gently. "But no, it had nothing to do with Jacquie. And if your husband had any idea, he didn't say anything to Mr. Hollingsworth about it. Not according to what Mr. Hollingsworth told me."

"So why—?"

"The estate," Mendoza said. "If your husband died, the business would go to Mr. Hollingsworth. But if your husband got divorced, his share of the business would become part of his assets, and the business would be audited for value. And while Mr. Hollingsworth had succeeded in hiding the embezzlement from your husband, he hadn't a hope of hiding it from an independent auditor."

"That's brilliant," I said.

"Thank you." Mendoza made a face. "It's a damn shame I won't live long enough to prosecute him for it."

"Don't give up. I still think they'll get us out of here and take us somewhere else before they kill us. Martha's grandfather built this house. She won't want to commit murder here."

"I hope you're right," Mendoza said, and leaned his head against the wall. All the talking looked like it had tired him. If he had a concussion, I didn't think he was supposed to go to sleep, though. And anyway, I had more questions.

"So I guess it was Farley who planted the overalls and knife in my garage during the funeral reception. And who tossed David's office."

Mendoza nodded. "He used the extension in your husband's office to phone in an anonymous tip that the knife was there."

"And what was he looking for?"

"Copies of original files," Mendoza said. "He kept telling you that they were identical to the files at the Music Row office, but they weren't. Among them were copies of files he had doctored. So if someone compared the copies to the originals, they'd be different."

Ah. Yes, that made a lot of sense. "So that's why he told me to get rid of them!"

Mendoza nodded. "And then, when he didn't find all the files he was looking for, he decided to make a trip to the penthouse, as well."

"That's my fault." I grimaced. "When I saw him yesterday afternoon, I mentioned that David had files downtown."

"He would have gone to the penthouse anyway," Mendoza said. "It wasn't your fault."

Maybe not. And since I didn't want it to be, I decided to take his word for it. "What about the fire?"

"You said it yourself," Mendoza said. "He told you to have a bonfire with all the old records. He assumed you had. He figured it would look like you'd gone to sleep with the fire still burning, and had been overcome by the smoke."

"So he was trying to kill me."

"He wasn't trying not to," Mendoza said.

"Why?"

He shrugged. "I have no idea. You'd be able to answer that better than me. Did you say or do anything that might have made him think you knew more than you did?"

Had I?

My brain was still fuzzy, and it took effort trying to put thoughts together. I spoke slowly. "I went to the office yesterday afternoon, looking for David's will."

Mendoza nodded.

"That's when I met Shelby. And a few minutes after she walked in, Farley showed up. I thought they were going to... you know."

Mendoza nodded.

"He asked what I was doing there, and I told him. And when I was going to leave..."

"Yes?" Mendoza said, his voice alert.

"It was weird. I almost got the feeling he was blocking the doorway. Like he wasn't going to let me leave. I knew that was silly, but..." But in retrospect, maybe not so silly after all.

Mendoza arched his brows at me.

"He asked what I had in my hand, and I told him it was insurance."

Mendoza smothered a laugh—part of me was glad he could still see the humor in the situation—and I said defensively, "It *was* insurance. Life insurance. A policy David had with me as beneficiary. I took it home so I could call the company tomorrow and tell them that David died. If nothing else, I get the million dollar payout."

"I hope you'll live long enough to enjoy it," Mendoza said, which wasn't very encouraging at all.

We stopped talking after that. As Mendoza pointed out, talking used more air than breathing, and we didn't know how long we'd be locked inside the vault. And anyway, we both felt bad. My head was still fuzzy from whatever Martha had put in my tea, and I'm sure Mendoza had a banging headache.

"I don't suppose you have your cell phone?" I asked after a while.

He cut his eyes to me. "There's no reception. I checked. We're locked inside a steel box."

"Thank you. I'm aware of that." I didn't need him to point it out every time I opened my mouth. "I thought maybe we could play a game, or something."

"I turned it off," Mendoza said, and closed his eyes again. "I didn't want to run out the battery."

Fine. Although if we died in here, fat lot of good conserving that battery would do.

He would have pointed that out. I didn't.

By Mendoza's Rolex, it was after ten when we finally

heard the sound of the door opening. Mendoza opened his eyes and lifted his head. I hadn't been sleeping, so I only had to look up.

After some whirring and clicking—the safety mechanism opening, I assume—the heavy door swung in. From outside, it looked just like a normal door. What I hadn't realized the first time I stumbled through it, was that it was four inches thick, reinforced steel.

Mendoza's gun came into the room, followed by Martha. At least I assume it was Mendoza's gun, since I had a hard time wrapping my brain around Martha owning one.

"Oh, good," she said brightly. "You're awake."

There was no response I could make to that, not without sounding either profane or inane, so I didn't try.

She wiggled the gun. "Come on. Up, up!"

I got to my feet. It was harder than I had anticipated. The room did a slow spin, and I put a hand to my forehead. Meanwhile, Mendoza seemed like he had some trouble, as well. He had to use the wall for support as he got slowly to his feet.

Martha tsked her tongue. "Theatrics, Detective?"

"You gave him a concussion," I said. "He's seeing double."

"Oh, dear." She sounded about as sorry as one would expect, considering that he was a man she had hit over the head with a crystal golf trophy this afternoon. "I suppose you had better help him then, Gina. I can't drag him."

"Where's Farley?" I asked, as I made my way across the room over to Mendoza, who was still leaning against the wall, looking winded. I had hoped that he was merely faking, that he had a cunning plan and was only pretending to be weak, until the moment he planned to make his move on Martha. But the way he draped a heavy arm across my shoulders and hung on, it was only too obvious that if anyone was going to have to come up with a cunning plan, it was going to have to be me.

And I was all out of cunning plans at the moment.

"Getting the car ready," Martha said.

Point to me. They were taking us somewhere else before they killed us. Maybe on the way there, I'd think of something.

We walked out of the office and into the hallway. I turned left, toward the front door, and got a poke in the ribs from the gun for my trouble. "Garage," Martha told me.

Uh-oh. Maybe they weren't going to take us somewhere before they killed us, after all. Maybe they planned to shoot us in the garage, and then load our bodies into the car and drive away.

I pushed open the door and helped Mendoza through and down the couple of steps to the concrete floor.

Farley's white BMW was parked in one of the bays, Martha's Cadillac in the other. The Caddy's trunk was open, and—I swallowed—lined with black lawn and leaf bags, the kind I had used to bag up the shredded files the other day.

Yesterday. Was it really only yesterday?

Mendoza staggered along beside me, one arm draped across my shoulders. He was dragging his feet, but I didn't know whether it was deliberate, to gain time, or because he had to.

"There," Martha said, gesturing with the gun.

"The trunk?"

"Yes, dear," Martha said. "I'm afraid it wouldn't make much sense to have you sit in the backseat."

No, probably not. Now the only question was whether she'd shoot us once we were inside the trunk, or whether they'd wait until they got to where they were going. If they did it now, they'd have to haul our dead weight back out of the trunk. And although they'd covered the inside of the trunk with plastic, there was a possibility that a drop of blood might find its way through to the trunk itself, where it would be enough to incriminate them.

Probably easier to lock us in the trunk alive and then make us climb out on our own before they shot us.

"Go on," Martha said, gesturing with the gun. "Shoo, shoo."

Farley was already behind the wheel, remotely opening the garage door preparatory to us heading out. The heavy door metal door started moving up along its track, rattling as it went. The noise almost drowned out Martha's voice.

"Go on, now. Stop dawdling."

It didn't drown out the command coming from outside. "This is the police. Drop your weapons and come out with your hands up."

The amplified voice was accompanied by two bright lights that flashed on, illuminating the interior of the garage and nearly blinding me. I threw a hand up to cover my eyes. Mendoza, meanwhile, dropped his arm from across my shoulders and threw himself at Martha.

I don't know whether she planned to shoot him or whether her finger just tightened on the trigger in surprise. Either way, the bullet whizzed by and buried itself in the trunk of the Cadillac with a *ping*. The gunshot itself was loud enough to shake my eardrums. Mendoza knocked Martha to the floor, flipped her over, and landed on her. Meanwhile, the voice outside continued to give instructions.

"This is the police. You are surrounded. Come out with your hands up."

"Gimme your belt," Mendoza said breathlessly, holding out a hand.

I untied it from around my waist and watched as he used it to tie Martha's hands behind her back.

"Get the gun."

No problem. It had landed a few feet away. I picked it up, gingerly, and brought it to him.

"Thank you." He plucked it out of my hand, and then grabbed my wrist and yanked me down. I landed next to him, on top of Martha, who gave out another *whoomph* as all the air left her lungs.

"Stay," Mendoza told me.

Sure. I made myself comfortable and watched as he walked over to the driver's side door and yanked Farley out by the arm. "On the ground. Hands behind your head."

It was quite masterful, especially as I knew his head had to hurt like hell.

From outside, the voice kept droning. "We are the police. You will be assimilated. Resistance is futile."

Mendoza snorted, and then raised his voice. "It's OK.

You can stop now."

"Oh, good," a voice said, non-amplified this time. "I was running out of ideas."

I stared at him. "Zachary?"

He grinned. "Hi, Mrs. Kelly."

"Zachary?"

"Yes, Mrs. Kelly."

"What are you doing here?"

"You didn't come back," Zachary said, "so I got worried. I knew where you'd gone, so when I got off work, I drove out here to make sure you were OK. And I saw the old dude—" he glanced at Farley, "get in your car—" he looked at Mendoza, "and drive away. That didn't seem right, so I followed him."

"Where did he go?" Mendoza asked.

"Bus station in downtown. He parked in the lot, went inside one side of the terminal and out the other, and hailed a cab. Cab dropped him back here. I figured you had to be inside the house somewhere, so I decided to wait. I figured they'd bring you out sooner or later."

Good thing they brought us out alive, I thought. Although I didn't mention that to Zachary. He'd done a fine job of saving the day, and telling him that had things gone differently, he might have saved a couple of corpses, would only be rain on his parade.

"Thank you," I said instead, and leaned in to give him a peck on the cheek. He flushed red, all the way to the roots of his hair.

Mendoza nodded. "Good job, kid. Help me load these folks into the back seat, and then you can take Mrs. Kelly home while I drive to the nearest cop shop."

"You don't need me to stay?" I asked.

He shook his head. "I'll get your signature on your statement tomorrow. You already told me everything that happened on your end."

"Head OK?"

"Fine," Mendoza said, probably lying through this teeth.

But his head wasn't my responsibility, and he was a grown man. He'd get himself and his head looked at when he was ready.

"I put my purse down next to the sofa in the parlor when I came in," I said. "I'm going to go get it, and then we can leave."

Zachary nodded. He was in the process of trying to haul Martha to her feet, so he probably had no breath left for talking.

I didn't even spare her a glance as I walked past her and into the house her grandfather had built. The house I sincerely hoped she wouldn't get to see again for the rest of her natural life.

EPILOGUE

"I'm thinking of becoming a PI," I told Diana a few days later.

We were sitting across from one another at a table at the Germantown Café, having lunch. And celebrating, after a successful meeting with Anton Hess and Judge Miller. Or successful for us, I should say; not so much for Anton, as the judge had decided that since David had played dirty and tried to hide assets from me, I was entitled to half of everything he owned, along with a hefty monthly alimony.

Of course, the fact that he was now dead complicated things. David's will had to go through probate, and his estate would be divided between Krystal, Kenny, and Daniel. My share would stay with me, but I'd get no alimony from a dead man. So while I wasn't a pauper, I wasn't exactly rolling in dough, either. I was looking for something I could do, that would help keep me in the style to which I had become accustomed while being David's wife. Or at least something that would keep some money coming in.

Diana stared at me. "Have you lost your mind, Gina?"

"Not at all," I said. "I'd be providing a valuable service. All those wives whose husbands are catting around, deserve to know the truth. And I think I'd like it. It was fun, following David around. If I become a PI, I get to do it for money."

"You had fun, following David around?"

I nodded. "Sure. And Jacquie and Nick." There was a certain thrill in sneaking along behind someone, wondering whether they'd spotted you or not. In trying to outwit them. It was the first time I'd been required to use my mind in years—the job of being David's wife having been singularly brainless—and I'd enjoyed it.

"Besides, I really feel that I could provide value. There are so many husbands out there, sleeping with their secretaries while their wives are at home, suspecting nothing. And there are so many husbands trying to cheat their wives out of their fair share in the divorce. A wife whose husband is banging his secretary as well as hiding assets, deserves to know the truth about what he's doing."

Diana took a sip of her cocktail. Once again, she was walking back to work, and I was driving. "How do you plan to do that? You don't know how to run a business."

"No," I said, "but Rachel does."

Diana put the glass down. "Your husband's admin?"

I nodded. "Farley fired her, you know. So he could bring in Shelby, the airhead who'd never in a million years realize he was embezzling."

Diana nodded.

"Rachel's husband died years ago. Heart attack in someone else's bed. That's why she had to go back to work and ended up working for David. So she has her own beef about cheating husbands. She's very organized, so she can run any kind of business, and she's been going through Farley's papers and figuring out exactly what he's been doing. After this week, she'll know all about hiding money."

"And she's willing to work for you?"

"Not just willing." I grinned. "She feels so bad because she didn't tell me what David was up to, or realize what Farley was doing, that she practically begged me to take her on. She thinks she could have prevented David's death if she'd only realized that the embezzling was going on."

Diana cocked her head. "Do you think she could have?"

Maybe, maybe not. "If she'd figured it out and had confronted him, he might have killed her instead. If she'd figured it out and told David... I'm not sure. Things might have turned out differently. But maybe not."

Farley had been willing to kill his oldest and best friend. He might have been willing to kill David under those circumstances, as well.

"And Zachary's going to be helping me," I added.

"The doorman from the Apex?"

"He wants to be a cop. After saving the day on Sunday, he's even more determined now. He thought working security at the Apex would give him a leg up on the competition, but working for a PI will be even better."

Diana took another sip of her drink. "How do you like living there? At the Apex?"

"I like it," I said. "It's nice. Centrally located. Safe. Nobody's going to burn it down."

She shook her head.

"And it's the perfect size. After David left, I realized just how big the house in Hillwood is. It was just me, and other than the funeral reception," and Mendoza, who didn't count, "I never had anyone visit. When David was there, at least we used to have his clients over for dinner once in a while. Or Farley and Martha."

"What's going on with them?" Diana wanted to know.

"They're in prison. Mendoza argued that they were a flight risk—they have plenty of money and nothing to keep them here—so they didn't get bail." I grimaced. "Martha's trying to push everything on to Farley. She had no idea that he'd had anything to do with David's death until I told her so on Sunday. She had no idea he'd broken into David's penthouse or torched my house. She had no idea he'd been embezzling. It all came as a shock to her, after thirty years of marriage, and she lost her mind for a few hours."

"Temporary insanity," Diana said.

I nodded. "She might even get away with it. She's playing it for all she's worth, anyway."

Diana smiled. "I take it you don't believe her."

"Not for a minute. She was in it up to her ears. Farley would never have dared to do anything without consulting her first."

I hadn't realized that at the time, but once I'd thought about it later, it made perfect sense. No, he wouldn't have cheated. He was completely devoted to Martha, who wore the pants in the relationship, figuratively speaking.

"It was probably her idea from the start," I said.

"Then let's hope the jury sees through her dignified Southern wife act, and sentences her as she deserves." Diana hoisted her glass. I hoisted mine, full of water. I was a little leery of tea just now.

We clinked and drank.

"So you'll be staying on at the Apex," Diana said when she'd put her glass down.

I nodded. "I like it there. No bad memories. Nice size. Lovely view. Once the contractors finish repairing the fire damage, I'm going to list the house for sale. And the convertible is already gone."

"I noticed that," Diana said, glancing out the window to where my new-to-me, smallish, black SUV was parked. "Used car?"

"The convertible wasn't good for following anyone around. Too conspicuous. Even Jacquie noticed it. If I'm going to be a PI, I need an inconspicuous car. Not shiny-new, not brightly colored. Nothing that anyone would notice." I gave my new ride a fond look through the window. "That's a Lexus, but not the most expensive kind. It's five years old, so it's not in perfect condition anymore. And it looks like half the other cars on the road. Nobody will notice me if I drive it."

She glanced at my head. "What about the hair?"

I put a hand to it, self-consciously. "I'll wear a wig."

The red was about taking back who I was. I wasn't giving it up, even to be a PI.

Diana—the blonde—nodded. "You're serious about this, aren't you?"

"Of course I am. I've already started studying for the PI license. The next exam is in a week." I dug in my purse and pulled out an oversized paperback. "This is the textbook."

Diana took a look at the title and arched her brows. "Private Investigating for Dummies?"

"It's what they recommended," I said. "I'm learning a

lot."

She smiled. "I'm sure you are. So when will you be open for business?"

I put the book on the chair next to me, with a fond pat. "I guess a couple of weeks after I know I've passed the exam and the license is official. So about a month from now. October 1st?"

Diana nodded.

"We already have an office. I'm taking over the Hollingsworth & Kelly building on Music Row. Someone has to. And it's the perfect size for us. An office for me, an office for Zachary, and an office for Rachel. Not to mention that it's a perfect location." And if I kept the pictures of Hank and Patsy and Jim on the walls, it would look like I'd been there forever, too.

"And a name?" Diana asked. "Do you have that?"

"We've been talking about it. Zachary wants to call it Spousebusters."

Diana chuckled. "He's young."

"It's cute. But probably a little too cute. We want to be taken seriously."

And I couldn't quite picture myself handing someone a business card from Spousebusters. "Rachel wants to call us Fidelity Investigations," I added.

"I like it," Diana said.

I nodded. "Me, too. Serious. Businesslike. And accurate. That's what we'd be doing. Investigating fidelity. Or infidelity."

"What's your suggestion?" Diana asked.

"I don't really have one. Although I was considering CheckMate."

"I like that, too. Cute, but not too cute. Right to the point. What's the problem?"

"There's already a PI firm called CheckMate. In New York."

"Different state," Diana said. "A thousand miles away. I'm sure private investigator licensing, like law and real estate, is state specific. Just because someone has incorporated a company by that name in another state, doesn't mean you couldn't do the same here."

"I know that. I just feel like I'd be copying."

"This isn't grade school," Diana said. "Copying's OK."

"There's a Fidelity Investigations out there, too. In Maryland, I think Zachary said. And a Fidelity Investigative Training Agency in Chicago. They contract with the government. Not sure I want to run afoul the government."

Diana shook her head. "What about Spousebusters? Is anyone using that?"

"Yes, but not domestically. In Australia. And don't think Zachary didn't point that out."

Diana grinned.

"We have some time to figure it out," I said. "First I have to pass the exam. Then we have to incorporate the business and work out all the details of the partnership. And then we have to actually dig up some clients."

"I can help you with that," Diana said.

"The incorporation?" Didn't we need a corporate attorney for that? "Aren't you too busy with your own share of cheating spouses to take on my business incorporation paperwork?"

"You have no idea," Diana said grimly. "I wasn't talking about your business incorporation, Gina. I could do it, but you're better off hiring someone who does it as a specialty. There are finer points I might miss. What I meant is that I can offer you some business."

"Oh. Good." She probably could, now that I thought about it. That hadn't even crossed my mind until now, but people probably talked to her about their suspicions of their spouses before they actually filed for divorce. And she could send them my way to find out whether their suspicions were warranted. "Thank you."

"Don't thank me yet," Diana said. "I want you to investigate Steven."

I blinked. "Your husband?"

She nodded.

"Your husband's cheating?"

"I don't know," Diana said. "But something's going on. And I want to know what."

Naturally. "Consider it done."

In fact, I'd start right now. This afternoon. As soon as we finished lunch. I wouldn't charge her, anyway, so whether I had a license or not at this point, didn't matter. There's no law to prevent anyone from following someone else around. Apart from the various stalking laws and such, but of course I wouldn't be stalking Steven.

Diana shook her head. "Get situated first. I want it all legal and on the up and up. Just come see me when you've passed your exam and have your license. He's not going anywhere in the next couple of weeks. And you only have a few days left to study."

Fine. "I appreciate it," I said.

"Don't mention it," Diana answered. "I trust you to tell me the truth."

"Of course."

"And to keep it confidential."

"Naturally."

She smiled. "So does Jaime know about this?"

"Mendoza? I haven't mentioned it to him." I hadn't seen him since Monday. He'd stopped by to get my signature, like he'd said he would, but that was the last time I'd seen him.

Which was as it should be. It had been a fleeting relationship rooted in circumstances, my lascivious thoughts about him notwithstanding. He had been investigating my husband's murder. It wasn't like we were friends. Or anything more.

"Let me know when you do," Diana said. "I'd like to be there. To see his face."

Uh-oh. "I guess he doesn't have a high opinion of private investigators?"

"You could say that," Diana said, grinning. "His wife hired one before the divorce. And slept with him."

"The PI?"

Diana nodded.

"Isn't that illegal?" The Private Investigating for Dummies book said it was. Everyone knows you're not supposed to sleep with your clients. It's a conflict of interest.

"Very. So not only did Jaime have to deal with this PI following him around and snapping pictures while his wife was suing him for child support, but then she ended up marrying the guy. So now Jaime's kid is being brought up by the guy who nailed him for adultery. He has good reasons to dislike the profession. And that doesn't count the professional ones."

Wonderful.

"I guess that's how you met," I said. "You represented him in the divorce."

"I represented Lola," Diana said.

"His wife?"

She nodded. "I often represent the wives. They like having a female attorney."

Since that was the reason I had hired her myself—aside from the fact that she had a reputation for being very good at what she did—I couldn't very well argue with that. In fact, I was hoping the same thing would hold true for female PIs. That women would feel more comfortable hiring me than a man.

"I just assumed, since the two of you seem to get along so well..."

"He's a nice guy," Diana said. "He knew it was his own fault that Lola divorced him. He tried to work things out with her, but by then she was sleeping with the PI and wouldn't have taken him back even if she could have trusted him again, and she said she couldn't. He didn't argue at all about the alimony. It's for Elias, and Jaime loves his kid."

I nodded. "Well, I don't expect I'll have much to do with Mendoza after this. The case is closed and he's moving on to the next dead body. One that won't have anything to do with me."

"Don't worry about it," Diana said. "I know where to find him. Maybe I'll just invite him to lunch and tell him myself, to make sure I don't miss the look on his face."

But then *I* would miss the look on his face.

Then again, considering his feelings about the PI profession, maybe that wasn't such a bad thing.

She leaned back and smiled. "You know, I'm proud of you, Gina. When you first called me and told me about David, I wasn't sure you were going to make it through this. But look at you now!"

Yes, look at me now. I had a new car, a new penthouse, an almost new wardrobe, new friends, and a soon-to-be new business...

"I've come a long way," I said, channeling that old Virginia Slims commercial. *You've come a long way, baby!*

Diana would probably remember it. She was older than me.

She grinned. "Let's drink to that."

"Let's." I lifted my water and she lifted her cocktail and we toasted.

And drank to that.

# # #

ABOUT THE AUTHOR

New York Times and *USA Today* bestselling author Jenna Bennett (Jennie Bentley) writes the Do It Yourself home renovation mysteries for Berkley Prime Crime and the Savannah Martin real estate mysteries for her own gratification. She also writes a variety of romance for a change of pace.

For more information, please visit Jenna's website:
www.JennaBennett.com

Made in the USA
Columbia, SC
03 June 2020